P9-CRW-225

THIEVES IN THE NIGHT

Grizwald motioned back to the other two. Reynolds and Manfried stepped from behind a boulder and moved past the horses toward the far end of the picket line, each carrying a saddle and bridle.

Somewhere in the night a coyote howled and waited for an answer. None came. But Grizwald saw something, someone, coming and whispered to the other two. They followed him around the line of horses toward the other side of the boulder near where Warren had fallen.

The night clouds had drifted past the moon now, shedding a soft light on the land below.

Adam Forrester approached the crumpled heap and recognized the unconscious face of Dell Warren. Forrester wore no side arm. He was about to reach down, pick up Warren's rifle and fire a shot to arouse the camp when the gun barrel touched the back of his head and he heard the cock of a hammer.

"Don't make a sound," Grizwald whispered. . . .

DOUBLE EAGLES

ANDREW J. FENADY

LEISURE BOOKS NEW YORK CITY

A LEISURE BOOK®

November 2002

Published by

Dorchester Publishing Co., Inc.
276 Fifth Avenue
New York, NY 10001

If you purchased this book without a cover you should be aware that this
book is stolen property. It was reported as "unsold and destroyed" to the
publisher and neither the author nor the publisher has received any
payment for this "stripped book."

Copyright © 2002 by Andrew J. Fenady

All rights reserved. No part of this book may be reproduced or transmit-
ted in any form or by any electronic or mechanical means, including
photocopying, recording or by any information storage and retrieval sys-
tem, without the written permission of the Publisher, except where per-
mitted by law.

ISBN: 0-8439-5061-7

The name "Leisure Books" and the stylized "L" with design are trade-
marks of Dorchester Publishing Co., Inc.

Printed in the United States of America.

Visit us on the web at www.dorchesterpub.com.

DOUBLE EAGLES

Preface

"Slaver's moon, Captain. Night's thicker'n tar."

"Patience, Mister Bogartis."

"*Patience?!* Sounds peculiar coming from the most impatient man in the U.S. Navy."

"Not tonight, Mister Bogartis."

"It ain't 'tonight' anymore, Captain. Figure it's just past midnight."

"Good. That makes it the Fourth of July."

"So it does, sir."

"And that means fireworks. Cannons loaded?"

"You bet, sir."

"Cannoneers at the ready?"

"Port and starboard, sir."

"Hand me that telescope," said Captain Thomas J. Gunnison. "And maintain strict silence until further orders."

"Yes, sir. And we await them further orders with gleeful anticipation." First Officer Beauford Bogartis

1

handed his captain the telescope, then added in a voice just above a whisper, "This time . . . by God . . . we'll get the dirty slave-tradin' sonofabitch."

"We'll get him, Mister Bogartis . . . by God or by gun."

Chapter One

The *Jubilee*, a three-mast merchant ship, lay anchored at the Bight of Benin, Gulf of Guinea, West Africa, in the early dark hours of July 4, 1856.

The *Jubilee* was taking cargo aboard.

Black cargo. Human cargo. Chained together.

Men clamped to a seemingly endless chain. Women and children, children old enough to work if they survived the crossing, were toggled to another chain.

Adam Forrester, the *Jubilee*'s captain, handsome with pistol-barrel eyes—round, dark, deep—and a smile lashed across a stormy but satisfied face, watched, flanked by two men. One tall and white. The other taller and black.

First Mate Kevin Connors, hollow-eyed, with a skull-shaped face, stood expressionless. Kambula, the African slave merchant, folded his huge arms across the wide plateau of his chest, which was covered by a bright purple and orange garment. His broad, shining face, a black basilisk, was punctured by a missing eye, the socket shrouded with lizardlike skin.

The three men stood silent amid the rattle of chains and the other sounds of their profession.

Men, women, and children, gleaming bodies, some with eyes bewildered, defeated—others defiant with tribal pride as ancient as history—were now shackled and chanting a dirge. A dirge, part sung, part spoken in Gullah, a language composed of West African tongues.

Men, women, and children, like cattle out of the dark continent, clanked aboard and disappeared into an even darker region—into the murky, yawning hold of the *Jubilee*—prodded by the slave traders, white and black.

From the green hills of Africa and the greener jungles, out of the veldt and the vast surface of desert sand, from the fertile riverbank soil and the craggy escarpments, for years Africa had provided the rest of the world with two of the continent's most profitable exports.

White ivory and black flesh.

Tusks torn from countless skulls of slaughtered elephant carcasses—and human beings taken by enemy tribes and mercenary black and Middle East merchants absent of conscience, whose only pursuit was profit.

Many parts of the world still coveted the elephant products. But the slave market had shrunk. Most civilized countries had abandoned slavery. And most countries, including the United States since 1809, had outlawed the importation of slaves.

As a result, the illegal traffic in slaves, though riskier, became more profitable for those who ventured the risk.

Captain Adam Forrester so ventured—and so profited. So far.

Other cargo, ivory, gold, tea, spice, almost anything, could be insured, but not the cargo carried aboard the *Jubilee* by Captain Adam Forrester. If that cargo was lost there was no compensation. And if caught, the consequences were seizure of the ship and prison for captain and crew . . . if convicted.

But the undetected completion of such a voyage spelled sky-high profit. So far all of Forrester's voyages had been undetected and exceedingly profitable.

He had agreed to pay in gold forty dollars a head for the 737 men, women, and children that made up his cargo. Forrester expected from eleven to twelve hundred dollars for each head put ashore.

Not all of the living cargo would live through the voyage. There would be "spoilage," as Forrester phrased it, up to ten percent on some trips. But that was part of the hazard of the trade.

By 2:30 A.M. the cargo was aboard and the hatches sealed. Off the mosquito-infected coast the tide was favorable.

Captain Forrester brought up a heavy leather pouch and placed it in the cradle formed by both the wide palms of Kambula's hands. The weight within the pouch produced a smile on Kambula's face.

"Until next time, my friend." Forrester grinned.

Kambula nodded, turned and walked toward the gangway that tilted from ship to wharf, and disappeared into darkness.

First Mate Kevin Connors grunted, then emitted a mirthless laugh.

"What is it that strikes you, Mister Connors?"

"That Kambula's supposed to be such a shrewd trader. . . ."

"And so he is."

"What if he knew you were willing to pay twice as much?"

"There's another way to look at it."

"How's that?"

Andrew J. Fenady

"For all I know, maybe he was willing to take half as much."

"Huh?"

"I'd say it all worked out fine—for all concerned—except for those down below. Wouldn't you agree, Mister Connors?"

"I agree with everything you say, sir."

"Well then, I say make ready to sail."

"Aye, aye, sir."

While the crew of the *Jubilee* made ready to sail, "those down below," as Forrester had called them, were chained and crammed together in darkness and confusion, a harvest of infamy, unaware of destination, or of the destiny of those who had been harvested before them.

As the dripping chain and anchor rose out of the water, Captain Adam Forrester struck a match, lit his cigar, and walked toward the helm of the *Jubilee*, leaving in his wake curling gray patterns of smoke that dissolved into nothing.

Chapter Two

Under the command of Captain Thomas J. Gunnison, the U.S. Navy frigate *Confidence*, an 86-foot ship of the line with a crew of 60, mounting 14 guns, floated in the silent darkness on the rim of a yeasty, curling fog bank.

In the last three hours Captain Gunnison had raised and lowered the telescope dozens of times, searching the night for a silhouette under sail.

The search had been fruitless.

Until now.

Once again Gunnison lowered the telescope from his sea-green eyes, this time with a smile on his face, a face fashioned like the prow of his powerful ship, leaning forward, wind-chased and confident. A face with the look of a hunter who had sighted his quarry.

First Officer Bogartis, a man who it was said could keep a steam iron afloat in a hurricane, had seen that look before, time and again. On seas, both shores of the Atlantic, north and south. In the Carribean. The Gulf of Mexico. In pursuit of pirates, smugglers, and enemies, foreign and American.

The look that meant prelude to action. Overture to danger—and mostly to victory.

"The *Jubilee*, Captain?"

Gunnison handed the telescope to Bogartis. His First Officer looked through it in the direction Gunnison had sighted.

"The *Jubilee*, Mister Bogartis. Keel heavy."

Gunnison withdrew a gold watch and chain from the vest of his uniform and pressed the stem of the hunting case, causing the lid to come open. On the inside of the lid there was a circular photograph of a beautiful, fair-haired woman. On the face of the watch the hands indicated 3:45.

Gunnison closed the lid and slipped the watch back into his pocket. Bogartis squeezed both ends of the telescope, pressing it into a shorter tube.

"We got him this time, Captain!"

"Not yet."

"You think he's spotted us?"

"You know Forrester. What do you think? Give the order to pursue, Mister Bogartis."

"Aye, aye, sir."

On the afterdeck of the *Jubilee*, Adam Forrester slapped the telescope into the chest of Connors and turned toward the helmsman as wisps of fog trailed across the lumbering ship.

"Hard a port! Hard a port!"

"Aye, sir," the man at the wheel replied.

"Head into that fog bank."

The helmsman spun the wheel.

"Mister Connors . . . open up the hold. All hands heave to!"

Double Eagles

Connors did not bother to reply. He was already shouting orders to the crewmen, orders that set them scurrying toward the hatches as the *Jubilee* abruptly changed course and plowed straight for the billowing veil of fog.

Adam Forrester knew his pursuer. They had met before, and always under adversarial circumstances. And he knew the consequences of capture loaded with the cargo carried by the *Jubilee*. He also knew the choice he had to make.

Loss of a fortune . . . or loss of his freedom.

Forrester had already made the choice.

Confidence dipped in pursuit, her prow cleaving the pulsing water under press of sail. Her thirty-one star flag fluttered unseen through the thick, starless sky. Her prey had disappeared into a cottony cloud of haze, into a dense moving blanket that blinded both vessels.

Two sightless ships in moist obscurity, wooden beasts floating under a dark gray overcoat dropped from a sullen sky—a prowling hunter seeking its skulking prey—both hunter and hunted, silent.

Until . . .

Distant screams.

Screams that became a continuous chorus. A deadly wail of those unwilling to die, squealing like pigs under slaughter, screams punctuated by the rattle of chains . . . then the plop, plop, plop of metal and flesh, a tangled mass of openmouthed men, women and children, lost souls plunging into the burgundy water below . . . into the grip of enveloping death.

Foaming and gurgling, the splash of iron and the surge of bodies, flailing . . . disappearing . . . helpless human cargo torn from the deck and dumped into the lapping crypt of the sea.

9

A wooden beast disgorging the contents from its belly and throat . . . like vomit.

Slavery had been a fiery issue since the United States Constitution was framed in 1787. The founding fathers sought to bank that fire and keep the states united by postponing the climactic solution to that issue with a series of compromises.

While slavery itself was not abolished, the importation of slaves was prohibited during the administration of Thomas Jefferson.

An African squadron was established to patrol the Atlantic and intercept the illegal slavers. But since the squadron was seldom composed of more than a half-dozen ships—among them the *Cyane, Hornet, Alligator, Adams,* and *Shark*—they served as little more than a wide-webbed sieve through which the slave-bearing schooners slipped with alarming regularity.

The whole of the southern American economy depended on laborers to work the plantations that grew cotton, tobacco, rice, and sugarcane. Slaves were the most economical laborers. Though it was no longer legal to import slaves, their offspring born in the United States were born in bondage.

For the nation the issue became conscience vs. economics—and for a nation founded on the principle of "all men are created equal," the outcome was inevitable.

But at this time the outcome was still in doubt, and in the meantime the Forresters of the sea plied their trade and took the risks. One of those risks was Captain Thomas J. Gunnison, whose ship had veered alongside the *Jubilee* as the night fog gave way to a gentler haze just before dawn—and as a shot rang out across the bow of the tranquil merchant ship.

"Ahoy, *Jubilee*! This is Captain Gunnison! We're coming aboard!" Gunnison's voice rang out.

"Hey, Tom!" Forrester replied. "That shot came too damn close."

"And we're coming closer."

Half an hour later the two ships were lashed gunnel to gunnel. Gunnison, Bogartis, and twenty-six armed crewmen of the *Confidence* were aboard the *Jubilee*. Bogartis and the rest were conducting the search as Gunnison stood by on the deck.

Forrester, in good spirits, had greeted Gunnison and the other intruders with a cynical smile.

"You know, Tom, among other things, you didn't ask for permission to come aboard."

Gunnison did not reply—not to Forrester. Instead he had turned to his first officer.

"Make a thorough search, Mister Bogartis."

Bogartis nodded to his crewmen, who took off in pairs, on and below deck.

"Would you care for a drink, Tom? I keep some private stock. The best Tennesse bourbon."

Gunnison did not respond.

"Then how about a good cigar? Made of the finest Virginia leaf."

Gunnison just stood silent, looking toward the east, where the sun would soon try to break through the receding fog.

Connors and the rest of the crew, unlike Forrester, were not in good spirits, a broiling potpourri composed of scalawags in assorted sizes and colors. They glowered at Gunnison as if he had stolen the contents of their purse—and he had. For them this aborted voyage might mean prison and definitely would mean loss of the bounty they would have shared from the sale of cargo. Never mind the loss of lives—that didn't matter a whit to any of them, not even to the black crewmen among them.

Andrew J. Fenady

They all sailed for one reason only, and had one allegiance only—to one god. Money. These were not musketeers on a mission. They were mercenaries without mercy. Unfeeling, except for the way they felt toward Gunnison now. And the way they felt, any one of them would as soon slit his throat as cut the rotten core out of an apple. They stood stiff-legged and quiet as Gunnison's men searched the ship and Adam Forrester smoked a good cigar made of the finest Virginia leaf . . . until First Officer Beauford Bogartis appeared from around the forecastle followed by other searchers from other parts of the ship.

"Hold's empty, sir," Bogartis reported to his captain.

"Oh." Forrester smiled and exhaled a patternless cloud of smoke. "Didn't I tell you, Tom, we're picking up our cargo at the Canaries."

"But we did find a few things, Captain," Bogartis said. "Course, we had to bust open a few doors and boxes."

"Speak up, Mister Bogartis."

"Two sets of cooking pots commonly known as slave coppers, a hundred barrels of bread, fifty barrels of rice, forty water pails, and other accoutrements usually connected with certain illegal commerce. They either neglected, or didn't have time to jettison."

"What about it, Forrester?" Gunnison said.

"Hardly a compelling case, Captain."

"When we first sighted you this ship was riding low in the water loaded with cargo."

"Who did the sighting?"

"I did."

"And so did I," Bogartis said.

"Really? Both of you . . . and from such a distance . . . and in all that fog . . ."

"We know what we saw, and so do you."

"You're mistaken on both counts, Tom. It's the two

12

of you against my word and the word of . . ." Forrester looked around at his crew and smiled. "The word of the forty-four decent, hardworking, honorable seamen who will all, every man jack of them, swear that this ship was sailing just as you boarded her."

"Then why did you run for cover?"

"Couldn't identify you through the fog. Thought you were pirates, didn't we, Mister Connors?"

"Aye, sir, we did."

"As I said before," Forrester grinned, "hardly a compelling case. Besides, I have a much more compelling case against you."

"For what?"

"For unwarranted interception, seizure, and destruction of private property. I would suggest we settle out of court. Wouldn't you agree, Tom?" Forrester's grin broadened.

Gunnison turned and walked toward the rail of the *Jubilee* as it floated alongside his own vessel. Bogartis and the other crewmen of the *Confidence* followed.

"I thought you'd agree, Tom," Forrester called out. "Maybe I'll come visit your ship sometime."

As Gunnison and his crew climbed back aboard the *Confidence*, Forrester tossed the butt of his cigar into the sea and called out even louder.

"Smooth sailing, Captain."

Gunnison, Bogartis, and the other crewmen were back on the deck of the *Confidence*. The lines that had been secured between the two vessels were loosened and retrieved. The two ships, still side by side, both under full sail, had begun to drift apart.

The sun was climbing above the watery horizon, and a morning breeze dissipated what had been a hugging bank of fog. Both ships groaned, and their tall masts dipped with the sway of their hulls.

"Well, Captain," Bogartis said. "Looks like he got away with it."

"Does it?"

"We don't have enough evidence to convict—"

"Evidence? Evidence, as you call it, is buried down below in that water, still chained together. God knows how many . . . human beings now food for the fishes . . ."

"We both know that, Captain. But the murderin' bastard's outmaneuvered us and there's nothin' we can do about it."

"You're wrong, Mister Bogartis. There's something I can do about it."

Gunnison pushed aside one of the cannoneers, reached out, and pulled the lanyard of a cannon, aiming directly at the *Jubilee*.

"Fireworks, Mister Bogartis. Fireworks."

The eleven-inch smoothbore Dahlgren erupted into the early light, sending a twenty-four-pound ball crashing into the hull of the slaver at the waterline. The gaping hole frothed and gurgled, sucking in water.

First Officer Bogartis and the rest of the crew stood stiff and stunned, but not as stunned as Forrester and his crew. Adam Forrester ran across the slanting deck, grabbed onto the rail, leaned out, and screamed toward the *Confidence*.

"Gunnison! Have you gone crazy!?!"

"Have you, Captain?" Bogartis inquired, still surprised, but evidently not disappointed.

"Sink her, Mister Bogartis."

"Captain, a shot's one thing . . . we'll say it was an accident, but you can't—"

"I said sink her, Mister Bogartis. That's an order!"

"Fire at will, men! Bring her down. Fire away."

The seven cannons on the port side of the *Confidence*

opened fire one after another as one missile after another exploded into the hull, rigging, sails, rails, masts, cabins, and galley of the *Jubilee*. Wood split, canvas ripped apart, and crewmen dove into the rolling sea as the seven cannons were loaded and fired again.

The bow took most of the firepower and the *Jubilee* pitched, then plunged forward and down into the foaming crests of waves, lifting the ship astern, fantail into the sky, where she paused for a last gasp and then slipped screaming into the sea.

"Lower away boats, Mister Bogartis. Pick up those decent, honorable, hardworking seamen out there."

"Aye, sir. Lower away boats, men! Hurry up, now! It's up to you men to save those murderin' bastards! Lower away!"

Forrester was not the sort of captain who would go down with his ship . . . nor would he be the last to leave it.

Captain Forrester had been the first to dive off the listing *Jubilee*, knowing there was no time to lower lifeboats. Diving in next to him was First Mate Connors, who had almost always been at his side since Forrester saved his life one night in Dakar when Connors was being attacked by two Arabs on a dark street. Forrester killed both Arabs with one shot apiece from his derringer. Forrester never inquired what the altercation was about, and Connors never volunteered. At the time, Connors wore a pea coat.

"You a sailor?" Forrester asked.

"I am that."

"Looking for a berth?"

"That I am."

"You got one." They walked away from the bodies of the dead Arabs toward Forrester's ship.

Since then Connors had been looking for an opportunity to repay Forrester in kind by saving his life. But Adam Forrester, up to now, had been master of his own ship and destiny and of the destiny of many others, including Connors. In fact, twice since Dakar, Forrester had again saved Connors's life—once in a whorehouse in Casablanca, and later on the *Jubilee*. A slave had got hold of a flensing knife and was about to bury it in Connors's back when Forrester smashed the black's skull with a belaying pin.

And now the two of them swam together, side by side, followed by other *Jubilee* survivors, toward the first boat that had been lowered from the *Confidence*.

Wet and shivering, Forrester stood on the deck of the *Confidence*, Connors next to him as the other survivors were still being helped up from the small boats.

"Well, Captain." Gunnison stood squarely in front of Forrester. "You said you might pay us a visit sometime. . . . Fourth of July is as good a time as any."

Forrester trembled and coughed.

"Sorry I can't offer you any Tennesse bourbon or—"

"You're crazy. . . ."

"Maybe."

"You killed some of my men. Sent 'em to the bottom."

"They're in good company down there."

"I don't think you realize what you've done."

"Sure I do. I just blew you out of the slavery business."

"No." Adam Forrester shook his head. "You just blew yourself out of the Navy."

Chapter Three

The General Court-Martial of Captain Thomas J. Gunnison had been in session three days.

On that third day, August 31, 1856, the odds were not in Gunnison's favor.

The Secretary of the Navy, James C. Dobbins, was a native of North Carolina. The Secretary of War, Jefferson Davis, was born in Christian County, Kentucky, and reared in Mississippi.

Franklin Pierce, elected President of the United States in 1853, though born in New Hampshire, was called "The Grand Compromiser"—and when it came to the issue of slavery, "The Gutless Wonder." Pierce could not afford to aggravate the South if he hoped to be re-elected, and he did so hope—fervently.

The court-martial was being held in the nation's capital, Washington D.C. George Washington, in 1790, had selected the exact spot of the "Federal City," later named in his honor. The city had been designed by

17

Pierre L'Enfant and laid out by Andrew Ellicott. Congress held its first session in Washington in 1800, and Thomas Jefferson became the first president to be inaugurated there.

In 1814 the British captured the city, sacking and burning most of the public buildings, including the White House—from which President James Madison and his wife Dolley fled with, among other items, the Declaration of Independence.

One of the structures that survived the siege was the building where Gunnison's court-martial was being convened forty-two years later. The building did not appear capable of surviving much longer.

During the weeks since the *Confidence* had dropped anchor in Baltimore carrying the survivors of the *Jubilee*, scores of Southern newspapers had railed against the "ruthless Yankee Captain's dastardly, unprovoked attack upon a helpless merchant vessel on the high seas"—a vessel whose registry happened to be Norfolk, Virginia.

Further militating against Gunnison's case was the fact that of the five judges comprising the court, one was a Californian and one a Connecticut Yankee, with the remaining three from Louisiana, South Carolina, and Georgia.

Gunnison's best hope, if it could be so called, was that the Chief Officer—designated as President of the Court-Martial—was Captain Garrett Merrill, the Connecticut Yankee, a man of impeccable character and integrity, devoted to naval tradition and justice.

The charges specified against Captain Gunnison included, as Forrester had predicted:

Unwarranted interception of the unarmed merchant vessel, *Jubilee*.

Illegal seizure and search of said vessel.
Destruction of private property aboard said vessel.

And finally, and most serious:

The sinking without warning of said vessel,
resulting in the deaths of three crewmen.

The latter charge might be interpreted by the court as
murder, for which the offender could be hanged if two-
thirds of the court so decided.

The lead prosecutor, Commander Hugh Bates, was a
posturing, perfumed peacock who had spent a good
portion of his forty-three years practicing his courtroom
conduct in front of mirrors. His tailored uniform con-
formed perfectly to his scant body. Try as he would to
lower the timbre of his scratchy voice, it nevertheless
tended to come across sounding like squeaking chalk on
a blackboard. Bates's naval career seldom voyaged beyond dry land, where he had commanded a flotilla of
desks. He had never heard enemy gunfire and seldom
walked the deck of a ship unless that ship was anchored
and some ceremony was involved.

Bates talked fast and attacked the opposition like a
hawk striking at a chicken. But Gunnison was no
chicken.

During those first three days Gunnison sat, a formidable monument of indifference to the strutting pop-
injay sawing the courtroom air with practiced motion
and rehearsed rhetoric. When Gunnison did move, it
was to look toward the entrance as if he expected someone to enter.

And he did.

Next to Gunnison sat his defense counsel, Captain
Lionel Graham, a man of large frame, a lionlike face

outlined by a mane of unruly white hair, with a navy
cloak covering his broad shoulders. Graham had lost
his left leg below the knee during a Mexican naval cam-
paign in 1848. The stump was fitted with a tapered
wooden shaft and he maneuvered with the aid of a pair
of aged pine crutches. Long ago, one of his officers had
dubbed him "The Sea Lion." The appellation fit in ap-
pearance and demeanor, and Graham had been so
called by friend and foe alike for many years. But as far
back as Tom Gunnison could remember, Lionel Graham always had been "Uncle Lionel," his father's best
friend.

During the War of 1812, it was Lionel Graham, the
youngest commander in the U.S. Navy, who introduced
General Andrew Jackson, the defender of New Orleans,
to the privateer-smuggler Jean Lafitte.

Graham had fought against Lafitte but had great respect for the buccaneer and negotiated a deal for his
amnesty if Lafitte's fleet from Barataria would throw in
with Jackson. The deal was struck and the British were
vanquished. "Old Hickory" Jackson went on to become
the seventh U.S. president. Lafitte, after a few years of
respectability, sent a note to the Sea Lion thanking him
for arranging the amnesty, but respectability was too
damn boring and he was going back to "the old ways
on the Spanish main"—and so he did until he disappeared from land and sea in 1825. President Andrew
Jackson had offered Captain Lionel Graham the job of
Secretary of the Navy, but the Sea Lion declined, pre-
ferring the deck of a ship to a desk in Washington. His
decision cost him his leg and forced him into retirement,
but it was a decision he never regretted.

Graham had come out of retirement to defend the son
of his best friend in the matter of the *Jubilee*.

Lionel Graham and Captain Jefferson Gunnison had

sailed, fought, and drunk side by side since near the turn of the century, until Jefferson Gunnison was killed in action.

And now Graham sat beside Tom Gunnison while Bates smiled and nodded toward Captain Adam Forrester, who sat upright in the witness chair and responded respectfully to Bates's respectful queries.

"Captain Forrester, where were you on the morning of July fourth of this summer, sir?"

"Aboard my vessel, the *Jubilee*, off the African coast."

"Were you carrying a cargo?"

"No, sir. We were heading toward the Canaries to pick up our cargo and make for Havana."

"And that's where you were attacked by Gunnison's frigate—"

"You're supposed to *ask* questions, Bates," Graham's voice boomed out. "Not make a statement . . . which is a lie anyhow."

"Your honor! Please!!" Bates moved with indignation toward Captain Merrill and the other court officers.

"Captain Graham, you know better than that," Merrill said.

"So does *he*," Graham responded.

"Rephrase your . . . question, Commander."

"Of course, sir." Bates moved back toward Forrester and smiled. "Would you please tell the court in your own words, Captain, what occurred that morning?"

Forrester told the court, in his own words, what occurred. None of the words was true—except for the fact that three of his crewmen died during the encounter.

"Thank you, Captain," Bates said somberly. "And my condolences on the loss of your crewmen . . . and, of course, for the loss of your defenseless ship under these regrettable circumstances. By the way, may it please the court, I offer a sworn and signed statement from the survivors of that crew, headed by First Mate Kevin Connors, verifying the events of that July fourth, as related by Captain Adam Forrester. Your witness, Captain Graham." Commander Hugh Bates bowed to the court, smiled, took his seat, and adjusted the shirt cuffs from under each of his coat sleeves.

Graham reached to pick up the crutches that leaned against the table in front of him and Gunnison.

"You're not going to get a word of truth out of him, Uncle Lionel," Gunnison said.

"I know that, son." Graham grunted as he rose and hooked a crutch under each arm. "But I'm gonna prod him some anyhow . . . do a little needlin'. Now, then." Graham spoke louder as he steered his way between crutches toward the witness. "You say your name's Forrester."

"If that's a question, the answer is yes."

"First name Adam? Like that fella in the Garden of Eden? That's a question too."

"Yes again."

"Do you believe that story about Adam and Eve, Captain Forrester?"

"That's what it says in the Bible."

"That's not what I asked you. Do you believe the story of Adam and Eve as written in the Bible?"

"I object." Bates rose to his feet. "I don't see the point to this—"

"Haven't got to the point and can't, if that little jackanapes doesn't shut up and let me get to it, Your Honor."

"You may proceed, Captain Graham . . . up to a point . . . but do get to it."

"Yes, Your Honor. Now then, Adam . . . Forrester, since you believe in the Bible, and you are a Christian . . . aren't you?"

22

"I am."

"You believe in heaven and hell?"

"Yes."

"You believe you have a soul?"

"Yes."

"That all humans have souls?"

"Yes."

"Blacks and whites?"

"How's that?"

"Do you believe that Negroes as well as white people have immortal souls?"

"Your Honor!" Bates exclaimed, and rose to his feet again.

"I'm getting there, Your Honor," Graham said. "Just a couple more questions . . ."

"You're heading toward breakers, Captain Graham. Be careful."

"I'll try to steer clear, sir." Graham moved closer to the witness chair. "Now then, Adam Forrester, we were talking about immortal souls, black and white. Let's just for a minute talk about your immortal soul." Lionel Graham reached out his hand, still leaning on both crutches, and took the Bible from the table near the witness stand. He held the Bible close to Forrester's face. "In the certainty that there is a heaven and hell . . . and in the knowledge that you will meet all the other immortal souls, white and black, before your maker . . . will you place your hand on this Bible and swear before almighty God to forfeit all hope of heaven . . . swear that you are not now, and never have been, a slave trader, and—"

"Your Honor, I object!"

"And that there were no Negroes—"

"I object!"

"No slaves aboard the *Jubilee* as you sailed from the African coast this last July!"

"Your honor!" Bates screeched. "I must protest!"

"You're out of line, Captain Graham." Merrill pounded his gavel. "And you know it."

"You and I both been out of line, Garrett, together sometimes."

"Well, this time we're not together, and that last question, if that's what it was, is struck from the record."

"So were them slaves." Captain Lionel Graham tossed the Bible back on the table and wheeled on his crutches away from Forrester. "I'm through with this . . . witness."

"Captain Forrester," Merrill instructed. "You may return to your seat."

Forrester rose, stepped away from the witness chair, and smiled as he walked past Gunnison, who looked back toward the entrance again.

"Commander Bates, do you have any further witnesses?" Merrill asked.

"No, sir. That concludes our case. The prosecution rests."

"Very well. Captain Graham, are you prepared to proceed with the defense?"

"You bet." Graham added, "Your Honor."

"Call your first witness."

"The defense calls First Officer Beauford Bogartis of the United States Naval frigate *Confidence*."

"Is First Officer Bogartis present?"

"He is, sir . . . I am, sir." Bogartis, seated in the first row, stood up.

"Uncle Lionel!" Gunnison leaned over, tugged at Graham's sleeve, and whispered, "Ask for a short recess."

"Why? What's the matter, Tom?"

Captain Thomas J. Gunnison pointed back to the courtroom door.

Two young acting midshipmen had just entered. Gunnison knew them both. One was named James Discant.

The other was Jeff Gunnison, Tom Gunnison's twenty-year-old son.

Even as Captain Merrill granted the recess, Gunnison was on his feet and moving toward his son. Both Jeff Gunnison and his friend James Discant showed the effects of the fast ride on horseback from Baltimore, where the training ship *Malta* had landed just a few hours ago, after its cruise.

When Acting Midshipman Gunnison had heard about the Fourth of July encounter, he had left a note for his father telling him that he would be back and with him as soon as the *Malta* returned. For days now, Captain Gunnison had thought of little else except having his son with him as he stood trial. The two had seen little of each other since Tom Gunnison's wife—Jeff's mother—Angela, died when Jeff was a baby. The infant went to live with his aunt Martha, Angela's sister, a teacher in Philadelphia. During all those years, Captain Gunnison had provided his son with everything he could need or want . . . except a father.

It was one voyage after another, with only short visits in between.

Jeff Gunnison had chosen to follow the Gunnison family tradition and was now in his third year as an acting midshipman at Annapolis.

"Jeff." Gunnison shook his son's hand and smiled. "It's good to see you."

"We haven't seen each other very often." Jeff did not smile.

"Not often enough. Thanks for being here."

"Sure, Dad."

25

"How are you, Jimmy?" Gunnison turned toward the other midshipman.

"I'm fine, sir," Discant replied.

"Come on, let's the three of us step outside."

They did, and stood to the side of the courtroom steps.

"You look like you had a rough ride, boys."

"So do you, Dad."

"I've had rougher, but everything's going to work out. It always does."

"Not always. From what we've heard, they've got a pretty strong case against you."

"Jeff, I'm not going to make any excuses to you or anybody else."

"I'm not the one you have to convince. It's that court in there."

"Uncle Lionel's got to do the convincing. I'm just going to tell the truth."

"You've always done that, Dad."

"I know that there are some things I haven't done, son, I—"

"Excuse me, sir," James Discant said. "I'll see you later . . . and good luck, sir." He moved back toward the courtroom, leaving Gunnison alone with his son.

"No matter how this comes out, Jeff . . ."

"Dad, I know you're set in your ways and have been for a long time. I don't expect you to change—"

"Captain, they're ready inside." It was Bogartis, standing at the doorway. "Hello there, Jeff." Bogartis pointed toward Captain Gunnison. "He said you'd get here." Bogartis grinned and walked inside.

"Jeff." Gunnison looked square at his son.

"Yes, sir."

"I wasn't going to say anything about changing my

ways. . . . What I was going to say is that no matter what happens, I'll always remember that you came here."

Both First Officer Beauford Bogartis's and Captain Thomas J. Gunnison's sworn testimony concerning the events connected with the sinking of the *Jubilee* varied in many respects from the testimony of Captain Adam Forrester—mainly in the respect of truth vs. lies.

Bates's cross-examination of Bogartis had been perfunctory and almost dismissive. His questions had mostly to do with distance and fog, regarding how low or high the *Jubilee* sat in the water before and after she was boarded by Gunnison and his men.

As to the "slave coppers," barrels of bread and rice and "other accoutrements usually connected with slave commerce," Bates emphasized that "usually" does not necessarily mean "always" and that there was no hard evidence, no proof of slave trading or anything remotely suggesting any illegal activity aboard the unarmed merchant ship.

Bates's cross-examination of Captain Gunnison was anything but perfunctory. This was Bates's time on center stage and he meant to give a memorable performance, one that would cast him as the premier prosecutor of the U.S. Navy and pave the way to promotion. What happened to the other people on that stage was of no significance or consequence. His only thought was of a new uniform, tailored to his exact specifications, a uniform with fancy braid and four captain's stripes.

As the cross-examination continued Bates became more frenetic, louder, and more aggressive, while Gunnison remained composed and unhurried, glancing occasionally toward his son, who sat on an aisle seat next to James Discant near the rear of the court.

". . . and it is your contention, then," Bates continued, "that there was a cargo aboard that vessel when you and your first mate sighted her with a telescope through the fog at a great distance."

"You can call it cargo. They were human beings."

"So it appears, then, that you and your first mate have identical stories."

"That's because it's the identical truth."

"So you both say . . . and *only* the both of you, against the sworn testimony of Captain Forrester, his mate, and his entire crew—those who survived—that swear the ship carried no cargo."

"It carried slaves that were thrown overboard."

"Did you . . . or anybody witness . . ."

"No, but it happened."

"Has your first mate, Mr. . . . ."

"Bogartis."

"Bogartis. Has he served with you a long time?"

"A long time, in war and peace."

"Yes, well, Captain, we are currently at peace, are we not?"

"Currently. But not for long, I don't think."

"It seems you were already at war with an unarmed merchant vessel, but let me ask, do you consider your mate, Mr. Bogartis, a loyal crewman?"

"Yes."

"Who will do what you ask?"

"What I *order*."

"And if you ordered him to lie about what happened . . . would he execute *that* order?"

"Why didn't you ask him?"

"Because I'm asking you."

"I wouldn't . . . and he wouldn't."

"Did you order him to fire on the *Jubilee*?"

"*I* fired first, then ordered."

Double Eagles

"You, *yourself,* fired the first cannon?

"I did."

"Isn't that uncommon?"

"So is slavery . . . and against the law."

"You had no proof, but you were judge, jury, and executioner. Your action killed three crewmen who did not deserve to die."

"Neither did those slaves, hundreds of them."

"Ah, yes, those phantom slaves that nobody has ever seen."

"And never will, because they were murdered."

"So you contend. Now, let me ask you, when you illegally boarded that vessel did Captain Forrester resist at all?"

"No."

"Did he not, in fact, offer you a drink?"

"Tennesse bourbon."

"And even a cigar?"

"Virginia leaf."

"Is that the conduct of a man who has something to hide?"

"He already hid it."

Bates shook his head and grunted. He looked toward Captain Merrill and the other officers of the court as if he didn't believe a word and they shouldn't either, then turned back to Gunnison.

"Now then, is it not true, Captain Gunnison, that you've had a personal vendetta against Captain Forrester for more than a decade?"

"I don't like him, if that's what you mean."

"No, that's not what I mean!" Bates spoke even faster and with more emphasis, biting on every word. "Isn't it true that your first encounter with Captain Forrester was when he commanded a ship called the *Flash*? A ship of the Texian Navy."

Andrew J. Fenady

"One of the gunboats that traded with the British and which were considered pirates by the U.S. Navy at the time."

"And in that encounter several of your crew were killed. You remember *that*?"

"I remember that I sank the *Flash* and that Forrester was tried for piracy and murder."

"Yes, then you'll also recall that during that trial war was declared between the United States and Mexico and Captain Forrester became an ally—"

"He's switched sides more than once."

"—that Captain Forrester was exonerated and proclaimed a hero!"

"Not by me. He was a pirate and a murderer. And now he's a slaver and a murderer."

There was a general reaction in the room, mostly favorable to Gunnison. However, Captain Merrill and the other officers of the court did not react.

Midshipmen Gunnison and Discant stirred slightly and looked at each other.

Tom Gunnison had removed his gold watch from his uniform pocket, pressed the lid open, and was looking not at the time but at the photograph of his wife. Bates continued to move as if stalking Gunnison.

"Let me remind you, Captain, that this court is convened to determine *your* guilt, not his.

"Guilt or innocence." Gunnison closed the watch and slipped it back into his pocket.

"Captain Gunnison," Bates's voice dripped with sarcasm as he pointed to the watch, "do you have an appointment?"

"That depends on them." Gunnison pointed to the five officers.

"Your Honor!" With an attitude of complete exasperation, Bates moved a step toward the officers in judg-

30

ment. "Would the court instruct the witness to answer the questions without levity?"

"Captain, you are so ordered." Merrill shrugged.

"Aye, aye, sir."

There was more laughter from the spectators as Merrill banged the gavel.

"I think I've had all I can bear from this witness." Bates wiped at his narrow brow. "And so, I believe, has the court. He is excused. The prosecution is prepared to proceed with summation."

What Bates had termed "summation" turned out to be a harangue that lasted the better part of an hour before he started to run out of wind.

". . . and there can be only one verdict in the case against Thomas Gunnison. Guilty! Captain Forrester, his crew, and his ship were the innocent victims of a man driven and consumed by vengeance." Bates looked toward Gunnison. "This man violated every known naval law. After stalking and giving chase, boarding without cause or authority, he took it upon himself to fire on a defenseless merchant vessel and sink it. And in the process of a cowardly attack three innocent men were killed! I repeat, there can be only one verdict."

Bates stepped toward Gunnison and, like a revolver, leveled his finger at the accused and held it pointed in midair.

"Gunnison is guilty as charged!"

Captain Lionel Graham, braced on crutches, finished summing up for the defense in a quiet but passionate tone.

". . . there has been a Gunnison in the United States Navy . . . well, as long as there has been a United States Navy. His father, and his father before him, served with honor to themselves and to the fleet in every war this country has ever a fought. A Gunnison was one of the founders of Annapolis."

Graham lifted his face toward the rear of the court-room.

"And Thomas Gunnison's only son, who is here standing by his father, is now a midshipman at the Academy." Graham approached Gunnison, then turned back toward the five officers. "Captain Gunnison has served in combat with distinction, with valor. During the Mexican-American War, after being wounded in action, he still carried out his mission, landing troops at Vera Cruz to reinforce the army of General Winfield Scott. Captain Gunnison has been decorated with the highest medal this nation can bestow."

The old captain placed a hand on the epaulet of Gunnison's right shoulder, then moved with great dignity toward the judges.

"And on that night, off the coast of Africa, Captain Gunnison was witness to murder. He has so sworn on his sacred honor. The murder of hundreds of innocent men, women, and children, flung to their deaths without mercy, without a chance—"

"I must protest!" Bates sprang to his feet. "If the court please—"

Captain Merrill pounded the gavel, but Graham continued.

"Captain Gunnison lowered away boats and gave orders to rescue all hands from the *Jubilee*. More consideration than murderers deserve."

"The defense has gone too far, Your Honor!" Bates protested. "This is not a summation! It is—"

"I'm just about done, gentlemen. Except for this . . . It is the duty of this court, this conscience of our great nation, to proclaim justice done by finding Captain Thomas J. Gunnison—on all charges—innocent."

Graham placed his gnarled hand on the Bible atop the table.

"I swear to you, my hand on this Bible, that Captain Thomas J. Gunnison is . . ."

"Guilty." Captain Garrett Merrill read from the verdict of the court-martial. "On all counts but one. The court finds that the charge of murder was not proved beyond the shadow of a doubt. But on all other counts—guilty. The court has taken into consideration Captain Gunnison's prior distinguished service in passing sentence. It is the sentence of this court that Thomas J. Gunnison is stripped of rank and dishonorably discharged from the United States Navy."

Chapter Four

Most of those still remaining in the courtroom after the verdict was read were quiet and slumped. Even the old building seemed to have sagged just a little.

There were exceptions. Bates and Forrester, along with Connors, stood smiling, nodding, shaking hands, and congratulating each other.

All the court-martial officers except Captain Merrill had left the room by the side door.

Captain Lionel Graham stood, braced by crutches, and took Gunnison's hand.

"I'm sorry, son. I did the best I could."

"Nobody could have done better, sir."

Captain Garrett Merrill approached Gunnison and Graham and extended his hand to the former officer.

"Good luck, Cap—Good luck, Mr. Gunnison."

"That was some verdict," Graham said, "that you and your boys came up with, Garrett."

"I had a hell of a time convincing three of those boys not to hang him."

"I can guess which three," Graham said. "Garrett, let's you and me go and get a drink."

"No, Lionel. Let's you and me go and . . . get drunk."

The two older men started off toward the side door. Captain Merrill turned back and spoke in a low, sincere voice.

"If I can do anything for you, Tom, just let me know."

"You already have, sir."

"And one more thing . . . If it means anything at all . . . I would have done just what you did."

"Thank you, sir. It means a hell of a lot." Gunnison picked up his cap from the table and moved to the aisle toward his son. Bogartis followed.

Jeff still sat in his chair staring ahead. Discant stood next to him and tried to smile as Gunnison approached.

"Well, Jeff," Gunnison put on his cap, "I guess—"

Jeff rose abruptly, looked at his father a moment, then turned his back and walked away.

"I'm sorry, Captain," Discant muttered. "He . . ."

"That's all right, Jim. You two look out for each other."

"Yes, sir." Discant hurried away after his friend.

"Tom."

Gunnison turned to face Adam Forrester. Forrester's mood was pleasant, friendly. Bates and Connors stood next to him. Neither of those two tried to mask his satisfaction as Forrester spoke and extended his hand to Gunnison.

"What the hell, Tom. The books are balanced."

Gunnison's look was neither pleasant nor friendly.

"Let's start all over." Forrester's hand was still extended. "Okay?"

35

Andrew J. Fenady

"Okay." Gunnison nodded slightly. Then he slugged Forrester, knocking him backward over a row of chairs, where he fell to the floor unconscious and stiff as a broomstick.

Connors didn't move. But Bates did, as fast as he could, out of range and out of the courtroom.

Gunnison turned and started to walk, not slowly, not fast, followed by Beauford Bogartis.

"Where do we go from, here, Captain?" Bogartis asked.

"What do you mean . . . 'we'?"

"The Navy quit you—so I'm quitting the Navy. Where do we go from here?"

"Where we've always gone, Mister Bogartis . . . to sea."

Chapter Five

Gunnison and Bogartis went to sea. The country went to hell.

At least it tried . . . and got close enough to smell the smoke. Gunsmoke.

It had been marching inexorably in that direction ever since it learned to walk—even before it was officially born on the fourth of July, 1776.

By 1856 the overture to the Grand Opera that would be called the Civil War already could be heard. Faint rumblings at first in the distance—rumblings that had their origins as early as 1619 when a Dutch ship with twenty African slaves aboard arrived at the English colony of Jamestown, Virginia.

But even a century before that, black plantation slavery had begun in the New World when Spaniards started importing slaves from Africa to take the place of American Indians who had died of overwork and exposure to disease.

Andrew J. Fenady

Under the U.S. Constitution all men were created equal—but not all free. The tolerance of slavery was part of the glue that allowed the states to remain united after the American Revolution. It made for an essential but uneasy unity. The uneasiness and disunity came to climax during the first decade of the second half of the nineteenth century.

In 1820 the Missouri Compromise had provided for Missouri to be admitted to the Union as a slave state and Maine as a free state, and western territories north of Missouri's southern border to be free soil.

At that time Thomas Jefferson wrote regarding slavery, "This momentous question, like a fire bell in the night, awakened and filled me with terror."

He was not alone in his alarm.

Abolitionists vowed to awaken the conscience of the entire nation—at least the northern half—by ringing the liberty bell day and night, until enough people would listen and respond with new laws, or with gunfire.

Abolitionist David Walker published a pamphlet titled "Appeal . . . To the Colored Citizens of the World," calling for a slave revolt. William Lloyd Garrison's antislavery newspaper, *The Liberator*, advocated emancipation. John Brown's cry for black freedom came from the barrels of rifles.

President Franklin Pierce's attempt to compromise, and balance the teeter-totter of north and south—freedom and slavery—fell apart in "Bleeding Kansas" and he failed to gain renomination of the Democratic Party. The convention of 1856 nominated, instead, James Buchanan of Pennsylvania.

Buchanan defeated John C. Fremont, the Republican candidate in 1856, but Buchanan's presidency was doomed to one term almost since its beginning. He was as much, or even more, spineless on the subjects of slav-

38

ery and a strong Union as Pierce. And the country had had enough of equivocation, evasiveness, and avoidance.

Abraham Lincoln stood for a strong Union and against slavery—and the country stood with Lincoln.

So ended the overture to the Grand Opera that would be called the Civil War, and the curtain rose on the bloodiest drama of a country not yet a century old.

The swelling rumble of discontent erupted into gunfire at Fort Sumpter on April 12, 1861—Confederate gunfire, aimed at the heart of the Union, and no longer was it only Kansas bleeding. South Carolina had seceded on December 20, 1860, followed by Mississippi, Florida, Alabama, Georgia, and Louisiana—then Texas, the biggest state, under the governorship of one of the nation's biggest men, Sam Houston.

But Sam Houston was against secession. Years before, when Texas declared its independence, Houston was named commander in chief of the revolutionary troops, the fighting Texians.

After General Antonio López de Santa Anna's overwhelming force defeated and burned the bodies of the Alamo defenders, Houston with 600 Texans crushed Santa Anna's army of 1,250, killing more than 600 and capturing the rest, including General Santa Anna.

Sam Houston was elected the first president of the Republic of Texas and led the movement for Texas to join the United States. And now he was governor, and in spite of his impassioned opposition, Texas voted to secede.

Houston warned his fellow Texans with his prediction of what was to come: "Your fathers and husbands, your sons and brothers, will be herded at the point of bayonet . . . while I believe with you in the doctrine of states' rights, the North is determined to preserve the

Union. They move with the steady momentum and perseverance of a mighty avalanche, and I fear they will overwhelm the South."

Another Southerner took the opposite stance.

Robert E. Lee had been the most distinguished officer in the United States Army. He had graduated from West Point at the head of his class in 1829. He had served with honor and glory in the Mexican War at Vera Cruz, Churubusco, and Chapultepec. He became superintendent at West Point and saw frontier duty in Texas.

It was Lee who commanded the detachment that suppressed the uprising led by John Brown at Harpers Ferry.

And it was Robert E. Lee who first was offered command of the U.S. Army at the outbreak of the Civil War. A monumental struggle ensued within himself—the Union or his native Virginia? He wrote to his sister, who lived in the North, "With all my devotion to the Union and the feeling of loyalty and duty of an American citizen, I can not raise my hand against my relatives, my children, my home. My Virginia.

"I hope I may never be called upon to raise my sword."

But, of course, Lee was called upon to raise his sword. He did so reluctantly but effectively.

Other Union officers born south of the Mason-Dixon line who decided to go along with Lee included Joseph E. Johnston, J. E. B. Stuart, P. G. T. Beauregard, T. J. Jackson, Jubal Early, and Albert Sidney Johnston. Once the flower of the U.S. Army, these officers made up a deadly bouquet now dedicated to the cause of states' rights.

Their dedication proved costly to the Union cause. Led by Lee, at first they seemed invincible, winning bat-

Andrew J. Fenady

40

tle after battle: Fort Sumter, Lexington, Belmont, Shiloh, Fort Royal, Bull Run.

The last months of 1861 and the first months of 1862 were crowned with victory after victory for the South.

Only at sea did the North prevail, because at the start of the war the South had no navy at all.

The Union possessed more than ninety warships. About half were sailing vessels, the other half steam-driven with nine-inch rifles on the gun decks and heavier weapons mounted on the spar decks.

Even so, it was a formidable task to try to blockade more than 3,500 miles of Confederate coastline and control the Mississippi and Tennessee Rivers.

The Confederates turned anything that could float into gunboats and did their best to build and buy a navy. But the South could never match the dozens of five hundred-ton "ninety-day gunboats"—built in less then three months, from keel-laying to commissioning—that were turned out by the North.

The Union's most telling naval action early in 1862 was not the victory over the South's ironclad *Merrimac*, but Flag Officer David G. Farragut's capture of New Orleans on April 12, 1862, seizing command of the Mississippi basin and bottling up the Confederacy's flow to the sea.

But the land battles and Southern victories took a heavy toll of the Union's men, matériel, and money.

The Southern cavalry and infantry and guerrilla contingents continued to drain the physical and financial resources of the North.

During the six years since his discharge from the Navy, Captain Thomas J. Gunnison had spent most of the time at sea. And while at sea, most of the time First Officer

Beauford Bogartis was at his side, or near enough to hear and execute Gunnison's orders.

Gunnison was always in demand, hired as captain by trading companies to sail ships into harbors that were too shallow, reefs that were too dangerous—haul cargo that no other captain would carry—and he received top dollar and a percentage of the profits from his voyages.

Even as a naval officer he had shown a streak of independence, but since his discharge that streak had become even deeper and wider, as he charted a course through the seas and through life, on his own terms.

He had left the past in his wake, never looked back, never reflected on what might have been.

The only pause on his course straight ahead was a letter from Captain Lionel Graham, written from his deathbed, bidding Gunnison "farewell until we meet again in heaven or hell, or some stormy sea in between."

Gunnison and Bogartis broke out a bottle of whiskey and drank it down in silence, then squeezed the cork back into the bottle and tossed it out to sea.

Through those six years, on land and at sea, Gunnison never mentioned his son's name and Bogartis knew better than to bring up the subject.

By December of 1862 there had been someone on Gunnison's sea trail for more than three months. The search led to San Francisco.

San Francisco—the cool gray city, gateway to the Orient, Alaska, Australia, the South Pacific, and around the Horn to all the ports on the east coast of the United States.

San Francisco—the largest natural harbor in the world, with enough room around the bay's four hundred seventy-five square miles to berth every ship afloat on the seas.

Spanish and English galleons had sailed past the

Double Eagles

Golden Gate as early as the sixteenth century, unaware of the fog-shrouded bay until 1775, when Captain Don Manuel Ayala, lost in the fog, steered his Spanish packet *San Carlos* into the bay and spent weeks surveying his wondrous find before sailing out again to spread word of the discovery to all the world.

Within a year, Captain Juan Bautista de Anza brought a boatload of settlers and named the colony Yerba Buena, because of the blanket of green mint that covered the hillsides. The two hundred inhabitants raised sheep and cattle and families until 1846, when the U.S. Naval vessel *Portsmouth*, under the command of Commander John Montgomery, landed an armed contingent ashore, raised the American flag, and proclaimed the territory a possession of the United States. The Spaniards were in no position to decline the proclamation.

In 1847 the town council officially named the village San Francisco, and within a year the population doubled. Then James Marshall found a glittering substance at Sutters Mill and unleashed a stampede of "forty-niners," who swelled the city to over twenty-five thousand seekers of fortune. They came by land and sea, Italians, Greeks, Scandinavians, Irish, English, and all breeds from all points of the compass.

And on a December day of 1862 there came a man named Justin Stewart, U.S. Navy Department—a tall, rope-thin man, well-dressed, white-haired, weary-eyed and pale—a man looking for Captain Thomas J. Gunnison.

Chapter Six

Justin Stewart, with brittle steps, walked along the bustling waterfront street as a newspaper boy hawked the news of yet another Confederate victory.

"Rebels rout Yanks at Fredricksberg . . . beat back Burnside! North suffers heavy casualties! Yanks withdraw!! Chronicle here. Paper, mister? Rebels rout Yanks!"

Stewart continued walking through the crowd, mostly men and most of them men of the sea, in uniform and mufti, toward the tall masts of sailing ships in the harbor and other vessels tied up along the wharf.

He paused near the bow of a merchant ship and took note of the name: *Phantom Hope*.

The gray-haired man adjusted his hat, then moved toward the gangway, where two men were descending side by side, one white, the other black.

As both men touched down on the wharf, a crewman called from the ship's rail.

"Mr. Joseph . . . Cookie . . . Will one of you bring me back a newspaper?"

Both men nodded. Stewart addressed the white man.

"Mr. Joseph, is it?"

"No. I'm Cookie. This here's Mr. Joseph—he's the second mate."

"Uh . . . I'm s-sorry," Stewart stammered.

"That's all right," the second mate replied. "Natural mistake. What can I do for you?"

"Well, I just wanted to verify something."

"Uh-huh," Cookie cackled. "Now that you've verified who's the mate and who's the cook . . . what else?"

"Is Captain Gunnison the owner and master of this vessel, *Phantom Hope*?"

"He sure as hell is. Isn't he, Mister Joseph?"

"And of other things." Mister Joseph nodded.

"Is he aboard?"

"He sure as hell isn't. Is he, Mister Joseph?"

"Not currently."

"Will he be back soon?"

"Depends on what you mean by soon. Wouldn't you agree, Mister Joseph?"

Mister Joseph nodded in agreement.

"What I mean is . . . would it be wiser to wait, or to . . ."

"Was I you, I wouldn't wait," Cookie said.

"Why not?"

"Because we won't be taking off for a few days . . . and in the meantime, Captain Gunnison's got business ashore. Ain't that so, Mister Joseph?"

"That's certainly so."

"Can you tell me where, gentlemen?"

"On the Barbary Coast." Cookie scratched on the stubble of gray whiskers sprouting out of his leathery face.

Andrew J. Fenady

"Could you squeeze that down geographically? *Where* on the Barbary Coast?"

"Well, let me see . . ."

"Perhaps I could persuade one or both of you to take me. . . ." Stewart reached into his pocket and withdrew a wallet.

"Save your money, mister," Cookie said.

"It would be worth—"

"Not enough. Both Mister Joseph and me is peaceable sorts . . . and there's no tellin' if Captain Gunnison is at war or peace right now."

"I don't understand what you mean."

"I mean," Cookie looked up at the sun, "it's hard to tell which saloon he'll be at about now. Wouldn't you say so, Mister Joseph?"

"So I'd say, Cookie." The black man smiled for the first time. He was over six feet in his sea boots, broad of chest, in a blue pea coat with two rows of six brass buttons tapering down to a narrow waist.

"Try the North Star, Mister. . . ." Cookie paused.

"Stewart, Justin Stewart. I'll do that. Pleased to have met you . . . both." Stewart turned, adjusted his hat again, and started to walk away . . . as if it hurt to walk, and it did.

"If he and the first mate, Mister Bogartis, ain't at the North Star," Cookie called out, "try the Pair-A-Dice."

"Thank you," Justin Stewart acknowledged without looking back. "Thank you very much."

As Justin Stewart turned from the wharf and the bay and headed toward the battalion of bars along the Barbary Coast, he thought to himself that only a little over three months earlier, in Baltimore, he had stood on a wharf and looked out across the Chesapeake Bay toward the Atlantic.

46

And today, just minutes ago, he had stood on another wharf—across the entire continent—and looked out across the Bay of San Francisco toward the Pacific.

Across the entire continent.

From the Atlantic to the Pacific.

Manifest Destiny.

A magnificent dream.

"Our great mission," Senator John C. Calhoun had said years before, "is to occupy this vast domain."

And as early as 1845 an article had appeared in an eastern newspaper: "Our Manifest Destiny is to overspread the continent allotted by Providence for the free development of our yearly multiplying millions. We will realize our Manifest Destiny."

From east to west the nation was one.

But not from north to south.

The magnificent dream had become a bloody nightmare. A nightmare that had torn the nation asunder and pitted neighbor against neighbor and brother against brother.

It was Lincoln's conceit that this nation could not endure half slave and half free.

And now the only way to put the nation together again was with the paste of blood.

But the engine of war also was fueled by guns, ammunition, and money.

And that was part of Justin Stewart's mission. He had crossed the continent by rail, by boat, and by stagecoach in search of the man who was essential in helping him carry out his mission. The search was coming to a conclusion now along a string of saloons on the Barbary Coast.

And the saloon industry obviously thrived as Justin Stewart made his way through the colorful parade of

men—and on this throughway, quite a few women, ladies currently on their feet.

He had stopped and asked for directions, which were
freely given, along with offers of entertaining diversion
at matinee prices. He accepted the directions gratefully
and declined the diversions regretfully—or so he said.

Stewart walked past the signs, the music, and the
barkers of various emporiums—the Dirty Doubloon,
the Breakers, the Hard Knot—then paused in front of
the North Star. He was about to enter, but before he
did, a sailor wearing the stripes of a first mate came
careening through the batwings of the Pair-A-Dice next
door.

This captured Stewart's attention. He watched as the
first mate lifted himself out of the gutter and shook himself off, then rushed back through the batwings,
wherein the sounds of knuckles against flesh, board
against bone, grunts, groans, and various unidentifiable
battle noises abounded.

Soon after, a bartender came flying through the same
batwings and landed where lately the first officer had
sprawled. But the bartender was unable to rise. The first
officer's face appeared above the batwings and grinned
with satisfaction.

"Excuse me." Stewart took a cautious step forward.
"Do you happen to be Mister Bogartis?"

"I do."

"My name is Stewart."

"Happy to make your acquaintance," Mister Bogartis
replied, and disappeared inside.

Justin Stewart thought it wise to take the precaution
of waiting in the street until the noises from the Pair-A-
Dice subsided.

It didn't take long.

When Stewart thought it safe, he entered, just in time

to see a big man dispatch a burly brute with a right cross, then grab another sailor, who swung a board as the big man ducked, lifted the swinger, and tossed him board and all into the back bar.

With that the brawl proceeded to wind down.

Mister Bogartis sat on a table and fingered a loose tooth. The big man looked around. There appeared to be no more to conquer.

Gunnison walked across the room toward Mister Bogartis. The captain was grayer, a stone heavier and untidier. His crew, a polyglot—American, Scandinavian, Mexican, and those of indeterminate breed—watched, smiled, and even clapped as their captain walk by.

Justin Stewart treaded his way through the wreckage, human and otherwise, and approached Gunnison as the captain took a gold watch from his pocket, flipped the lid, and checked to make sure the timepiece was still ticking. It was.

"You'd be the one," Stewart said.

"Which one?"

"The one called Gunnison. Captain Thomas J. Gunnison. Late of the U.S. Navy."

"About six years late." Gunnison put the gold watch back into his pocket.

"Justin Stewart." Stewart extended his hand. "U.S. Navy Department."

Gunnison looked at Bogartis, then shook hands with Stewart, whose hand was delicate and enervated.

"You're somewhat off course, aren't you, Mr. Stewart?"

"I don't think so," Stewart replied. "And neither does Gideon Welles."

"Who's Gideon Welles?" Bogartis inquired, still working at the tooth, now with his thumb.

"Secretary of the Navy," Gunnison said. "Mister

49

Stewart, this is Mister Bogartis, my first officer."

"Yes." Stewart nodded. "I've already had the pleasure of his acquaintance just outside the . . . threshold of Pair-A-Dice."

"Did you just happen to pass by?" Gunnison smiled.

"No, Captain—I've come thousands of miles to find you and your ship. Some of your crew gave me directions, very good directions, and here I am."

"Would you care for a drink after such a long journey?"

"Not here, but may we go back to your ship and talk . . . business?"

"If it's U.S. Navy business, I think you're wasting your time . . . but my time's not all that important, so let's go."

"Very good."

Gunnison started toward the threshold of Pair-A-Dice, followed by Stewart, Bogartis, and the rest of the crew. The bartender was making his way through the batwings and wiping some leaking blood away from his broken nose.

"You leaving, Captain?" the bartender asked.

"Business, Jake." Gunnison reached into his pocket, withdrew a wad of money, and put it into Jake's palm. "This ought to cover the drinks and damage."

"Yeah, except for my nose. But you're always welcome at the Pair-A-Dice, Captain . . . and you too, Mister Bogartis." Jake tucked the wad of money under his apron and into his pocket.

Chapter Seven

They arrived at and walked up the gangway in the same order—Gunnison, Stewart, Bogartis, and the rest of the crew in various stages of sobriety and disrepair.

Mr. Joseph and Cookie were on the deck waiting.

"Good afternoon, Mister Joseph." Gunnison greeted his second officer. "Everything in order?"

"Good afternoon, sir," Mister Joseph responded. "Everything in perfect order." Then he smiled as he looked toward Justin Stewart. "I see you found him."

"In 'paradise.'"

"Cookie," Gunnison said. "We might have a guest for supper tonight."

"Aye, sir."

"And make up something special. Mister Stewart represents the U.S. Navy Department, and he's come a long way to chew the fat of confabulation."

"Aye, aye, sir."

* * *

51

Andrew J. Fenady

Captain Gunnison's cabin was appointed just about the way Justin Stewart expected, except for the number of books on the shelves. Many more than he expected. History, poetry, Shakespeare, mathematics, science, Darwin and the Bible, along with too many others that Stewart did not take time to note.

Gunnison brought forth a bottle and three glasses from the sideboard and placed them on his desk. He started to pour.

Justin Stewart coughed and breathed irregularly. He rubbed at his chest as inconspicuously as he could manage. He didn't manage very well.

"Drink, Mister Stewart?"

"I'd better not."

"Might clear up that . . . congestion."

"It might at that." Stewart looked at Bogartis, then back to Gunnison as the captain half filled the three glasses.

"Sit down, Mister Stewart. You can talk in front of Mister Bogartis. Besides being the first officer, he has an interest in this vessel."

All three took a glass and sat, Gunnison behind his desk.

"Confusion to the enemy." Gunnison grinned.

"An appropriate toast, Captain." Stewart sipped while Gunnison and Bogartis each took a hearty swallow. "Let's get down to business."

"Let's." Gunnison poured again.

"I . . . that is, the government, our government, wants to charter this vessel for a voyage with a certain cargo around the Horn to Baltimore."

"When?"

"Immediately."

"That soon?"

"Yes."

52

"Well, I'm sorry, but I already have a charter."

"I'll take care of that. The government will."

"What's the cargo?"

"The cargo is two thousand Henry rifles and enough ammunition to probably win the war."

Gunnison finished his drink again, and so did Bogartis. This time Bogartis poured.

"Why don't you haul it overland?" Gunnison asked.

"Winter. The mountains'll be impassable to the north, and the Southern Route is, well, the Southern Route."

"Why my ship?"

"Because, number one, this ship's of Mexican registry and the Confederate corsairs aren't as likely to attack a vessel flying the Mexican flag as they are an American ship."

"Number two?"

"Because you're the best sailor on the west coast—"

"Any coast." Bogartis interrupted.

"—and you've rounded the Horn a dozen times."

"Fourteen." Bogartis grinned. "Tom knows the name of every wave between here and the Horn."

"What terms do you . . . does the government propose?"

"Twenty thousand in advance. An additional twenty thousand when the cargo is delivered."

Gunnison and Bogartis looked at each other and drank again, simultaneously.

"The cargo will be put aboard at night. The entire mission must be shrouded in secrecy. And I will be a passenger aboard the vessel."

"I don't want to sound skeptical, Mister Stewart, but it's a long voyage and you don't look like you're quite up to the trip."

"Don't you worry about that."

"I won't so long as I get the advance money."

"You will."

"Good."

"I cannot stress, Captain, what this means to the country, to the . . ."

"You don't have to beat any drums, nor wave any flags, Mister Stewart. We've got a deal, and I'll live up to my end of the bargain."

"One more thing, Captain . . ."

"Just one?"

"Yes. You must agree that a small contingent from the Navy will come aboard as escorts."

"I agree . . . so long as *I'm* the captain."

It was past midnight, and winches strained as the cargo was being loaded. Gunnison and Bogartis glanced at each other and noted that certain crates were heavier than others, but said nothing while Justin Stewart stood beside them on the deck of the *Phantom Hope* and steeled himself against the damp, fog-glutted night.

The loading procedure was under the command of Second Mate Joseph, who issued commands in a calm but authoritative demeanor.

"Mister Rankin, ease up on that line or you'll miss the hatch by two feet."

"Aye, sir."

"Your Mister Joseph appears to be quite competent," Stewart observed.

"He's not my Mister Joseph," Gunnison said. "And yes, he is quite competent."

"Isn't it unusual for a Negro to be an officer?"

"He's an unusual Negro, or maybe he isn't. That's one of the things your Mister Lincoln's fighting for."

"How do you mean?"

"I mean Mister Joseph is a former slave . . . a runaway. Made his way to New Haven, appropriately enough—that's where we met. Asked for a job . . . any job."

"Was he a sailor?"

"They don't have many sailors on plantations. Nope. But he figured he was better off at sea than on land . . . and so did I."

"So you made him a second mate?"

"Nope . . . seaman helper. But he worked his way up. . . . Could barely read, but he borrowed every book in my cabin—mathematics, science, astronomy, even poetry. Took him almost five years, but he got there, learning and working. All I did was give him the same chance as anybody else."

"Captain Gunnison . . ."

"Yes?"

"I think the United States Navy made a great mistake—"

"We all make mistakes." Gunnison pointed to the wharf. "What the hell is that?"

Pulled by teams of straining horses, two heavily loaded wagons covered by tarps, and with two naval officers and several sailors aboard, groaned then creaked to a stop alongside the *Phantom Hope*. The two officers debarked and approached the gangway.

Mister Bogartis looked at Gunnison as the pair of officers walked up the gangway toward the deck.

Lieutenant Jeff Gunnison and Ensign James Discant stepped aboard Captain Gunnison's ship. Discant saluted.

"You don't have to salute me, Mister Discant," Gunnison said. He looked at his son, then at Stewart. "Did you know about this? About my son being one of the naval escorts?"

"I did."

"And you didn't see fit to mention it?"

"I didn't. Does it make a difference?"

"Not to me."

"And not to the Navy Department. That's all that matters. That and the cargo."

"Fair enough." Gunnison pointed to the lead wagon on the wharf. "What's in there?"

"Cannons. Two of them." Jeff spoke for the first time.

"The other wagon?"

"Balls," Jeff said. "Cannonballs."

"These two officers have compiled a fine record together," Stewart observed. "And I'm told they've been friends for a long time."

"That's right." Gunnison nodded. "Jim's been like a second son. He . . . well, I'm sure they'll do their duty. All right." He pointed to the wagons again. "Get that stuff aboard. We'll leave in forty-eight hours with the tide." Gunnison looked into the eyes of his son. "Anything else?"

"Yes." Jeff paused for a beat. "I would have preferred another captain."

"You might have a preference," Gunnison said. "But you don't have a choice."

Less than twenty-four hours later, a single-mast dinghy with two men aboard, Hiram Able and Joshua Bender, approached a sailing ship, *Corsair*, anchored in the darkness outside the bay. A frigate flying no flag.

Bender waited in the dinghy as Hiram Able made his way aboard and toward a man who stood in the shadows.

"Captain?"

"Yes."

"The *Phantom Hope* sails with her cargo tomorrow night."

Double Eagles

Captain Adam Forrester stepped out of the shadows and was joined by First Mate Connors.

"So do we." Forrester smiled, struck a match with his thumbnail, and lit a fresh cigar.

Chapter Eight

The course, south by southeast. The sunlit ship, *Phantom Hope*, had been at sea six days, rushing under full sail of three masts, with the wind at her quarter and all sheets to starboard, leaving a milky foam in her wake.

Far behind there was something else in her wake. A hunter stalking its unsuspecting prey, floating high in the water without cargo in her belly, but hungry to devour what lay in the hold of the ship it tailed.

The *Corsair* was too far behind to see or hear the white puffs and the sounds of cannon fire erupting from the heavily laden *Phantom Hope* as she caught the wind and forged ahead.

Again and again the pair of cannons were loaded and fired at an imaginary enemy at sea.

Captain Gunnison, Mister Bogartis, and Justin Stewart watched as Lieutenant Jeff Gunnison, with Ensign James Discant at his side, drilled the crews, barking commands, adjusting elevation, firing and loading faster.

Each carronade fired a 68-pound shot, weighed just 3,600 pounds, and was an inch short of five feet. Since it was light, it needed only four men to handle it, mounted high on the ship, with a sliding carriage that allowed it to be trained through a wide arc.

The advantage of such carronade was that it allowed small ships, merchant ships, frigates, and suchlike to carry a punch out of proportion to their size.

Each gun was primed, with handspike men trained to left or right. Then came elevation, lock cocked, and on command, the trigger line was pulled with "suitable jerk."

"He's fired more cannonballs on this voyage," said Mister Bogartis, "than Andy-by-God-Jackson did all his life. What the hell's he shootin' at?"

"He won't be shooting much longer, Mister Bogartis." Gunnison looked up at the sky, then out over the green horizon. "The sea's turned stormy."

"Good," said Bogartis. "I'm going deaf."

"And I'm going below," said Justin Stewart as he coughed, rubbed his chest, and walked away.

The cannonading ceased as the *Phantom Hope* crashed through fierce breakers. The ship, pressed under by wind and sea, leaped up and out across the endless expanse.

Captain Gunnison pointed above and gave command to shorten sail as the vessel swayed and pitched.

Even before his captain's command, and after all the years and all the voyages together, Mister Bogartis knew what the captain wanted and went about the necessary business of making ready to weather one more storm.

* * *

Each night since the voyage began there was an empty chair at the captain's table.

Seated were Captain Gunnison, First Mate Bogartis, Second Mate Joseph, and Ensign Discant. Absent tonight, and every other night, Lieutenant Jeff Gunnison. The lieutenant ate supper alone in the cabin he shared with Jeff Discant.

Throughout the voyage father and son had not exchanged a dozen words, and then only when necessary.

A couple of times Justin Stewart tried to force conversation between the two by asking some question regarding the North–South conflict or the cargo, the voyage, or anything that came to mind at the moment when the two men were together. But each time Jeff slipped away, managing never to speak directly to his father.

Mister Bogartis, as he had done since the trial, steered clear of the storm clouds that hovered around the two men.

Those at the captain's table had just about finished supper, and Cookie was pouring more coffee all around.

There was a bottle with six fingers of whiskey in front of Gunnison. He emptied the bottle into his cup, rose, and left the cabin, cup in hand.

The sea was calm. The night had two moons—one in the star-splattered sky and another dancing on the starboard waters along the Tropic of Cancer.

Gunnison looked from the moon in the sky to the moon in the sea, sipped from his cup, and thought of the night his son was born. One of the few nights he had managed to be at home since his wedding, one of the times between voyages. The baby was born strong and healthy. Angela almost died. Gunnison had knelt at her bedside and prayed, vowing to God and to her, even though she was unconscious, that if God made her well, if she survived and regained her health, he would give up the Navy, give up the sea . . . and stay with her always.

When she did get well, Gunnison told her of his vow to God and to her. But Angela only smiled, kissed him tenderly, and said she could not speak for God, but for herself, she wanted the man she married, a sailor who went where he belonged, and when he returned their time together would be more precious—she did not want some sailor who was marooned in the dry dock of regret.

Their time together was more precious than they realized, and shorter. Much shorter.

"Captain? Are you all right, sir?"

It was a sailor named Rankin who spoke. Alan Rankin. He had been aboard the *Phantom Hope* for three voyages. A quiet man, somewhat older than the rest of the crew, maybe fifty, who kept to himself mostly, but did his work and did it well. And a man who somehow seemed to be nearby when any of the rest of the crew needed help of any kind. He was not a big man but had an inner strength, a tender strength, and a comforting voice with words worth listening to.

"How's that?" Gunnison looked at Rankin.

" 'The waters are hidden as with stone, and the face of the deep is frozen.' So is your face, Captain. I only asked if you were all right, sir."

"I'm quite all right, Mister Rankin, and that will be all."

"Yes, sir." Rankin started to turn.

"Mister Rankin. That quotation . . . from the Bible, isn't it?"

"Yes, sir. Book of Job. The Voice Out of The Whirlwind. Good night, sir."

"Good night . . . and thank you, Mister Rankin."

61

Andrew J. Fenady

Gunnison took the last sip of whiskey from the cup and saw that James Discant stood nearby. He had obviously watched and heard what had happened.

"Are you going to inquire after my health too, Mister Discant?"

"Captain . . ."

"Because if you're of a mind to, don't bother."

"I don't mean to interfere sir. . . ."

"Then don't."

"It's just that I understand your point of view, sir."

"Do you?"

"I think you were right and the court was wrong."

"My son doesn't."

"But you don't know what it's been like for Jeff."

"Go ahead and tell me."

"It was a terrible burden for him to go on at Annapolis. . . ."

"Must've been real hell."

"He could have quit. That would have been the easy way. But Jeff's not a quitter. He chose to go on with a name that . . ."

"Say it . . . that's been disgraced."

"I was with him more than once when someone said something and he . . ."

"Defended my honor . . . or was it dishonor? It would have meant a lot more if he had just shook hands after the trial." Gunnison looked down at the empty cup. "But then I guess from his point of view that would've been asking too much."

"You know that he finished at the top of his class. He'll make a great officer . . ."

"And a gentleman?"

"Someday Jeff'll change his mind about you, sir."

"Who gives a damn?!" Gunnison turned, empty cup in hand, and walked away, his face still frozen.

*   *   *

From the storeroom below, Gunnison had procured a fresh bottle of whiskey, Tennessee bourbon, but something had been preying on his mind since that night in San Francisco when he watched the cargo being loaded aboard the *Phantom Hope*.

In the hold of the ship, he set the bottle on top of a crate, then placed the cup upside down on the nape of the bottle. He took a knife out of his pocket, opened the blade, and cut the rope holding fast one of the long crates, then pried open the lid.

He took out one of the long guns, one of the dozen Henrys that were in each crate. A beautiful—if you could call a gun that—well-balanced rifle, the latest model. He cocked, then clicked the trigger of the Henry—a .44-caliber, fifteen-shot type that weighed nine and a half pounds with a brass breech.

This was one of the thousands of rifles that had been shipped west to the army forts built to protect the settlers and teach the Indians respect and rectitude for their white brethren.

When the war broke out between the North and South, the Union needed all the manpower that was available. Many of the forts were abandoned and the settlers and Indians were left to their own devices. Thousands of Henrys, still crated, were left behind in warehouses.

Now the North needed those rifles to teach respect and rectitude to its Southern brethren. Hence the long voyage around the Horn to some yet-to-be-determined battlefields.

Captain Gunnison set the Henry back in the box, sealed up the lid, then turned and moved toward a crate with a different configuration.

Since the beginning of the bargain, Justin Stewart had

Andrew J. Fenady

revealed information to Gunnison in dribs and drabs, one dollop at a time. Captain Gunnison felt there was still more to be revealed—and that that revelation lay in some of the other crates.

Chapter Nine

Something was wrong.

The morning dawned bright and brisk and the wind swept the face of the ocean clean. The waves flashed and rippled in clear weather along the hull of the *Phantom Hope*, but something was wrong, and Captain Gunnison knew it as he emerged from his cabin onto the deck.

He rushed toward Rankin, who was at the helm. Bogartis and Mister Joseph were right behind him, then Jeff and Discant.

"You're off course, Mister Rankin!" Gunnison barked.

"The wheel's locked, sir. Something's fouled up the rudder!"

"Ship off starboard!" the lookout hollered from above.

Gunnison and the rest of the crew on deck turned as Justin Stewart appeared from below. Gunnison grabbed

Andrew J. Fenady

a telescope from Bogartis and sighted to starboard.

By now the ship could be seen with the naked eye, but through the telescope Gunnison could see the Stars and Bars being hoisted and make out the frigate's name.

"Confederate!" Gunnison shouted. "The *Corsair*."

"That's Forrester's ship!" Stewart exclaimed.

"Sir," Rankin called out. "We can't maneuver."

"Mister Bogartis," Gunnison said. "Get a rope. I'm going down there."

"Captain . . ."

"Get a rope, Mister Bogartis!"

Lieutenant Jeff Gunnison moved quickly toward the cannons on deck, with Ensign James Discant right behind him.

Captain Gunnison removed the watch and chain from his pocket and handed them to Cookie.

"Hold this."

On the deck of the *Corsair* Forrester grinned and lit a cigar. Connors stood next to him as the ship drove straight ahead with the wind astern.

"Fish in a barrel." Forrester inhaled the smoke. "Prepare to fire."

"Aye, sir."

The *Corsair* advanced, now maneuvering adroitly as the *Phantom Hope* plowed ahead in a defenseless straight course. Gunnison, holding a long knife, was being lowered by a rope to the waterline, then below. The *Corsair* fired the first volley as her sails flapped and fluttered.

The battle was joined as guns from both ships erupted. The *Corsair* had more and heavier cannon. The *Phantom Hope* was hit just above the waterline, then again, splintering the mizzenmast. But the *Hope*'s two cannons were more accurate, even without benefit of

66

maneuver. Cannonballs smashed into the *Corsair*'s deck.

Below water at the *Hope*'s stern Gunnison struggled to loosen, untangle, and cut the heavy netting twisted into the rudder. A cannonball exploded nearby, rocking the *Hope* and Gunnison. He surfaced, breathed deep, and dove again.

The netting was hopelessly twisted and entwined. Gunnison pulled and cut at the tangled shroud, and at the same time clung to it as the ship lumbered forward, rocking from the effects of the *Corsair*'s firepower. After more than three minutes below the surface he had made little progress freeing the ship's entangled rudder.

Gunnison felt his lungs tighten, ready to explode. Still he slashed through the water at the coiled netting that collared the rudder. Again and again, with all the strength that was left, he cut and tore away at the web that snared the ship . . . until the netting was freed from the rudder and washed away.

His head throbbed, his eyes bulged, and his lungs pleaded for air, as he let loose the knife and upsurged with both hands and legs to the surface.

On the deck of the *Phantom Hope* Rankin felt the ship respond to his turn of the wheel.

"Mister Bogartis!" he called out. "He's done it! She's free!"

"Hard to port!" Bogartis ordered, then turned to Jeff. "I'll bring her alongside for you, Lieutenant. Give 'em hell!"

The ship came to, and rolled in the long sea. Canvas flapped and boomed, and the halyards slacked and jerked taut.

The next volley from the *Corsair* came nowhere near the eluding ship.

"Fire!" Lieutenant Gunnison commanded.

Both guns hit their marks. The mainmast of the *Corsair* cracked and splintered, sails ripping apart. Wood and canvas crashed onto the deck. Men fell bleeding. Some died, including the helmsman, as the ship lurched then loafed with the wind, disabled, devastated.

Forrester spit out the cigar and raced to the wheel. It failed to respond. The *Corsair* was dead in the water.

Gunnison swam hard and fast until he grabbed hold of the rope still dangling from the *Hope*'s deck, and hollered up to Bogartis and Cookie leaning over the rail.

"Hoist away!"

Mister Joseph held on to the line as both Jeff and Discant rushed up next to Bogartis and Cookie.

"Mister Joseph," Bogartis said, "get that damn fool up here. The rest of you lend a hand." Bogartis took the watch and chain away from Cookie. "Here, give me that before you drop it overboard."

Bogartis held the timepiece and looked at Lieutenant Gunnison and Ensign Discant.

"Good shooting, boys. Andy-by-God-Jackson woulda been proud of you."

Captain Gunnison climbed over the rail, helped by Mister Joseph and Cookie. He wiped at his face as his son approached, followed by Discant.

"Are you all right, sir?" It was Discant who asked.

Gunnison nodded as his son spoke to him.

"I can sink her."

"No." Gunnison looked out toward the disabled Corsair.

"Why not?"

"Because we'd have to take aboard survivors . . . prisoners. We already got our hands full." Gunnison took his watch from Bogartis, who looked at the two young officers and grinned.

"Sir," one of the crewmen approached and addressed

the captain, "Mister Stewart's been hit. I don't think he's going to . . ."

"Let's get him down below. Mister Bogartis, Jeff, in my cabin."

Justin Stewart, barely conscious, near death, lay in Gunnison's bunk as the captain leaned over him. Bogartis and Jeff stood by.

"Captain . . ."

"Yes, Mister Stewart, I'm here. Jeff, close that door."

"What?" The lieutenant looked puzzled.

"I said close that door."

Jeff Gunnison obeyed.

"Captain . . ."

"Mister Stewart, I'm sorry we don't have a doctor aboard, but you'll be all right. . . ."

"No, I won't. . . . You were right . . . I won't finish the voyage, but you . . ."

"We'll get through."

"Something . . . I've got to tell you . . ."

"About our cargo?"

Stewart nodded.

"The rifles?" Jeff took a step closer.

"No . . . more important."

"The gold," Gunnison said.

"Yes . . . the gold."

Jeff looked at his father, then back at the man in the bunk, who struggled to speak.

"Listen . . . 768,000 double eagles . . . minted in San Francisco . . . never circulated . . . fifteen million dollars . . . government desperate . . . needs to finance war . . . never mind guns and ammunition . . . get gold to United States . . . that's your mission . . . you hear . . . Capt . . ."

Justin Stewart was dead.

"I hear," said Captain Thomas J. Gunnison.

Chapter Ten

December is the month of shortest days and longest nights. Darkest nights. But that December of 1862 was made up of the darkest days and nights since the revolution of 1775—and the bleakest.

He had been elected as the sixteenth president of the United States, and for a time it looked as if he might be the last president of the United States—as that nation was conceived.

In 1860 Abraham Lincoln's tall shadow fell across Washington, D.C.

Another, darker, deadlier shadow fell across the length and breadth of the nation and plunged the country into an Armageddon of uncertainty and despair.

The founding fathers had created a nation that had no precedent. Instead of the people being answerable to the government and its leaders, the government and its leaders were answerable to the people.

"We the people of the United States, in order to form

a more perfect Union . . . ," the Constitution began, but by the time Lincoln was elected the people were no longer united and some states had already repudiated the framework of the founding fathers by seceding, and by punctuating their right to secede with gunfire.

The Confederate cause for secession had, so far, also been punctuated by a series of victories for the South and setbacks for the Union. During the past few months:

Jefferson Davis had been inaugurated as permanent president of the Confederate government, officially dividing the nation.

Lincoln had removed General George B. McClellan as Federal General in Chief and had yet to find a winning commander for his army. The Union Army's command had gone from General Winfield Scott to General George McClellan to General Ambrose E. Burnside to General Joseph Hooker to General George Gordon Meade, but none had matched the winning wizardry of Robert E. Lee and the South's other general officers.

Lincoln had called for three hundred thousand three-year enlistments, but the enlistments were slow to materialize, and antiwar and anti-Lincoln sentiments had materialized.

The Second Battle of Bull Run ended in a Federal rout.

Lee reached Frederick, Maryland.

Jackson captured twelve thousand Union troops at Harpers Ferry.

Stuart destroyed Chambersburg, Pennsylvania.

Lee defeated Burnside at the Battle of Fredericksburg.

Sherman's attack on Chickasaw Bluffs above Vicksburg was repulsed.

And during a bleak winter day a meeting took place

in the office of the president of what remained of the United States.

Abraham Lincoln stood looking out the window behind his desk. The others in the room, all cabinet officers, were Secretary of Treasury Salmon P. Chase, Secretary of War Simon Cameron, and Secretary of the Navy Gideon Welles.

The tall man at the window had been heralded and hailed as a Mid-Century Messiah by many and cursed and damned as the Abolitionist Ape by almost as many.

The war had worn on his face and mind and on his soul, but his resolve was as fierce and unbending as it had been at the beginning, no matter what the cost.

"Unfortunately, gentlemen," Lincoln said, still looking out at the lightly falling snow, "military striking power is determined by the economy." He turned and faced the three men seated in the room. "Valor and devotion are not enough to win a war."

"Mister President . . ." Simon Cameron, the Secretary of War, started to comment, but the President continued, paying no heed.

"If so, the South already would have won. Gentlemen, proliferating casualties have reached every community, touched nearly every home. And still the war profiteers are numerous and blatant, while people find the burden almost too much to bear."

"Mister President." Salmon P. Chase, the Secretary of Treasury, rose from his chair. "During the past year industry was not geared to run out the demands of war and we were forced to make heavy purchases abroad. The treasury is depleted, our credit exhausted."

"I know full well, Mister Chase," Lincoln picked up a stack of papers off his desk, "from reading your detailed reports." He let the stack drop back onto the desk.

"We've issued greenbacks," Chase went on, "but if

they're not backed by gold reserve they'll soon be next to worthless."

"I understand." Lincoln nodded. "Now, have you any good news from the Treasury Department, Mister Chase?"

"I hope so, sir. That's why I've asked Mister Welles to sit in. We've hatched a little scheme."

Chase removed a gold coin from his pocket and placed it on the President's desk. Lincoln picked it up.

"A twenty-dollar gold piece." Lincoln smiled. "It's a start, Mister Chase, but one double eagle is hardly enough to tip the scales." He put the coin back on his desk.

"No, sir. But gold is where you find it . . . and you find it in the west." Chase took up the coin again and held it between his thumb and forefinger. "There are close to eight hundred thousand more of these double eagles, minted in San Francisco."

"That's a long way away," Lincoln said.

"But right now they're on their way to the Treasury, and *that* could tip the scales for just long enough."

The President obviously became more interested. Lincoln looked at Gideon Welles.

"Where does the Navy come in, Mister Welles?"

Welles rose and took a step toward the desk and the President.

"The gold is aboard a ship bound for Baltimore."

Simon Cameron sprang to his feet and glared from Welles to Chase.

"A ship!? As Secretary of War, I should have been consulted."

"Would you have agreed, Mister Cameron?" Chase asked.

"No! Definitely not!"

"That's why you weren't consulted," Chase replied as Lincoln smiled.

"How many naval vessels are involved?" Cameron demanded.

"None," Welles replied calmly. "Only a single merchant ship, but with a small naval contingent aboard, plus a representative of the Navy Department, Justin Stewart—"

"I know Stewart," Cameron said. "He's a sick man."

"He's a good man . . . and so is the captain of the *Phantom Hope*."

"*Phantom Hope*?" Lincoln mused. "Aptly titled, and who is the captain?"

"Thomas J. Gunnison," Welles answered.

"Gunnison!" Cameron shuddered. "Why, that man was thrown out of the Navy!"

"That was the Navy's mistake," Welles replied. I served with his father, and Tom Gunnison served with me. I've seen him face danger, risk death for his men and his country. He is against slavery and devoted to the Union."

"I know that to be true, sir." Secretary of Treasury Salmon P. Chase approached Lincoln. "And sometimes valor and devotion *are* enough to win the day."

"Mister Chase," Lincoln smiled again, "you Connecticut Yankees are supposed to be a cautious breed."

"We are, sir. But if I have to throw caution to the wind, I'd want that wind to be at Gunnison's back."

President Abraham Lincoln moved to the window and looked out as before.

"Well, gentlemen, for the time being, it seems that the *Phantom Hope* is our last, best hope. Let's pray that the wind *is* at Captain Gunnison's back."

*   *   *

Captain Gunnison stood by the rail near the body of Justin Stewart, which was wrapped in a shroud atop a plank held by four crewmen near the edge of the ship.

They were all there, even the helmsman, who had locked the wheel to course. First Mate Bogartis, Second Mate Joseph, Lieutenant Gunnison, Ensign Discant, Cookie, Rankin, and the rest. They had all removed their hats and stood in respectful silence as the captain spoke.

"Unto Thee we commit this soul until that sure and certain day of resurrection when the sea shall give up its dead—and they will be judged every man according to his works. The Lord giveth, the Lord taketh away. Blessed be the name of the Lord." Gunnison looked around at the crew and ran his thick fingers through his hair. "I . . . uh . . . found a rosary among his possessions—Mister Stewart's, that is—and put it in his pocket. I didn't know him very long, nor very well, when it comes right down to it . . . except that he was a good man who loved his country. I guess that he was Catholic . . . and I'm not, so . . . if there's any among you who, well, can say anything that . . . might give him some comfort, please . . . do so."

There was a pause as the crewmen looked from one to another. Then one of the men, Alan Rankin, moved a half-step closer to the body of Justin Stewart. Rankin crossed himself three times and spoke in a soft but clear voice.

"Hail Mary, full of grace. The Lord is with thee. Blessed art Thou amongst women, and blessed is the fruit of thy womb, Jesus. Holy Mary, mother of God, pray for us sinners, now and at the hour of our death. Amen." Rankin stepped back into the line of crewmen.

Captain Gunnison nodded to the men holding the

Andrew J. Fenady

plank. The plank was tilted and the shrouded body was given to the sea.

"That's it, men." As the crew started to disperse, Gunnison put on his cap and turned to Bogartis and Jeff. "Now, the next thing we got to do is jettison the guns and ammunition."

"Sir . . ." Ensign Discant blinked in surprise and disbelief.

"We're taking on too much water," Gunnison went on. "Have to lighten weight."

"We sure as hell do," Bogartis said. "And fast."

"But Captain . . . ," Discant started to protest.

"Won't be long," Gunnison went on, "before Forrester makes temporary repairs and rigs canvas."

"That's what the sonofabitch'll be up to, all right," Bogartis agreed.

"We've got to get to San Angelo, make our repairs, and get the hell out."

As Lieutenant Jeff Gunnison nodded, Discant couldn't constrain himself any longer.

"But the guns, Captain . . ." Discant turned to his fellow officer. "Jeff! The guns and ammunition! Our orders are to get them to—"

"Just a minute, Jim." Gunnison looked at his son. "Jeff, you better take Ensign Discant aside and explain about the . . . cargo."

"Sure." Jeff nodded. "Come on, Jim."

As the two young naval officers walked away, Bogartis smiled.

"Well, I better get to it. What a pity. Such lovely guns, those Henrys."

"That's right, Mister Bogartis. And you better keep a hundred of those lovely Henrys and plenty of ammunition . . . just in case."

76

"Aye, sir." Bogartis grinned. "I was going to do just that, Captain."

"Mister Joseph!" Gunnison called out.

"Yes, sir." The second mate responded from nearby.

"All the sail you can muster, Mister Joseph. South by southeast."

". . . those were Stewart's last words: 'never mind the guns and ammunition . . . get the gold to the United States . . . that's your mission.' "

"Fifteen million . . . My God, Jeff, this ship's a floating gold mine!"

"Well, my father was right about one thing. This ship won't be floating much longer unless we lighten the load and raise the keel line."

"And you think he knew about the gold before Mister Stewart told him?"

"I know he did. I've got to admit there's nothing goes on aboard this ship he doesn't know. He might even know what each of us is thinking."

"What are you thinking, Jeff? I mean, about him? Have you changed your mind? Even a little? You know he saved this ship . . . and us . . . all our lives, by what he did."

"Including his own."

"Yes, but nobody else went down there."

"I never said he wasn't brave, but . . ."

"But what?"

"Just let it go, will you, Jim?"

"Is that an order, sir?" Discant smiled.

"If that's what it'll take to do it." The lieutenant also smiled, then turned as he heard the sounds off the stern.

Crates of guns and ammunition were being thrown overboard.

Both of the young officers walked aft where Captain

77

Gunnison stood next to Mister Bogartis, who was supervising some of the crew who were lifting, then heaving the crates into the sea.

They all watched as the string of crates floated for just a short time, then began to sink.

"They look like coffins out there," Mister Bogartis observed. "Don't they, Captain?"

"I guess a lot of Southern troops will stay alive because we didn't deliver them," Ensign Discant said.

"That's one way to look at it." Captain Gunnison nodded.

"What's the other?" Jeff asked.

"Those guns could've shortened the war and saved a lot more lives . . . on both sides."

"There's still the gold," Lieutenant Gunnison said. "That'll help end the war."

"You're right, Lieutenant," Captain Gunnison agreed, as he turned and walked away. "And that part of the cargo we will deliver . . . just as sure as the turning of the earth."

The rest stayed and watched until the last of the coffinlike crates sank beneath the wake of the *Phantom Hope*.

Chapter Eleven

The *Phantom Hope* lay anchored in the harbor at the Port of San Angelo, Mexico. Lines fast. Sails folded. The gaping hole in her starboard keel still evident just above the waterline.

The ship had been in the harbor for less than half an hour, but word had spread as soon as the vessel was spotted outside the breakwater.

Men, women, and children began gathering on the wharf, and now a mariachi band played and serenaded the ship, which still flew the Mexican flag.

Some of the crew tossed coins at the children, who scrambled to retrieve them, then hollered for more. Purveyors of all manner of merchandise maneuvered across the area redolent of food and flowers. The air was rife with scents; the smell of tacos, tortillas, and frijoles mingled among the fragrances of lilies, roses, and wine. Dogs barked and scampered along with cats and even chickens across the wharf.

An ornate black carriage, pulled by a team of perfectly matched white horses, driven by a man in uniform with an armed guard sitting next to him, turned onto the wharf and approached the *Phantom Hope*. The crowd cheered and separated, allowing passage for the carriage and the four uniformed horsemen who escorted the phaeton.

Some of the onlookers chased after the carriage with shouts and laughter, waving and cheering.

"Captain Montego! Captain Montego!"

"*Viva* Montego!"

"*Viva capitán!*"

The carriage came to a stop near the ship's gangway. One of the horsemen already had dismounted and was opening the carriage door.

Some of the women and children began to throw flower petals into the air and toward the carriage as they cried, "*Viva* Montego!" "*Viva El Capitán!*" "*Viva* Rosario Montego!"

Captain Rosario Montego stepped out of the vehicle and waved a salutation as his boots touched the wharf. He was a smiling, middle-aged, mustachioed man in resplendent white naval uniform from head to heel, complete with twin pearl-handled revolvers. He had a dark face with much darker eyes, and on his left cheek a saber scar that added a note of dash and danger.

From the deck Captain Gunnison, Bogartis, Jeff, and Discant watched as the bemedaled man made his way toward, then up the gangway.

"Who is that, sir?" James Discant inquired.

"That," Gunnison grinned, "is the captain of the Port of San Angelo. A friend."

Stepping onto the deck and also grinning, Captain Montego executed an exaggerated salute toward Gunnison.

"Permission to come aboard, Captain?"

"Permission granted, Captain, with extreme pleasure." Gunnison returned the salute.

"My friend!" Montego exclaimed, and thrust both arms around Gunnison, whose arms went around Montego, completing the *abrazo*.

They parted and slapped each other's shoulders.

"Captain Montego, you know Mister Bogartis."

"Welcome, *señor*."

"*Gracias*, Captain."

"This is Ensign Discant," Gunnison continued, "and . . . Lieutenant Jeff Gunnison, U.S. Navy."

"I can see the resemblance." Montego smiled. "Your father is a great friend and a great man. This welcome," he pointed toward the crowd on the wharf, "is for him and his ship."

"Thank you, Captain," Gunnison said, "and you've probably noticed that the ship is in need of repairs and so is the crew."

"We will see to the needs of the ship, and the crew, especially my friend . . ."

But Montego's friend was looking elsewhere, in the direction of the lady who had just stepped aboard from the gangway.

And almost immediately everyone else was looking. That was not unusual whenever and wherever China Lil appeared.

She wore a straight green dress, although nothing was straight about China Lil except her attitude. She seemed taller than she actually was, because of the way she stood and moved, seeming to glide rather than walk.

Her face was beautiful and unsunned, of indeterminate age, maybe thirty-five, maybe forty, but it didn't matter. Her thick hair was black as a raven's wing, her lips redder than scarlet ribbons, but her eyes and everything she wore were green, green as the jade necklace that circled her slender throat.

Her voice was lutelike through a slight, confident smile.

"Hello, stranger."

"Hello, Lil." Gunnison nodded.

"When I came aboard to see you off, I promised to come aboard and welcome you back, remember?"

"I remember. Uh, Miss China Lil, this is my son, Jeff."

"He's not as . . ." China Lil looked at the lieutenant. ". . . tall as you said."

"He's still growing." Gunnison smiled.

"Good. I like tall ships, tall men, and tall . . . drinks. And speaking of drinks, Captain Montego, you were talking about looking after the needs of the ship and the crew, especially your friend. . . ."

"Yes." Montego grinned.

"Well, he's my friend too, and in honor of my friend and his friends, there will be a little celebration at China Lil's." She turned to Gunnison. "Will you . . . and your friends be there?"

"They will . . . and I will."

"Good. Tonight the party is on me."

China Lil turned and glided toward the gangway as everyone watched and savored her departure.

"Well, my friend," Captain Montego said, turning back to Gunnison, "see you all tonight, then, at China Lil's. *Adiós*."

Nobody paid much attention as Captain Rosario Montego departed.

"If you don't mind, Captain Gunnison," Jeff said, "I think we'll skip the celebration tonight."

"I do mind. These are very gracious and respectful people. It would be very ungracious and disrespectful to decline their invitation. And you, both of you, as representatives of the U.S. Navy, will be there. Is that understood?"

"Yes, sir!" Ensign James Discant smiled. "Sir, may I ask you a question?"

"Go ahead."

"That lady, China Lil . . ."

"What about her?"

"She doesn't look . . . Chinese."

"She's not."

"Then why does she call herself that?"

"She had to call herself something."

"Uh-huh . . . Strange."

"Mexico is a strange country."

A strange country.

Beautiful and bountiful. Fierce and unforgiving. Since time remembered, a battlefield, and worth fighting for. Rich soil in vast areas. Thick forests. Deep natural harbors. Flowing rivers. Jagged mountains ingrained with silver and gold. A favorable climate. But in places, arid deserts defying all that breathes and moves.

A thousand years before Christ, the Olmecs, Mexico's first civilization, thrived in areas later called Tabasco and Vera Cruz. They were followed by other Indian cultures, more advanced—much more advanced and civilized than their Indian brethren in North America: Teotihuacan, the Zapotecs, Mixtans, the Maya, Toltecs, and the Aztecs, who ruled the largest and most advanced empire Mexico ever saw until the arrival of Hernán Cortés in Vera Cruz in 1519.

Cortez had fewer than 400 soldiers, 16 horses, and little artillery aboard 11 ships. He burned the ships and never looked back until he had conquered all of Mexico for Spain.

So passed the next three hundred years, filled with

blood and revolution, until the rebel leader Vicente Guerro gained independence for Mexico in the Treaty of Córdoba, September 27, 1821.

A little more than two decades later the Mexican general, President Antonio López de Santa Anna, lost half of Mexico to the United States in a war that ended in 1848.

Shortly after that a giant made himself known and respected in the land of bloody revolutions, and that giant, a leader who was not a man of great size but of great principle, was an Indian from Oaxaca named Juárez—Benito Juárez.

President Juárez infuriated the wealthy conservative class by liberalizing the constitution and instituting land reform, setting off another bloody conflict that still raged as his country plunged deeper and deeper into debt. And even now Napoleon III, one of the major lenders, threatened to name Archduke Maximilian of Austria as the emperor of Mexico.

Ironically Mexico's strongest ally in the present conflict was its former enemy, the United States. President Abraham Lincoln looked with sympathy toward his neighbor to the south. But Lincoln was in no position to render aid, or to enforce the Monroe Doctrine in case of European intervention, because President Lincoln was involved in a bloody fight to preserve his own country.

It was into this arena, this cauldron of conflict, that Captain Thomas J. Gunnison had landed his ship *Phantom Hope* in the Port of San Angelo, Mexico.

A strange country.

Ensign Discant finished buttoning the tunic of his dress uniform. Lieutenant Gunnison sat on the lower bunk of their cabin. He wore his uniform's dress pants and shirt, but the tunic lay on the bunk beside him.

"Better get a move on, Jeff."

"Who the hell does he think he is?"

"Well, you might be able to forget the fact that he's your father—I presume you're talking about Gunnison, *pere*—but don't forget he's also the captain of this ship and according to the agreement Stewart signed, he's in charge of this little expedition and . . ."

"Does the expedition include a drinking fest at China Lil's?"

"I guess if he says so, it does. Besides, it might be . . ."

"Be what?"

"Oh, I don't know—informative . . . enlightening . . . and just plain fun."

"Fun! Watching him and that green . . ."

"Oh, ho! Is that what's bothering you?"

"Hell no! I don't give a damn what he does, so long as we get the g—the cargo to Baltimore . . . with or . . ."

"Without him?"

"If we have to, we—"

There was a knock on the cabin door.

"Come," Jeff said.

The door opened. Captain Gunnison stood there in an immaculate blue blazer with four stripes on each sleeve, fresh trousers, and shiny, new, uncreased black boots.

"You two about ready?"

"Yes, sir." Discant smiled. "We were just talking about the voyage around the Horn, sir. You know . . . about what our chances are."

"Part of our chances depend on Forrester and his plans. As for the other part, well, they don't call it Cape Horn the Terrible for nothing. There's two hundred days of gale and a hundred thirty of cloudy sky. The rest of the year is strong winds and rough seas. Besides fixing the keel, we'll need new sails—stiff ones made out of double-o canvas—waterproof tarps, and bolted timbers over the hatches to keep from getting swamped. Last year five out of every eight ships didn't make it, stove in by rollers or rocks. It's no place for indecision. That's why the captain's every order will be obeyed instantly, otherwise . . ."

"Otherwise what?" Lieutenant Gunnison asked.

"Otherwise I consider it mutiny—and I hang mutineers, Lieutenant. Be ready in five minutes."

"Yes, sir." Ensign Discant gulped.

Chapter Twelve

China Lil's was resplendent with colors, mostly green of every shade, and with streamers and flowers. A band. Senoritas, and sailors from the *Phantom Hope*. Most of the crew looked like gorillas with shaves, the ones that had bothered to shave. Cookie sat at the far end of one of the tables braced by two senoritas, buxom and buxomer. Two of the sailors, Mister Joseph and Alan Rankin, were absent. Captain Gunnison had granted their request to stay aboard and maintain vigil on the ship.

Gunnison was at the head of the longest, grandest table, flanked by Captain Montego to his right and China Lil on his left. She wore a different, silkier green dress but the same jade necklace. Gunnison had seated his son and Discant next to their hostess. The lieutenant had not spoken a word to her since their arrival over an hour ago, except for a polite hello and an occasional nod in response to her occasional remark to him.

Andrew J. Fenady

Captain Rosario Montego laughed and drank, sometimes rum, sometimes tequila, and monopolized Captain Gunnison's attention with vivid reminiscences.

"How long since your last voyage here, my friend?"

"Nearly a year."

"That long?" Montego laughed. "It seems like yesterday. Do you remember that night at the Golondrina when the captain and the crew of the *Paloma* thought they . . ."

"Yes, I remember." Gunnison nodded. "Captain, I have to ask you something. I need a favor. . . ."

"You who have saved my life, not once, but three times, once when I was *borracho*, and twice sober, have but to ask."

"*Bueno*. There's a ship coming this way, the *Corsair*. . . ."

"Forrester." Montego became serious.

"We had a little recent . . . run-in. The *Corsair*'s been damaged." Gunnison pointed to his son. "Thanks to him."

"The apple does not fall far from the orchard." Montego grinned. "What can I do?"

"Send out some of your fastest sloops. Let me know when you sight her."

"This is important to you?"

"Very important."

"Done! That's it?"

"That's it."

"Ah!" Montego laughed. "But tonight we are just beginning . . . tonight . . ."

"Gentlemen." Jeff rose. "I wonder if you'll excuse us." He looked toward Discant. "Ensign Discant and I have some business aboard ship. We—"

"You hear that, my friend!" Montego prodded Gunnison. "Business! Youth is not what it used to be. In our time . . ."

"I'll see you both to the door!" China Lil rose and looked at the young officers.

"Thank you," Jeff said. "That's not necessary."

"As your hostess, I insist. It's an old Spanish custom, isn't it, Tom?"

Gunnison nodded.

China Lil glided toward the door followed by the two men.

At the entrance she paused and spoke to Discant.

"Would you excuse us for just a few moments?"

"Of course." He smiled at Jeff. "I'll wait outside."

"No, please . . . go to the bar and have a nightcap. I'd like to walk out in the garden with the lieutenant. We won't be long."

Ensign Discant nodded and walked away.

The garden, cooled by the ocean breeze and bathed in the fragrance of flowers, seemed an anachronism beside the pagodalike café. China Lil walked only a few steps before turning and facing the young lieutenant, her moonlit eyes looking directly into his.

"You do look like your father."

"Funny. He used to say I looked like my mother. But then, I don't imagine he talked much to you about my mother."

"More than you imagine."

"Between . . . drinks?"

"Between a lot of things. I want to tell you something. . . ."

"You don't owe me any explanation, and neither does he."

"No. Gunnison doesn't explain. You either take him as he is, or . . ."

"Walk away? That's what I did. Until now, when I have no choice."

"Jeff . . . years ago, along the beach he found a girl . . . bloodied, beaten, and . . . well, never mind the rest. He took me to a place where they took care of me. When I tried to tell him who I was and what happened, he smiled and saved me the humiliation by saying he already knew. . . . He said that I was a princess from Cathay, kidnapped by pirates, and had managed to escape far away across the sea. Not long after that, while I was still getting well, he came to this place." She pointed to the café. "It was called the Scarlet Palace then, and owned by a brute named Red Morgan. How he found out what this man had done to me I don't know. He never told me and I never asked. There was a poker game that came down to the two of them with the stakes getting higher and higher, until it was Gunnison's ship against the Scarlet Queen. Morgan laughed and put down four queens. He stopped laughing when Gunnison laid four kings on top of them. The next morning Morgan was found hanging from that tree," China Lil pointed, "and Gunnison said to me, 'Princess, there's your palace, sorry it's not in China.' "

"And you've been paying him back ever since."

"I could never pay him back for what he did for me, but I try, because . . . I love him, and while he could never love me in the same way, sometimes he . . . he needs me . . . and Jeff, even though he tries not to let it show, there's something . . . someone he needs even more."

"Is that the end of the story?"

"No. Nobody can say exactly how it will end. But there's one ending you'll never have to be concerned about."

"What's that?"

"You'll never have a stepmother."

Captain Thomas J. Gunnison did not return to the ship that night—nor for the next three days and nights.

Chapter Thirteen

During that time the *Phantom Hope* was undergoing repairs by the crew and by Mexican workers provided by Captain Rosario Montego.

Bogartis and Mister Joseph never left the ship. Neither did Jeff Gunnison and Ensign Discant.

New planks were cut to size, fitted to replace the jagged hole torn just above the waterline, then painted.

Torn sails were thrown away, and even the sails in good condition were replaced with stiff double-0 canvas. The decks were scrubbed and polished.

Jeff Gunnison and Discant had the gun crews clean and check both cannons, and thanks to the efforts of Captain Montego, a new supply of sixty-eight-pound shot was brought aboard to replace what had been spent in practice and in the engagement with the *Corsair*.

The larder had been filled with fresh fruit and airtights for the voyage.

Captain Gunnison's absence was never mentioned.

But with each passing day, then hour, Lieutenant Gunnison grew more restless, until the afternoon of the third day when Mister Bogartis was walking on deck with Cookie and Jeff caught up to them.

"Mister Bogartis. Just a minute, please, Mister Bogartis. . . ."

Bogartis stopped, looked back. Cookie had an idea of what was coming and kept going. Bogartis looked up at the blue sky.

"Nice weather."

"Never mind the weather nor the friendly natives. This ship is ready to sail."

"So?"

"So, when's . . . when's Gunnison coming back?"

"Damned if I know. I'm just the first mate."

"And he's supposed to be the captain. . . ."

"But I'll tell you one thing."

"What?"

"I'm not going after him."

"He hasn't been aboard ship for three days."

"I noticed that. Maybe he's got a lot of catching up to do."

"Catching up with what?"

"Why don't you ask him?" Bogartis smiled. "He's right behind you."

Gunnison stepped on deck, freshly shaved—and whatever he had been doing, he was all business now. Jeff appeared somewhat off guard.

"I was just saying to Mister Bogartis—"

"Never mind that," Gunnison snapped. "The *Corsair*'s been sighted."

"Great thunderin' hallelujah!" Bogartis grinned.

"How far out?" Jeff asked.

"Not exactly out. Heading for the harbor of Salina.

93

Mister Bogartis, not a word to anyone until I say so. Jeff, my cabin. Now."

Gunnison had taken off his jacket and rolled out a map of Mexico on his table. His face was grim and determined, his voice strong and authoritative. He pointed to the map with a quill as he spoke.

"Now, most likely he'll finish up repairs at Salina, wait for us to move out, and hit us with—"

"We'll be ready."

"No we won't," Gunnison said.

"What?"

"That's what he expects. We've got to do the unexpected."

"What do you mean?"

"I mean—"

There was a knock at the cabin door and Bogartis's voice.

"Captain."

"Come in, Mister Bogartis."

Bogartis opened the door, stood at the entrance and smiled.

"This better be important, Mister Bogartis."

"That's up to you to determine, Captain. Your partner's here."

Both Gunnison and Jeff were surprised—Jeff the more surprised.

"I didn't know you had a partner."

"Silent partner. Fellow named Henri Lessuer from New Orleans. Put up the money for the *Hope*. Didn't know he was in town."

"Well?" Bogartis said.

"Show Mister Lessuer in."

Bogartis's smile turned into a mischievous grin as he opened the door wider and stepped aside.

"*Miss* Lessuer."

Miss Lessuer walked past Bogartis and into the captain's cabin as if she owned it. She was about twenty-two, an overwhelmingly beautiful creature with the bluest eyes and reddest hair on land or sea, an inviting, willowy body, the kind of body that any man whom she walked past would turn to make sure he saw what he saw. She wore a tight, red summer skirt that shimmered as she moved and matched her hair, and a soft blue blouse that shimmered even more and matched her eyes. Those eyes swept from Captain Gunnison to Lieutenant Gunnison and back again to Captain Gunnison. Her voice was low and as inviting as her walk, almost.

"You can call me Dominique. My father did . . . when he thought about it." There was just the slightest spice of a southern-belle carmel lilt in that voice, but with strength and independence.

"Where *is* your father?" Gunnison asked.

"He died in bed . . . holding a bottle of bourbon in one hand and a *señorita* in the other."

"Those were the only two good habits he had." Gunnison smiled.

"You're right. I didn't like him and I don't like you. . . ."

"That was meant to be funny."

"This isn't . . . and I don't like you," she continued, "*but* he was my father and you are my partner."

"Like hell."

"I've got the papers and his last will and testament to prove it in any court of law." Dominique Lessuer looked back at Jeff. "Who's this?"

"Close that door, Mister Bogartis."

"From the inside or out, Captain?"

"You stay here."

"Yes, sir." Bogartis closed the cabin door and stayed.

"This is Lieutenant Jeff Gunnison," the captain said.

"Gunnison, son of Gunnison?" Dominique smiled.

Both Gunnisons nodded.

"I can . . ." She looked the lieutenant up and down. ". . . see the resemblance."

"Thank you," said Captain Gunnison.

"I didn't necessarily mean that as a compliment. . . . Any of you have the makings of a cigarette?"

"No. But I can provide you with a cigar." Gunnison pointed toward a humidor on his desk.

"Thanks, no."

"All right, then, just what else do you want?"

"First," Miss Lessuer further appraised Lieutenant Gunnison, then looked at Captain Gunnison, "passage aboard the *Phantom Hope* out of Mexico."

"The *Phantom Hope* isn't leaving Mexico—at least not for a long time."

Jeff reacted and took a step toward Gunnison.

"But we've got to—"

"Our friend Forrester out there," Gunnison pointed toward the bay, "is waiting for us to make repairs and head for international waters, then hit us with everything he's got."

"But we've got orders . . . the cargo . . ."

"I know the orders, Lieutenant. We're going to take the cargo off the *Hope*, freight it across the isthmus overland to Vera Cruz . . ." Gunnison crossed the isthmus on the map with a quill. ". . . put it aboard another ship, and make delivery."

"Well, then, it looks like I'm going to have to change my plan." She reached into the divide of her blouse, produced a cigarette that was already rolled and a match, ignited the match with her thumbnail, and lit up.

"I see you sometimes smoke your own cigarettes," Gunnison said.

"Only when I have to." She inhaled and tossed the match into the brass spittoon on the floor. "It looks like I'll have to go overland with you."

"Like hell. You're not going anyplace with us."

"We're partners. Half this ship is mine. I've got to protect my interest."

"You can sail your half anywhere you want, partner."

"You know there are worse partners than me. Suppose I decide to sell my half of the ship to somebody else?"

"You'll find the market for ships these days is tenuous." Gunnison placed the palm of his left hand at her elbow, escorted Dominique Lessuer to the door, opened it, and pointed to the passage. "I'm sure you can find your way out, partner."

"I can find my way out of a lot of places." She dropped the cigarette on the floor, stepped on it, and kept on walking.

Gunnison closed the door. The second he did, Jeff exploded.

"You're not fooling me, *Captain*!"

"I'm not?"

"This is just a ruse so you can save your damn ship!"

"Well, the truth is, I did think about saving my ship, but that's not the whole of it." Gunnison walked to his desk and obtained a cigar from the humidor.

"What is the whole of it?"

"The only chance we've got," Gunnison bit off the end, lit the cigar, and smoked as he talked, "is to slip away while Forrester thinks we're still making repairs and get a big start. By that time we'll be halfway to Vera Cruz."

"Sounds logical." Bogartis nodded.

Andrew J. Fenady

"It would, to you," Jeff said.

"Listen," Gunnison went on. "Before you know it, there's liable to be a fleet of Confederate ships out there against your two guns."

"I guess so, but . . . how do we know we can make it across the isthmus?"

"Made the trip once before when I had trouble with a ship. Didn't we, Mister Bogartis?"

"We did."

"I don't trust both or either of you."

"That hurts." Mister Bogartis sighed. "Hurts."

"I think you lied, deluded me into coming here in the first place. . . ."

"Think what you will." He puffed. "Doesn't change things."

"And maybe you're lying now. Maybe you want to get us out in the wilds, get rid of us, and steal the gold."

"Maybe I do. But me and the gold are going. If you stay here . . . I've already got rid of you." Gunnison took another puff. "Lieutenant, you've got no choice."

From the deck of the *Phantom Hope* Captain Gunnison and Captain Rosario Montego watched as the cargo of crates was being transferred, under the supervision of Mister Joseph and the watchful eyes of Lieutenant Gunnison and Ensign Discant, into four heavy-duty wagons on the wharf.

"Thank you, my friend," Gunnison said, "for your help in procuring the necessary equipment on such short notice."

"*De nada*. We will have a farewell drink tonight?"

"That we will."

"Till then." Montego started toward the gangway.

As the heavy crates were being loaded onto the wagons, Discant wiped the sweat from his brow and turned to Jeff.

"I'm just not sure, Jeff."

"About what? Making the trip overland?"

"That's right. We don't know what we're getting into. I trust your father, but that crew outnumbers us five to one. If they find out what we're carrying . . ."

"We've got to make sure they don't find out."

"I'd feel better if we could take those cannons along."

"Too damn heavy, and I'm not sure what good that would do out there."

"I just don't like it."

"Neither do I. But like the man said, we've got no choice."

"See you this evening, gentlemen." Captain Montego smiled and saluted as he walked past.

Dominique Lessuer leaned against a bale on the dock and smoked a cigarette. She had been watching and waiting near Captain Montego's carriage. Her wait was over.

"Excuse me," she said, and moved toward the captain as he approached. "You are Captain Montego?"

"I am." Montego bowed.

"I'm told you are the captain of this port."

"At your service, *señorita.*"

"My name is Dominique Lessuer."

"I heard you were here. My condolences . . . I knew your father."

"Everybody did. Can you tell me, Captain, who is the richest man in San Angelo?"

"*Señor* Don Carlos Alvarez."

"Where is he located?"

"He has an office at the plaza. You can't miss the sign."

99

"Thanks."

"This is my carriage. May I take you?"

"No, thanks."

"Very well." Montego started toward the carriage, then paused. "*Señorita* Lessuer, you are a very beautiful young lady. A caution. I would not put too much faith in what Don Carlos says."

"I don't put much faith in what anybody says."

"My friends." At China Lil's, Captain Montego raised his glass to those seated at the table: Gunnison, China Lil, Jeff, Discant, and Bogartis. "*Vaya Con Dios.*"

They all drank.

"And allow me to give you some good advice," he added.

"Go ahead," Gunnison said.

"Don't go!"

As Montego spoke, Jeff noticed Dominique Lessuer being escorted to a corner table by a well-dressed, middle-aged man he did not recognize. Jeff motioned to his father.

"Looks like your partner's found a friend."

"Looks like."

"Yes." Montego nodded. "Miss Lessuer asked me about Don Carlos this afternoon. She wanted to know who was the richest man in town."

"I hope you warned the young woman," China Lil said.

"I told her," Montego shrugged, "to be cautious."

"That is Lessuer's daughter you told me about, isn't it, Tom?" Lil asked.

"The one and only, far as I know."

"She's beautiful." China Lil rose. "I think I'll go over and make sure she's cautious."

The men all stood for a moment as China Lil left the table.

"Gentlemen," Montego said as they sat. "I was serious when I said don't go."

"What do you expect us to do," Gunnison smiled, "stay here until the war is over?"

"Which war are you talking about? Yours or ours? Ours has been going on for over forty years." He looked at Jeff and Discant. "Yes, since long before you were born. During that time fifty-two governments have come and gone. And now Benito Juárez's government is in peril."

"What's that got to do with us?" Discant asked.

"There is a rumor that Louis Napoleon is sending an expeditionary force to invade Mexico."

"We're a long way from Mexico City," Jeff said, and took a sip of his drink.

"Yes," Montego agreed. But marauders calling themselves everything from guerrillas to generals on both sides are ravaging the countryside, killing and looting—"

"Well," Gunnison interrupted, "you've got your war and we've got ours. Anyway, we've got orders." He looked at Jeff. "Haven't we, Lieutenant?"

"Yes, we have." Jeff nodded. "And we're going to carry them out."

"Can't those orders wait?" Montego grinned.

"Nope," said Gunnison.

"Well, then." Montego shrugged. "To orders!"

They all drank again.

"Don Carlos." China Lil smiled as she approached the corner table. "It's good to see you and . . . your friend." She extended her hand.

Don Carlos rose, took her hand, and nodded toward Dominique.

"Thank you. May I present Miss Dominique Lessuer. Miss Lessuer, this is the fabled China Lil, the grandest lady in all Mexico."

"You flatter me, Don Carlos."

"Impossible."

"I'm very pleased to meet you, Miss Lil," Dominique said. "You, too, might have known my father."

"When he was in town he was a good . . . customer."

"I'm sure he was."

"As a matter of fact," Don Carlos cleared his throat, "Miss Lessuer and I were just discussing some business involving her father."

"Well, then, I'll leave you both to your business," China Lil smiled, paused a moment, and added, "and Don Carlos, please give my best regards to . . . your wife." She turned and walked away slowly.

"Oh, yes." Don Carlos sat, and acted as if he hadn't heard China Lil's last remark. "Where were we, *señorita?*"

"We were at your office this afternoon when you said you would think it over and give me your answer here tonight."

"Oh, yes."

"You already said that, *señor*. Well, we're here, so tell me. Will you buy my half of the *Phantom Hope?*"

"Well, you see, these days, what with how things are on the high seas, the business of shipowning can be very . . ."

"Tenuous?"

"I was going to say hazardous . . . and there is another consideration."

"What's that?"

"Captain Gunnison." Don Carlos nodded toward Gunnison's table. "Having a partner like him can be even more . . ."

"Hazardous?"

"Unpredictable. You can never tell what a man like that will do . . . or not do."

"So I'm finding out. I . . . I could lower my price."

"Price has very little to do with it."

"Then does that mean your answer is no?"

"I would like more time to think it over. *Señorita* Lessuer, I wish I could persuade you to stay in San Angelo. I could make your life here very . . . comfortable."

"For how long?"

"For as long as you like."

"You mean for as long as you like. Besides, what about the war?"

"What about it?"

"Suppose the other side wins?"

"For me there is no other side. I am a supplier. I supply both sides. The outcome is of no consequence."

"Or concern?"

"My concern is commerce."

"Just business, is that it?"

"Also," Don Carlos leaned closer, "pleasure."

"And that's where I come in." She, too, leaned closer for just a moment, then withdrew. "Where does your wife come in?"

"My wife and I have an understanding."

"But you and I don't." Dominique looked toward Gunnison's table, where China Lil was just sitting down. "Don Carlos, I am flattered by your proposal, but I have to make other arrangements. However, in prospect of future considerations . . ." Once again she leaned closer. ". . . there *is* something you can do for me. . . ."

The men all rose again as China Lil took her seat next to Gunnison.

"Is she trying to sell him my half of the ship?"

"I'm not sure about that." China Lil smiled. "But I know what *he's* trying to sell."

"The *señorita* is a very desirable dish," Montego said. "And Don Carlos has a voracious appetite."

"Well," Jeff rose, "it's getting late, and this is our last night to sleep aboard the ship. . . ."

Ensign Discant also rose.

"Right," Gunnison said, "I'll be there in just a while."

"You will?" Jeff said as if he didn't quite believe it.

Gunnison didn't see fit to answer.

"Miss Lil," Jeff turned toward her, "I hope that story you told ends well for you."

"Thank you. I hope it ends well for all of us."

After the two young officers left, Montego leaned close to Gunnison and whispered so no one but Gunnison and China Lil could hear.

"You and I are like brothers. What's in those crates?"

"Birds, brother."

"What kind of birds?"

"Eagles."

Half an hour later Gunnison and China Lil stood in the garden looking at the sky.

"Isn't that the North Star?" She pointed.

"And Venus close by. It's a good night for sailing."

"But you won't be sailing for a long time to come, will you, stranger?"

"Not for a long time. . . . Maybe . . ."

"Maybe what? Maybe never? Is that what you're saying?"

"I'm not saying anything."

"I don't expect you to. You know that by now. And I know that the odds are against you ever getting to Vera Cruz."

"You can never tell about odds."

"Not with you. At least we've had the last three days. . . ."

"Maybe not the *last*. But just in case, I want you to know something—"

"Something I don't already know?"

"I left some papers with Captain Montego. In case something happens on the way to Vera Cruz, my half of the ship and some other things . . . go to you."

"Tom . . ."

"Let's let it go at that."

"But why not to your son? To Jeff?"

"If I don't make it, the odds are, neither will he."

"What if he does?"

"If he does, he's got his life, his career in the Navy. He's got a future."

"And you don't think I have?" She smiled.

"Well, the saloon business is pretty risky. You ought to get out of it as soon as you can."

"You're one to talk about risk."

"But hang on to that necklace." He touched the jade on her neck.

"I always will."

"Well, the shortest farewells are the best."

"Not always." She moved closer. As close as she could.

Chapter Fourteen

Somewhere at sea, beneath the North Star with Venus close by, the *Corsair* lay at anchor, waiting.

The lookout had spotted what the *Corsair* was waiting for and had alerted the captain.

A small Mexican vessel pulled alongside with two crewmen aboard and an old captain.

"Captain Forrester!?" the old captain shouted. "Adam Forrester!?"

"I'm Forrester," came the response from the deck. Forrester stood there with his cigar and with First Mate Connors standing next to him.

"I have a message for you." The old captain held up an envelope.

"Bring it up," Forrester called back.

"First, *señor*," the old captain waved the envelope, "I was told you would pay two hundred pesos."

"Who's it from?"

"*¿Quién sabe?*"

"All right." Forrester smiled, puffed, and looked at Connors. "Bring it up and I'll pay."

"No, *señor*. First throw down two hundred pesos . . . then send down someone to pick up the message."

"You're very cautious, old man."

"*Sí, señor*. That's how I lived to be an old man."

Chapter Fifteen

Four wagons, pulled by six-ups, creaked and groaned under the strain of the weight, as the caravan moved along one of the Creator's most rugged and complex creations—the Mexican terrain. Dull, flat, monotonous in places where the devil had stomped the dust off his boots—craggy, colorful, and spectacular in other parts of the vast and varied landscape.

A hot, nomad wind whispered around boulders and through forlorn trees and jagged rocks that sheltered unseen creatures who waited for the coolness of the night—a coolness that would not come for hours yet.

At the fore of the contingent rode Gunnison, Bogartis, Mister Joseph, along with Jeff and Discant.

Gunnison and Bogartis had shed most of their sea attire in favor of land boots and riding clothes. Gunnison had procured a vaquero hat, a red bandanna, a blue cotton shirt with canvas vest, and bugger red pants around which circled a cartridge belt holstering a Colt

.44, and in his rifle boot was one of the Henrys.

Mister Bogartis still wore his sea cap. So did Mister Joseph.

The naval personnel who rode right behind them were still in uniform, but unbuttoned to accommodate the hot weather, all except Jeff and Discant, who were strictly regulation—so far.

The caravan was strung out over a couple hundred yards, with the crew of the *Phantom Hope* interspersed alongside.

Cookie drove the third wagon, which also served as the chuck wagon.

Everyone in the caravan knew that the crates aboard the wagons were inordinately heavy, but the contents were known only to Gunnison, Jeff, Discant, and Mister Bogartis, who muttered as he rode alongside Gunnison.

After almost a mile of mutterings Gunnison could take no more.

"Mister Bogartis, what're you mumbling about?"

"About my ass."

"What about your ass?"

"Too damn long on this broomtail."

"That's a fine horse. Montego provided us with nothing but the best. Besides, we're just getting started."

"Yeah, well, my ass is getting sore and I'm getting horsesick."

"You'll get used to it, and so will your—"

"I'm used to water. I want to see some water, not these pissy streams. I want to see some salt water—and lots of it."

"You will, Mister Bogartis, in Vera Cruz."

"How far?"

"Just a couple hundred miles, remember?"

"I remember, all right, but that was different. We was travelin' light. At the rate those wagons are movin', it

109

might as well be a couple thousand miles."

"Patience, Mister Bogartis."

"Yeah, the last time I heard that you got us court-martialed, *remember*?"

"I remember."

"This time," Bogartis went to mumbling again, "he's liable to get us all killed. . . ."

"What did you say?"

"Nothin'."

"Didn't sound like nothin'." Gunnison smiled. "What about you, Mister Joseph?" he asked. "How're you doing?"

"I was on land a lot longer than on sea, sir."

"On horseback?"

"Mule, sir. Somebody else's. I'll ride back and check on the crew if it's all right with you, sir."

"Go ahead."

Mister Joseph wheeled his horse and headed back along the contingent.

"You know what I wish?" Bogartis said after they had ridden farther.

"What?"

"I wish," Bogartis nodded toward the covered crates in the wagons, "them eagles could fly and take us along with 'em."

"Go easy on that 'eagle' talk, Mister Bogartis."

"Nobody heard . . . except our two Navy boys here."

"Let's keep it that way. I don't—"

"Captain!" Bogartis pointed.

"I see it."

"You mean her!"

Jeff and Discant also had spotted *her* and moved closer to Gunnison, as he and Bogartis rode toward the familiar figure ahead.

Dominique Lessuer leaned aslant in what shade there

was from the scrubby tree, rolling a cigarette. Her red hair sprawled beneath a wide-brimmed hat. She wore a soft cotton blouse and breeches tucked into black boots.

No horse. No carriage. No escort. Just Dominique Lessuer running her pink tongue along the clean white cylinder of a cigarette. On the ground near her were a trunk and suitcase.

Gunnison signaled back for the caravan to hold up. Then he and Bogartis, along with Jeff and Discant, reined in close to her.

Despite the heat and the surroundings, she appeared as fresh as a spring garden. The faces of all four men looked like they were viewing a mirage. But all four men knew that Dominique Lessuer was real enough in this time at this place.

Too real.

"Hello, partner." She smiled at Gunnison. "I told you I could find my way out of a lot of places . . . including San Angelo."

"What was the fare?" Jeff asked. "And who got paid?"

"The fare was a promise . . . that I don't intend to keep." She looked from Jeff to his father. "And Captain Gunnison, your son has a salacious mind."

"Salacious?" Gunnison smiled. "You must have gone to school some."

"In France."

"That figures."

"At any rate, it looks like we're going in the same direction." She pulled a match from her blouse, thumbed it afire, and lit up.

"We're going in opposite directions," Jeff said.

"I don't think so."

"Look," Jeff pointed to the stationary wagons, "you're wasting a lot of our time."

Andrew J. Fenady

"No, you are. Because when it's said and done you wouldn't leave me here."

"Why not?"

"Have no horse."

"We'll give you one," Jeff said.

"Have no food."

"We'll give you some," Jeff said.

"Have no weapon."

"I don't think you need a weapon." Captain Gunnison looked her up and down.

"Might be a rattlesnake around," she said.

"Might." Gunnison nodded. "You could give it first bite and still win."

"No matter what you say, Captain, I'm coming along."

"Out of the question." Jeff adjusted the brim of his officer's cap even though it didn't need adjustment.

"But I am." She smiled.

"What makes you so sure you're coming along?" Captain Gunnison asked.

"Two things. You can't just leave me here."

"And?"

"And I'm going to make you a proposition you won't turn down."

"Won't I?"

"Get me out of Mexico and you can have my half of the *Phantom Hope*."

"That," Gunnison looked at Bogartis and back to Dominique, "is an interesting proposition."

"For ten thousand dollars."

"Still interesting."

"Well?"

"Mister Bogartis," Gunnison said, "put her on a wagon."

"I'd rather ride a horse."

"Put her on a horse."

"This isn't some cotillion," Jeff protested. "She's liable to get killed."

"Yes." Gunnison smiled and rode toward the wagons.

The *Corsair* lay anchored in the harbor at the Port of San Angelo, Mexico, not far from the *Phantom Hope*. Lines fast. Sails folded. The *Corsair* had been repaired, but evidence of the sea battle was still apparent. She flew no flag.

This time there had been no celebration. No mariachi band. No food. No flowers.

However, Captain Rosario Montego was waiting on the dock as Adam Forrester, along with Connors, stepped off the gangway onto the wharf.

And this time there was no *abrazo* with the greeting.

"I am Rosario Montego, Captain of the Port."

"Adam Forrester."

"Yes, I know."

"This is First Mate Connors."

"How long do you intend to be here?" Montego made no acknowledgment of the introduction.

"That's hard to tell."

"What is your business here?"

"Well," Forrester smiled, "that's hard to tell too. Might be selling. Might be buying. Might be trading . . . depends."

"On what?"

"The market conditions."

"What is the ship's registry?"

"Confederate States of America. This is a neutral port, isn't it?"

"You know it is."

"Yes, I do."

"May I inquire where you are going from here? I mean, in San Angelo."

"Why not? You could follow me anyhow. I understand there's a gentleman named Don Carlos Alvarez in San Angelo who deals in . . . anything."

"That, *señor*, is true."

"I'm going to make a deal with him for some equipment. Anything else, Captain?"

"No. That will be all for now . . . Captain."

While Adam Forrester conferred with Don Carlos, Montego conferred with China Lil, and later the two of them and a man named Roberto watched as Forrester, Connors, and most of the crew of the *Corsair* were at the stable and corrals owned by Don Carlos. They were in the process of selecting horses and equipment for a journey. Obviously not a sea journey.

"Roberto," Montego said, "you are the best rider with the fastest horse in San Angelo."

"*Sí, capitán.*"

"You take that horse and ride as fast as you can. Catch up with Captain Gunnison and deliver this envelope. This is vital."

"Vital, *capitán*?" Roberto took the envelope.

"Important."

"Life and death," China Lil said.

"*Sí, señorita.*"

"In this other envelope is the money we agreed upon, two hundred pesos."

"*Sí, capitán,*" Roberto smiled and took the second envelope.

"And you'll never have to buy another drink at my place as long you live," China Lil added.

"*Sí, señorita.*" Roberto grinned.

* * *

The caravan had lumbered on for more than an hour since Dominique Lessuer had selected a horse to her liking, an appaloosa mare named Chita.

Dominique and Chita rode between Gunnison and Bogartis, Jeff and Discant just behind her.

"When do you want to sign the papers?" she asked Gunnison.

"What papers?"

"Agreement on the sale of the *Phantom Hope*."

"Later . . . tonight, maybe."

"All right," she said. "I'll write up the agreement."

"*I'll* write it . . . you just sign it."

"Okay, until then we're still partners."

The caravan continued to lumber on.

Roberto had already covered half the distance to the caravan. He rode with the speed and dust of the pre–Civil War Pony Express riders. He weighed no more than a hundred and twenty-five pounds and sometimes less. He had not even waited to tell his wife, Margarita, who had borne him three children in five years and who was bearing yet another in a few months. He had taken a small sack of grain for his horse, Macho, and some jerky for himself, filled two canteens, mounted up with the two envelopes tucked inside his shirt, and rode so Macho's hooves barely touched the ground. It had been a long while since he had possessed two hundred pesos at one time. When Margarita saw all that money her face would light up like a sunbeam. And Roberto intended to take up China Lil's offer of free drinks as soon as he returned to San Angelo.

Two men on horseback, with rifles already out of their scabbards, had reined up at the lip of the canyon and squinted at the racing horseman approaching the pass below.

The two Mexicans, Andres and Beka, looked at each other then back toward the pass.

"That's a good-looking horse," said Andres. "And fast."

"Let's go get it." Beka grinned.

"Too damned fast. We can't catch it. Shoot the rider. Much easier."

"You're right," Beka agreed.

Both men took aim with their single-shot, bolt-action rifles.

Both shots went off at the same time. One shot hit the rider's chest. The other shot hit the horse's chest. Both rider and horse buckled, somersaulted, and landed on the ground a dozen feet apart.

Both dead.

"Goddammit!" Andres hollered. "You hit the horse!"

"No!" Beka hollered louder. "You did!"

"Now what?"

"Let's go down and see what he's got on him." Beka shrugged. "That horse is no good to nobody."

"Except buzzards."

Andres and Beka went through Roberto's pockets, finding a few coins, then they discovered the two envelopes inside his shirt. Andres tore open the slim envelope first.

"Looks like a letter."

"Wonder what it says."

"I don't know and I don't care," Andres exclaimed. "Look at this!" He had ripped open the second envelope and held up the money. "Over a hundred pesos!"

"Two hundred," Beka beamed. "I can't read, but I can count."

"What do we do? Tell General Carvajal?"

"I tell you what we do. One hundred for you, one hundred for me, and we tell nobody."

"If he ever finds out, he'll cut off our *cajones*."

"He'll never find out, because you won't tell him, I won't tell him, and," Beka pointed to the dead man on the ground, "he can't tell him."

"You make good sense."

"Damn right."

"You know something?" Andres said.

"What?"

"He was riding like hell toward something."

"So?"

"So maybe we ought to find out what."

"We will, but not as fast as him."

"Something else . . ."

"What?"

"I still think it was your shot that killed the horse."

"We'll never know. All we know is we got two hundred pesos." Beka stuffed his share into his pocket.

"What about them?" Andres pointed to the dead man and animal.

"Buzzards." Beka shrugged.

The slim envelope and message that Andres had dropped drifted away with the hot wind back toward San Angelo.

The sun had just begun to dip from its noon arc but still blazed down on the level table of land flanked by pitted hillocks, still sending heat waves across the spanning horizon, with Gunnison, Dominique, and Bogartis leading the way. The shadows of the caravan were growing longer as they dragged behind.

"When do we eat?" Bogartis asked.

"When we find some shade," Gunnison said.

"That might not be till dark."

"You could miss a couple of meals, Mister Bogartis. Looks like your beam's expanded some lately."

"Yeah, well it looks like I'll be a bag of bones by the end of this voyage," Bogartis said, and then muttered, "Chances are we'll *all* end up bones. . . . Thought I seen buzzards back there . . . feathered sonsofbitches . . ."

There was some commotion toward the rear of the caravan. One of the wagons, the last one, had come to a stop. Alan Rankin, who had been riding alongside that wagon, now galloped past the other three, the crewmen, and the naval contingent, toward Gunnison.

"Captain."

Gunnison reined up as Rankin approached.

"Captain Gunnison . . ."

"What is it, Mister Rankin?"

"We lost part of the load on the last wagon."

"How's that?" Gunnison and Bogartis looked at each other as Jeff and Discant drew closer to Rankin.

"It's," Rankin pointed back toward the wagons, "Miss Lessuer's trunk that we strapped aboard. . . ."

"Oh, that." Gunnison was obviously relieved. "Is that all? The hell with it."

"What do you mean the hell with it? Strap it back on," Dominique commanded.

"You will not, Mister Rankin. Those wagons are over-loaded as it is."

"But my clothes! Some of them are from Paris. . . ."

"We're a long way from Paris, partner. You won't need any evening gowns around here."

"We made a deal. . . ."

"The deal was to take you, not your wardrobe, but I'll tell you what I'll do."

"What?"

"We'll take a ten-minute rest." Gunnison removed the gold watch from his pocket and looked at it. "You've got that much time to go through both satchels, keep what'll fit in the suitcase, and put it back on the wagon.

But the trunk and the rest of the stuff stays."

"I will not!"

"You've got ten seconds to make up your mind—otherwise, we just keep going."

"You big bastard!"

"Yes, ma'am, seven seconds."

"I won't!"

"Five seconds."

"That's all I have in the world."

"Two seconds."

"I will not go on without that trunk."

"Up to you." Gunnison closed the lid and slipped the watch back into his pocket. "Time's up. Let's move on, Mister Bogartis. . . ."

"No!" Dominique shouted.

"What do you mean 'no'?" Bogartis said.

"I mean all right." She looked at Gunnison. "You son-ofabitch!"

Jeff smiled as she wheeled her horse.

"You too!" she hollered when she rode past him.

Chapter Sixteen

Along with the conquistadores from Spain came conversion to Christianity in the form of the Catholic Church.

For more than two thousand years the civilizations and cultures of Mexico, like those of rest of the world, had feared and worshiped many gods.

But with the coming of Cortés came the missionaries, with their Bibles and crosses . . . and the teachings of Christ.

It had taken many centuries to build the great cathedrals of Rome, Paris, and the rest of Europe. In the last two and a half centuries, along with teaching the Sermon on the Mount, the missionaries had managed to construct churches of more modest means than those on the continent, but still with crosses of gold, valuable icons, and estimable adornments to grace places where españoles—Spaniards born in Spain; crillos—Mexican born, but with Spanish blood; mestizos—Spanish and

Indian; and indigenes—the native Indians, all gathered
to worship the Father, the Son, and the Holy Ghost.

To worship and pray in refuge and peace.

But at the church of Saint Brendan, a dozen miles
ahead of Gunnison's caravan, there was neither refuge
nor peace.

Saint Brendan's was being sacked.

Bandoleroed guerrillas looted the church, taking
whatever they could. Hands ripped a gold cross from
the altar and crosses from other places; icons, jeweled
vestments, candleholders, and even candles were also
taken.

Three nuns kneeled near the altar and prayed as more
than a dozen armed intruders laughed and scavenged
and smashed the stained glass windows.

An old priest, Father Dominic, stood with both hands
upraised, pleading with one of the men, Vega, who
turned toward him with a heavy gold crucifix in one
hand and a gold chalice in the other.

"Please, I beg you, by all that's holy! You cannot do
this! You must not! You can't desecrate . . ."

As Father Dominic moved toward Vega and dropped
to his knees with hands now clasped, a man on
horseback rode through the open doors of the church,
past some of the guerrillas and the nuns, his horse
stomping close to the altar.

"General Carvajal!" Vega laughed.

General Prospero Carvajal, a big man wearing a hat
similar to that of General Santa Anna, parts of some
undetermined uniform crisscrossed with two bandole-
ros and pistols on either side, reined up the huge black
stallion. He glanced at the kneeling nuns and, seeing
that they were old, turned his attention to Vega.

"General Carvajal," Vega repeated, grinning. "The
padre here says we can't do this."

Father Dominic rose from his knees and faced the man on horseback.

"He says," Vega held up the crucifix and chalice, "he says we dese . . . desecrate . . . what do you say, my general?"

"I beg you . . ." Father Dominic placed his hand on the flank of Carvajal's horse.

"I say proceed," the general said.

"In the name of God . . ."

"No." Carvajal's horse was fractious, snorting and prancing as Father Dominic drew away. "In the name of President Benito Juárez."

"Juárez would never sanction such sacrilege. Never!"

"Harsh times call for harsh measures. Hold still, horse!" Carvajal's face, brown and flat, with black beads of eyes beneath almost continuous eyebrows and thin lips that slashed downward, looked at the priest. "The government needs money to finance the fight against the enemies of our people."

"And the people need their churches to pray."

"Let them pray," Carvajal wheeled his stallion, looked around, then back at the priest, "in less elaborate surroundings."

"The Lord . . ."

"The Lord will still watch and listen to them." Carvajal laughed.

"Yes, even as he is watching and listening now." Father Dominic again moved close to the general's horse and lifted his hands toward the reins.

Carvajal's boot dislodged from the stirrup, he kicked the priest's chest, sending him onto the floor.

"The time will come when you will regret this," the padre said.

"The time has come for us to leave—us to our business and you to your prayers."

"I'll pray for your soul . . ." Father Dominic said as he struggled to his feet.

"Do that, padre . . . *adiós*." Carvajal waved to his men and spurred his horse.

As Vega started away from the altar the priest tried to grasp the crucifix from him. Vega swung the heavy cross, slashing a sharp edge across Father Dominic's forehead and spurting blood from the priest's brow into both eyes.

Vega walked up the aisle as General Carvajal rode through the arched doorway and down the stone steps of Saint Brendan.

"What the hell is that?" Beka pointed from his horse toward an object far ahead.

"I don't know. Let's go see."

What they saw after they rode ahead, dismounted, and examined the object was an open trunk containing women's clothing, with other feminine attire strewn all around on the ground nearby.

"I never saw something like this around here," Beka said.

"Or anyplace else." Andres held a petticoat up to his nose and inhaled. "Never smelled anything like it, either."

"Melena would give anything for all this."

"What's she got left to give?" Andres laughed. "The general's already got it all."

"How do we carry it back to camp?"

"We don't. Put it all inside and close the lid. Let them send a wagon for it."

"That's what we'll do," Beka agreed.

"We got something else to do first. We find out who dropped this and . . ." He winked.

"And what?"
"And what else they got."

The caravan passed by Saint Brendan's from a great distance, too great a distance to see the damage—and kept moving.

General Carvajal rode into camp followed by his men, who carried the loot from the church.

The general's temporary headquarters was isolated within a meadow between the shoulders of a mountain range. Years before it had been the village of some forgotten tribe, forgotten and abandoned until Carvajal decided it would be the hub of his operations until he had removed all that was worth removing from the surrounding area. Then he and his army would find another strategic camp from which to forage.

As Carvajal and the rest of the men dismounted, the women of the camp who cooked, cleaned after the men, and serviced their needs, turned from their labors and went to greet them, some with open arms, others with bottles.

The woman who greeted Prospero Carvajal was taller and more favorably proportioned than the rest, her face and features more Spanish than Indian, and dressed with cleaner clothes and brighter colors. She stood out from the others like a daffodil among corn husks, with a beauty not supernal but of the earth. She approached with a pelvic walk. Between pearl-white teeth she pulled the cork from a whiskey bottle, spit it away, and handed the bottle to Carvajal.

"Ah, Melena. You always know what I want, don't you?"

"And when you want it," Melena said, smiling as Carvajal drank. She pointed to Vega with the cross and chalice and the other men carrying the results of the raid. "It looks like you got religion."

"Religion that melts into gold bars. Some for Juarez and some for . . ."

"General Carvajal."

"We share and share alike. That is the way of the army."

"Your army."

"Melena." He took another deep swallow from the bottle. "You know what I want now?"

In the vast beige terrain the four-wagon caravan and the riders on horseback raised puffs of dust clouds as they made their way northeast.

Andres and Beka, on their bellies by a boulder, looked down at the passing pilgrims.

"I wonder . . . ," Andres said.

"Wonder? Wonder what?"

"What's in those wagons. Something heavy."

"Not dresses." Beka nodded.

"How many on horseback you count?"

"Too many."

"Not for Carvajal."

"We got a lot to tell him. And don't forget, something not to tell him." Andres patted his pocket with the pesos in it.

"I think one looks like a woman, with those two in front."

"We'll find out sometime."

"Hmm. But not now."

"Now, like good soldiers, we make our report to the good general."

Andres and Beka crawled backward, then rose behind the boulder and moved toward their two horses.

* * *

They had already come across the dead bodies, man and horse. Forrester had fired two shots and the battalion of buzzards reluctantly took to the air and circled in the distance, waiting for the intruders to depart so the black birds could return and finish their repast.

Two of the crewmen from the *Corsair* vomited, and most of the rest turned away at the sight of what was left of the corpses.

Forrester, Connors, and one other crewman, Mase Grizwald, did not turn away. Grizwald was a big man, a hard man, with a pitted face, who once commanded a ship himself, and who came aboard the *Corsair* only until he could avail himself of another command. He was not averse to commanding the *Corsair* if anything happened to the current captain and first mate.

From the condition of what was left of the bodies, man and horse, it was impossible to determine the cause of death. Nor were the crewmen curious enough to investigate.

"All right," Forrester had said. "Let's move on."

"Sir . . ."

"What is it, Rink?"

Johnny Rink cleared his throat. He was barely eighteen, a Texas hardscrabble farm boy who could barely read or write, thin, with a scarecrow face and long arms dangling.

"Well, sir . . . ain't we gonna bury 'em?"

"We're going to move on."

"Be all right, sir, if I stay behind and do it? I mean, just the . . . the man. I'll catch up to y'all, sir."

"It'll probably take you too damn lo—"

"I'll stay and help him, sir. It won't take us long. We'll catch you."

Dell Warren was one of the heirs to a beautiful Virginia plantation who, unlike his three older brothers, had declined the opportunity of being an officer on land for the prospect of serving the cause at sea, where there was a need just as great.

"Very well, Mr. Warren," Forrester said. "But see that you catch us within the hour."

"Aye, sir." Both the young sailors nodded.

"What're you going to dig with?"

"Got my knife, sir." Warren pulled a seven-inch flensing knife from his belt.

"Got my Bowie, sir." Johnny Rink withdrew the fifteen-inch weapon from its sheath.

"One hour," Forrester repeated.

That had been more than four hours ago. Since then, after Johnny and Dell had concluded their Christian deed and caught up to Forrester and the crew, they had made another unexpected discovery in the wilderness, and were now examining the contents of the trunk left behind, first by Gunnison and Dominique and then by Andres and Beka.

Forrester had given the order for the men to dismount, stretch, and relieve themselves while he and Connors opened the trunk and poked at the contents.

Forrester was not surprised by what they found. While he was making his deal with Alvarez, Don Carlos had told him that when and if the captain caught up to Gunnison and his crew he might find an attractive addition to the expedition. One of his men had taken a Miss Dominique Lessuer and some baggage several miles out toward Vera Cruz in advance of Gunnison's departure. Don Carlos did not confide the details of the deal he had made with the lady, but there was a lascivious grin on his face in the telling. He did mention that he had never met anyone quite like her and eagerly anticipated meeting her again. Meanwhile—he smiled as

127

he said it—she had left him something to remember her by.

When Forrester had told the crew that they were going to abandon, at least temporarily, the *Corsair* and proceed by land, there were grumblings among the men. Some, led by Mase Grizwald, asked to know the nature of the overland mission.

"I signed on as a sailor and for a share of the bounty we take from U.S. ships, not to slog across Mexico."

"You signed on to obey orders, Grizwald, and you'll obey my orders, or else."

"Or else what?"

"The penalty for disobeying an officer's orders on sea—or land—is death, and you will address that officer as 'sir.' Get back to your horse and mount up." Grizwald had done just that, but there was the look of murder in his eye as he obeyed. He had not spoken another word since they left San Angelo.

"Well," Forrester closed the lid of the trunk, "the buzzards won't want any of this. There's a couple of hours of daylight left. Let's get mounted."

The weary animals pulling the four heavy wagons had slowed even more, and no amount of urging, by voice or whip, could prod them into moving faster.

The sun was settling behind the saw-toothed peaks to the west, taking daylight with it. Gunnison looked to the rear and saw the wagons falling farther away.

Mister Joseph and Alan Rankin were at the tail of the expedition in a vain effort to hurry the tired animals along.

"I hope the captain finds a spot to camp before sundown," Rankin said. "These animals—"

"He will," Mister Joseph said, interrupting.

"That church some miles back must've had a well with water."

"I saw you looking that way. You must be Catholic like the people hereabouts."

"Why do you say that?"

"Well, on shipboard, when we were burying Mister Stewart, and the captain asked if anybody knew . . ."

"Oh, yes."

"I haven't been in a church for a long time, have you?"

"No. No, I haven't." Rankin's heels kicked into the flanks of his horse and he moved forward, ahead of Mister Joseph.

Dominique still rode the Appaloosa between Gunnison and Bogartis, with Jeff and Discant close behind.

"These Mexicans must have groins made out of lead," Dominique remarked.

"What did you say?" Gunnison looked at her.

"You heard me—groins made out of lead. These damn Mexican saddles are hard on the crotch, don't you think?"

"Well, I . . ."

"I'm used to an English saddle, or even a Western, but this damn contraption could cripple anybody's joint. I think I'd rather ride bareback."

Gunnison glanced backward at Jeff and Discant, who had both heard and were grinning. Mister Bogartis seemed to blush through his whiskers. The seamen were used to plain talk from saloon girls and street women, but coming from this creamy-complexioned Southern belle they were at a loss for the proper response to her sudden observation.

"You can ride up on a wagon anytime you choose," Gunnison suggested.

"Hell no, that's hard on the—"

"Look, lady. It was your idea to come along. Nobody promised you first-class transportation, and I'd just as soon skip any anatomical complaints . . . unless you're asking somebody to give you a rubdown."

" 'Somebody' better not try—not unless it's my idea . . . and I've got no such notion." She looked back at the two young officers. "At least, not yet."

"It's still a long way to Vera Cruz," Jeff said.

"I like the conversation better back there." Dominique smiled. "Excuse me, Captain." She let the Appaloosa drift back between the lieutenant and ensign.

"Why don't you two loosen a few buttons and get comfortable?" Dominique unfastened another button on her blouse; that made three. "This isn't some dress parade we're on, you know."

"Isn't it?" Discant smiled.

"You two ever been to Paris?" Dominique asked.

"No."

"No."

"You'd like it. I'm not sure Paris would like you. You two go everyplace together?"

"Only when we're ordered to."

"Are you following orders now? Were you ordered to follow," she pointed to Gunnison, "him?"

"You ask a hell of a lot of questions, Miss Lessuer," Jeff said.

"Only when I'm bored, and so far this trip is pretty damn boring. You notice that?"

"Let's hope it stays that way," Jeff added.

"Something else I noticed. You want to know what it is?"

"I can live without it."

"Looks like you can live without your father. That's what else I noticed. You two don't talk much to each other, do you? Seems like you, Lieutenant, speak only when you're spoken to when it comes to him. Afraid he'll spank you?"

"If you say so."

"Well, I guess I shouldn't have said that. You two probably have your reasons, and it's none of my business. But after a while, out here, you've got to say something . . . don't you think?"

No answer.

"I guess you don't. Maybe I'll just talk to my horse from now on. Chita," she said to the Appaloosa, "what do you think of the unpleasant situation between the states?"

No answer.

"You know," Bogartis whispered to Gunnison, "what that partner of yours said about these saddles is true. Think I'd rather be keelhauled than—"

"Mister Bogartis." Gunnison pointed ahead. "There's some."

"Some what?"

"Water."

There was a shallow, slow-moving stream in the distance bordered by a squad of scrubby oaks along the banks.

"You call that water?" Bogartis rose in the saddle to get a better look. "Why, it ain't even hardly wet."

"Wet enough to fill up our canteens and the livestock. Good place to camp."

"Anyplace is, where I can get off this hammerback."

Mister Joseph had ridden up alongside.

"Looks like we made our first port, Mister Joseph," Gunnison said.

"Pass the word. We camp here tonight."

"Aye, aye, sir." Mister Joseph nodded.

"I don't know about you people," Dominique said,

and swiped the dust off her blouse, "but I'm going to take a bath."

"Is that an invitation?" Gunnison grinned.

"No, definitely not. And most of these sea wolves look like they never heard of soap."

Chapter Seventeen

It was a long, winding way from the Mexican-American War, just over a dozen years ago, to this night at Carvajal's camp, and to the many other camps and "Carvajals" who called themselves generals, colonels, captains, patriots, or, closer to the truth, guerrillas.

On November 19, 1846, James K. Polk, President of the United States, had named Major General Winfield Scott—also known, because of his flamboyant uniforms and military zest, as "Old Fuss and Feathers"—commander of an expedition whose mission it was to seize the port of Vera Cruz, march to Mexico City, and settle border and other disputes between the two countries.

It took until February 2, 1848, and the Treaty of Guadalupe Hidalgo to officially terminate resistance and hostilities. In between it took the outpouring of gunfire and blood—from the successful siege of Vera Cruz to the 260-mile march toward Mexico City and the battles of Buena Vista, Cerro Gordo, Jalapa, Contreras, Churubusco, El Molino, and Chapultepec, where on September 14, Mexico City's mayor and other officials surrendered Mexico City to General Winfield Scott while a band of U.S. dragoons played "Yankee Doodle Dandy."

But it had taken a great many Yankees, officers and men, to win the war. And many of those Yankee officers and men weren't Yankees anymore. They were Rebels fighting against their former comrades for the cause of the Confederate States of America.

And the officers and men of the Mexican Army had split into even more splinters, serving dictators and presidents that came and went until the advent of President Benito Juárez from Oaxaca, a president who was determined to unite all of Mexico against all enemies, foreign and domestic, and create a government patterned after that of its former enemy, the Unites States of America.

Prospero Carvajal was also from Oaxaca, but there the resemblance to Juárez ended. Juárez was of the people and for the people. Carvajal was of, and for, himself. A young soldier in the Mexican-American War, he had succeeded more by cunning than courage, deceit than devotion, profit than patriotism, in organizing a band mostly made up of scalawags, back-shooters, and looters of which, he, being the worst, naturally was the leader.

In the name of reform and the ideal of independence, they plundered and pillaged, especially the rich, since the rich provided more profitable plunder than the poor.

They also raped.

Prospero Carvajal had, years before, raped Melena. That's how their union began, and since it was found to be satisfactory on both sides, continued until this night as they sat around the campfire eating goat and drinking whiskey and wine.

But Melena was not the first in her family to be raped.

Decades earlier, her mother, a peon, was looked upon favorably by Don Miguel Domingo, an españole born in Castile who owned a huge ranch in Tacatecas. The fact that Don Miguel had a portly wife and three children was of no consequence or consideration. He took the young woman to bed and, when she became pregnant, provided her with a suitable husband—a peon, of course—and continued to bed her whenever he was so inclined.

The product of Don Miguel's illicit liaison was a daughter named Melena, who blossomed with much of the bearing and looks of her Castilian heritage.

Before Melena was sixteen her uncredited father began to cast curious glances in her direction. Melena's mother had become almost as portly as Don Miguel's wife, who had now borne him a total of six children.

What might have happened next is only conjecture, because of what did happen.

Prospero Carvajal and his band of raiders attacked, looted and burned Don Miguel's ranch, and in the encounter Carvajal looked favorably upon the sixteen-year-old girl who stood apart from the other flat-faced peons.

Rape or no, Melena was constrained to leave the life she had led, particularly since that life no longer existed now that the ranch was burned and Don Miguel was dead.

She became not just one of the women of the camp, but General Prospero Carvajal's woman. He did have others, but none quite like the one who sat next to him tonight, ate goat, drank wine, and listened to Andres and Beka make their report.

Vega, who was second in command to Carvajal, but with no real authority, sat close by, drinking from a bottle and stealing glances toward Melena's breasts plunging almost to her waist as she sat.

"First," Andres reported, lying, "we find a trunk with women's clothes—"

"A woman's clothes," Beka interrupted. "All the clothes belonged to one woman. Coats, dresses, and things she wears underneath."

"Expensive clothes," Andres added.

"Clothes not from Mexico."

So far Carvajal was not paying much attention, but Melena was.

"What's the matter with you?" she said. "Why didn't you bring it back? The trunk with the clothes."

"Too heavy to carry," Andres answered, then looked to Carvajal. "Maybe you want to send a wagon back and get it. . . ."

"Will the dresses fit me?" Melena asked.

"I don't know." Andres shrugged. "We didn't try them on."

"Why didn't you bring back something so I could try it on?"

"Because we were in a hurry to find out who dropped it . . . while there was daylight," Andres said, very pleased with his answer.

"Did you?" Carvajal asked.

"Yes."

"Well?"

"Well what?"

"This report," Carvajal said, "is going to take longer than the war. Goddamm it, did you find out who dropped it?"

"Yes," Andres nodded, "four wagons, loaded heavy, with about forty men on horseback . . ."

"And a woman, we think."

"They must be crazy," Carvajal said, "to travel here."

"Some of them looked like they wore uniforms," Andres noted.

"What kind of uniforms?"

"I don't know," Beka said. "Not like anything I ever saw."

"Guns and rifles?" Carvajal asked.

"Yes."

"Maybe they're not so crazy." Carvajal shrugged.

"I want that trunk," Melena said.

"Never mind the trunk."

"I want it!"

"You'll get it . . . and maybe more, much more. Where are they now?"

"Tonight they camp by the stream," Andres said.

"They move to the north and east," Beka added.

"Maybe Vera Cruz," Andres suggested.

"They'll never get there." Carvajal drank and smoothed a palm across Melena's breast.

"I don't think so, my general." Vega smiled as he watched his general's moving hand.

"We can always use horses and guns," Carvajal said, "and whatever is in those wagons."

"A woman too, I think," Andres reminded him.

"Do we wait for the rest of our army?" Vega asked.

"They won't be back for days." Carvajal removed his palm from Melena.

"We will take care of them ourselves. Whatever they're carrying must be worth a hell of a lot to have so many guarding it."

"And to risk coming across here, my general."

"You're right, Vega. They had to have come from San Angelo . . . maybe from a ship. Andres . . . these uniforms you saw—could they be from a boat? A navy boat?"

Andres shrugged. So did Beka.

"Well, besides the horses, guns, and whatever else they're carrying, we'll have some new uniforms to wear."

"What about the trunk? I need something new to wear. Everything I've got is so old and worn you can almost see through it."

"I like to see through it." Carvajal laughed.

"What about *them*?" Melena pointed at the men, starting with Vega and making a circle. "You want them to see through, too?"

"All right, all right! You'll get your trunk. But first we get what's in those wagons."

"When, my general?" Vega asked.

"*Mañana.*" Carvajal already was rising, with a bottle in one hand and with the other pulling Melena to her feet.

As the two of them walked toward their hut, all the men's eyes were on Melena. By the light of the campfire they could almost see through the gossamer material that clung to the swells and dips of her undulating body. What they couldn't see through, they could imagine. And they all used their imagination. Especially Vega.

And there was one time when he used more than his imagination.

Months before, at another camp, when Carvajal was away, Vega no longer could bear to look at Melena, her beautiful, almost patrician face, the swaying breasts, narrow waist, and long, inviting legs—to look and do nothing.

He had drunk just enough to ignite his lust and ignore the consequences. He had watched as she slept naked without Carvajal next to her. She turned from her side, revealing the full glory of a body unlike any Vega had ever touched or seen before. He could not, nor did not, think of what would happen to him afterward. He thought only of what it would be like to take her. To have her. And if he had to, kill her and run away, or kill her, blame somebody else, and kill him too . . . leaving them side by side, unable to testify against him. Whatever it took, he would take her.

With Tarquin's ravishing strides, he stiffened, screwed up his alcoholic courage, and was upon her—but only for a moment, only until the knife slashed across his throat, leaving a thin red line, and the sharp point pressed just under his Adam's apple.

He trembled, sobered, went limp, and pleaded. He was sorry. Never again. If she spared him . . . didn't tell Carvajal . . . didn't tell anyone . . . he vowed he would never touch her . . . or even look upon her. . . . He would do whatever she commanded as long as he lived . . . he swore by his dead mother . . .

In that first instant Melena's survival instinct was to kill the sniveling bastard, but another, more cunning instinct told her that even a sniveling bastard might sometime be of more use to her alive than dead.

She took Vega up on his vow—neither would say anything to anyone. She would spare his life in return for servitude. She knew that Carvajal at any time might find another, younger, more desirable woman. A woman who would take her place. A woman who had to be disposed of. At that time Melena would use Vega, maybe even give him what he had wanted this night, in order to get rid of the younger, more desirable woman that neither Carvajal nor she had yet met.

Since then Vega had been careful about what he said and how he looked at Melena.

Still, knowing what was happening in Carvajal's hut

as the rest of them sat around the campfire, Vega couldn't help thinking about her.

The fingers of his hand touched the thin white scar at his throat, a scar concealed by the stubble of black whiskers, a scar that remained as the only real memento of a mad moment that almost cost him his life. . . . And still he thought of her.

There was a strange, unreal stillness at the campsite along the stream where Gunnison had chosen to spend the first night of the journey across the cauldron that was called Mexico.

An uneasy quiet.

Maybe because the crew and the animals were tired. More tired than usual. Much more.

Maybe because of the uncertainty.

Instead of sailors on a ship, a ship they knew and could command, a ship they could direct—shorten sail, change course, seek harbor in case of storm—they were strangers in a strange land. A land of treacherous terrain, where most of them had never journeyed before. A land where they were unfamiliar with friend or foe—and couldn't tell them apart.

Most of the *Phantom Hope*'s crew had no particular allegiance to any country. Their home was the deck of whatever ship they sailed on at the time. They were citizens of the sea.

And one ship on one ocean was just about as good as another.

Gunnison, to them, was a better captain than most, a captain who paid top wages and split a fair share of his profits with them, but when it came right down to it, just another captain of just another ship.

And now they found themselves not aboard a ship with a cargo and destination that they knew, but in a foreign, unfriendly country where an unseen enemy could strike from any direction at any time, night or day.

These were the thoughts of most of the crewmen, thoughts they kept to themselves in the strange, unreal stillness of the campsite.

Chapter Eighteen

And in the strange, unreal stillness, Dominique sat by the stream, still wet, clad only in a short, flimsy chemise, her long lovely legs illuminated by moonlight, half submerged in the water.

She rolled a cigarette.

Dominique Lessuer lit the cigarette, tossed the burnt match into the stream, and took another puff.

"Why don't you come down and get a better look?" she said to no one in sight.

Silence.

"Come ahead, sailor boy. I won't bite you." She ran the finger of her left hand through her damp, red hair, which seemed even redder in the moonlight. "Your dad said he'd give a snake first bite, remember?"

Jeff Gunnison stepped out from behind the tree.

"That's better." She inhaled. "Well?"

"Well, what?"

"Don't you recognize an invitation when you hear one?"

"Invitation to what?"

"Talk about old times."

"We haven't got any old times."

"We never will have, if we don't start sometime."

"I can't figure you out."

"You're not supposed to. I'm the mystery woman. But you'd have a better chance if you came closer."

Jeff moved toward the stream and Dominique.

"I've heard that redheads were reckless, but lady, you take the prize. . . ."

"What *is* the prize?"

"It could be you," he pointed back toward the camp. "If somebody took a notion. You know those sailors aren't exactly knights in shining armor."

"Oh . . . so that's it."

"That's what?"

"Your excuse. You're actually Galahad, protecting the fair, defenseless lady."

"Not exactly, I'm . . ."

"Well, you're certainly not Mordred, nephew and betrayer of King Arthur. I'm going to call you Galahad. Sit down, Galahad, or are you afraid you'll get that uniform dirty?"

"It's been dirty before." Jeff sat on a rock. He couldn't help looking at the tantalizingly assured figure of the young woman stretched out just inches from him.

"Go ahead. Take a good look. We're used to *voyeurs* in Paris. They're harmless."

"Like the man said, this isn't Paris . . . and some voyeurs aren't as harmless as others."

"Are you talking about the crew . . . ," she nodded toward the camp, ". . . or yourself?"

Andrew J. Fenady

"I'm talking about being . . . reckless."

"Sometimes you talk too much."

"Then I'll just say good night." He started to rise.

"No. Sit down . . . Galahad. Please."

Jeff sat.

"You know," she said, "we've got something in common."

"We do? What?"

"Fathers."

"Everybody's got a father . . . well, most everybody."

"But not like ours. Mine was a rascal, a scoundrel . . . and yours . . ."

"What about mine?"

"You tell me."

Silence.

"You won't, will you? Well, I guess that's up to you. But I think *they* had something in common."

"Being scoundrels?"

"Something else."

"What?"

"Honesty. Whatever my father was, he never deceived me, or anybody else. He was tough and independent, and he could charm the fangs off a snake, but he never went back on his word . . ."

"Or his country?"

"The court-martial . . . I heard about it."

"Everybody has."

"That's what's eating you, isn't it?"

"It's not exactly easy to swallow."

"You think it's easy for him? From what I heard, he did what he thought was right and . . ."

"Blackened the name of Gunnison."

"Maybe it isn't just black and white, maybe—"

"Maybe we'd better get back. You got any clothes . . . I mean, with you?"

144

She pointed to a pile on the other side of the rock.

"Not as many as when I started out, but . . ."

"But enough to get back to camp. Put 'em on. I'll walk you back."

"Sure." She flipped the butt of the cigarette into the water. "Galahad."

Mister Joseph and Alan Rankin sat near each other at one of the campfires. With a sailor's needle and strong thread Rankin mended a jagged tear in a shirt he had taken off. Mister Joseph was carving at a piece of wood.

"May I borrow that?"

"What?" He looked up from his carving.

"That knife . . . for just a minute. The thread's too tough to bite off, and I left my knife in my saddlebag."

"Sure." Mister Joseph handed the knife to Rankin, handle toward him.

Rankin cut the thread and returned the knife, also holding it by the blade.

"Thanks."

"Anytime. Say, you did a pretty good job on that shirt." He smiled.

"We had to do all our own sewing at—" Rankin caught himself and didn't finish.

"Where?"

"At . . . home."

"I see . . . and where—"

"What's that you're carving?" Rankin asked.

"Well, I carved one like it before. It turned out to be a cross. I guess this will too."

"A cross? What for?"

"The other one was for my daughter."

"Your daughter? I didn't know you had a family, Mister Joseph."

"Why wouldn't I? Because I was a slave? Even slaves have families . . . as well as feelings."

"Please, excuse me. I didn't mean to offend you."

"No. I'm the one who owes the apology, Mister Rankin. Why should you know anything about my family? I've never talked about them."

"Are they . . ."

"And I'd prefer not to talk about them now . . . if you don't mind."

"Of course not. I suppose each of us has things he'd prefer to keep to himself. That doesn't mean," Rankin extended his right hand, "we can't be friends, does it?"

Mister Joseph smiled and held out his right hand.

"Well, Galahad, here's my castle. And the crimson-haired lady thanks you for the safe escort." They stopped beside one of the wagons, where Dominique's suitcase had been set underneath. "I'd ask you in for a flagon of wine, but I have no flagon and no wine . . . but thanks to you I still have my innocence."

"Yeah. About as innocent as Cleopatra."

"You had to say that, didn't you, you sonofabitch."

"I'm sorry."

"I'm not. We both know where we stand . . . and where we don't." Dominique Lessuer stooped to her knees and crawled under the wagon without looking back.

Captain Gunnison sat alone at another campfire looking into the flames, a tin cup in one hand, a whiskey bottle by his side.

He had seen his son and Dominique walking together from the direction of the stream. They looked like a romantic couple in the moonlight, but Gunnison didn't think there was much likelihood of romance between the two of them. Oil and water. Fire and ice. Even worse, hydrogen and oxygen.

But romance was the furthest thing from Gunnison's mind. His mind was on Vera Cruz . . . and fifteen million dollars' worth of double eagles . . . and the possibilities . . .

Mister Bogartis approached, muttering.

"Are you talking to me?"

"No, I ain't talkin' to you."

"Then who the hell are you talking to?"

"I'm talkin' to a hooty owl up in a tree. Hooty owl's got sense. We ain't."

"Well, there isn't any hooty owl, nor any tree anywhere near this spot . . . except down by the stream. So go down there and talk."

"That way you can't hear me."

"So you are talking to me."

"I guess so."

"Well, what're you saying?"

"I'm sayin' that firm footin' don't agree with me— that's what I'm sayin'."

"All right, so you said it."

"Even the air smells different on land. It don't smell healthy."

"Well," Gunnison lifted the whiskey bottle and an extra cup beside him, "this doesn't taste any different on land. Sit down and have a drink."

"It does." Bogartis sat. "But I will."

Miles to the southwest Forrester's camp, smaller, and with fewer men and only one light wagon to carry supplies, was settling in for the night.

But the men in the camp, the crew of the *Corsair*, made up of an even coarser congregation than that of the *Phantom Hope*, were not exactly settled. They, too, were unaccustomed to, and unsatisfied with, circumstances that prevailed. Better dirty weather aboard ship than a clear night on strange land.

When Forrester spoke, or Connors commanded, they continued to respond with "Yes, sir," but the "Yes, sir" lacked the snap on land that prevailed at sea.

They were slower to respond and surly in their obedience. Grizwald had set the example by moving just a beat behind the norm and never quite looking an officer in the eye when that officer spoke.

"I don't like it, Captain," Connors said quietly to Forrester as the two of them stood near the wagon, away from the others. "It's that damn Grizwald. That hogface is stirrin' up trouble just as sure as that moon's up there. Think I ought to stick a shiv up his—"

"Now, Mister Connors," Forrester blew a smoke ring into the windless night, "belay that. We're going to need every man jack of these bastards. They're just a little skittish yet. They'll settle down."

"Tell you the truth, Captain, I'm a little skittish myself. You know I've never questioned you, Cap—"

"I know that, Mister Connors. And you've got a right to wonder what I'm going to do. I'm doing a little wondering myself . . . about Gunnison."

"He outnumbers us, maybe two to one."

"But he's got something I want, and I'm going to get it."

"How?"

"Don't know yet. But we couldn't get it if we stayed in San Angelo. Once we spot him, we'll just keep following him until we get our chance . . . maybe not till Vera Cruz. But I'll get what I'm after one way or another—and you'll get your share." Forrester smiled.

"I know that, Captain."

"Get some sleep. We'll move at first light."

"Aye, sir."

But Grizwald was planning to move before that. And in a different direction.

He had primed two of the crewmen to go with him.

The first, Reynolds, had served under him before as first mate. When sober, Reynolds was an able seaman, but somehow he seemed to have an inexhaustible supply of rum secreted somewhere, a supply into which he frequently dipped. The same was true on land. Since leaving San Angelo he had had a slightly unfocused look in his eyes.

The second, Manfried, was a notch above a moron and a rung beneath a rogue. He would follow whoever talked to him last and promised him most. Today it was Grizwald.

Earlier in the day, when they had stopped to rest the animals and feed them grain, Grizwald had made his case to both of them.

They were off, Grizwald said, marching in some fool's parade trying to catch up to and defeat a bigger, better-equipped force while exposing themselves to bandits and the devil knows what in a treacherous country that nobody knew—and for what? Nobody knew that either.

While the camp slept, the three of them would take their horses and enough water and supplies to get back to San Angelo. Forrester would not follow them, and when they got back to the port, the *Corsair* would be there waiting for a new captain and first and second mate.

"We'll need a crew," Reynolds said.

"We'll get one in San Angelo. There's more sailors there than rats in the cellar."

"Who does that ship belong to?"

Andrew J. Fenady

"Not to Forrester. He's abandoned it. We're claiming it in the name of the Confederate States of America." Grizwald smiled. "Until we get out to sea, then we claim it for ourselves and go into business."

"What kind of business?"

"Whatever makes us a profit. It's better than going up against Gunnison and who the hell knows what else. What do you say?"

They said yes.

Johnny Rink had been on first watch at the camp when a figure approached out of the dark.

"Johnny?"

"Yep. Who is it?"

"Warren. Dell Warren."

"Good evenin'."

"It is so far. Get some sleep, Johnny. My turn to stand guard."

"Tell me something, will you, Dell?"

"If I can."

"What're we doin' out here?"

"I can't . . . tell you that is. I guess nobody knows except Captain Forrester and maybe Mister Connors—and they're not confiding in us."

"Con . . . fide . . . ing?"

"Telling us," Warren said. "Sooner or later, we'll find out."

"This isn't turnin' out the way I figured."

"Ours not to reason why, Johnny. Hand me that rifle."

Gunnison was refilling the two glasses when Bogartis cleared his throat and nodded toward Jeff and Discant, who were walking nearby toward the spot they had staked out for the night.

"Why don't you ask 'em over for a drink?"

150

"Why not? Say, gentlemen," he called out. "Come over here a minute, will you?"

They did, and stood side by side.

"Relax, fellas. You look like you're at attention. Sit down, have a drink—it's been a long day. We've got a couple of extra cups, haven't we, Mister Bogartis?"

"We have."

Jeff hesitated, but Discant smiled and sat, tugging at the lieutenant's sleeve as he did. Jeff also sat while Gunnison poured.

"Confusion to the enemy," Gunnison toasted, and then drank.

"Speaking of the enemy, sir." Discant glanced around. "It's quiet so far."

"So far ain't far enough," Mister Bogartis said.

"You think Captain Montego was exaggerating?" Discant drank and looked at Gunnison.

"About what?"

"Guerrillas. War. Danger."

"From what I know about him, and I've known him for some time, Montego is not prone to exaggerating . . . when it comes to things like that. No, I don't think things'll stay . . . quiet."

"What about your crew?" Jeff asked.

"What about them?"

"I've been thinking. There are ten of us in our contingent, counting Jim and me."

"So?"

"So, you've got forty in your crew—"

"Counting Mister Bogartis and me."

"But how many of those forty can you count on in case of an attack?"

"You saw them fight on the *Phantom Hope*."

"That was at sea. They had no place to run. No chance to run. On land it could be different."

151

Andrew J. Fenady

"It could."

"How many?"

"I've been thinking about that too. I'd count on Mister Joseph, Cookie, and Rankin. As for the rest, half aren't even U.S. citizens. They'd fight to save their lives . . . but not our cargo—they don't even know what it is."

"Should we tell them?" Discant asked.

"I don't think so."

"Why not, sir?"

"Well, greed is a curious thing. It can throw even a good man off balance. If they know, we might have a fight on our hands before we met anybody else."

"Mutiny?" Discant looked from Jeff to Gunnison.

"It's been known to happen, and for a lot less than . . . well, for a lot less. Let's just keep things as they are for the time being."

"Yes, sir." Discant nodded.

"Yes, sir," Jeff repeated as he rose. "Thanks for the drink."

"You're welcome. I hope we have one in Vera Cruz," Gunnison said.

Two night clouds drifted slowly across the sea of sky, sailing in front of a thousand blinking stars. The first cloud floated beneath the milky moon and continued on its celestial journey to nowhere. The second cloud hit the moon, wrapped its vapors around the circle, and covered the night with a shroud of darkness except for the light of the blinking stars.

Dell Warren stood guard at the near end of the picket lines where the horses were tethered. He had been looking up at the sky watching the amorphous cloud envelop the moon, then looked around at the raw, enduring landscape of Mexico, barren, brown, and unforgiving, and thinking of how different, under that same sky and moon, the scene was even now in his native Virginia.

Virginia, with soil rich, dark, and fertile—verdant Virginia, with hospitable earth that provided its sons and daughters with all their wants. Where Dell Warren's father and his family before him had worked with care and pride for more than a century.

The Warrens of Virginia.

There were Warrens there ever since there was a Virginia. And there was a Virginia before there was a United States. Virginia played a major part in the creation of the United States. Washington, Jefferson, Madison, Henry, Monroe. Would there have been a Declaration of Independence, a Constitution, a United States, without these Virginians?

Since the birth of Virginia, the Warrens had been there. Soldiers of the soil. Warrens had fought and bled and died in the French and Indian War, the Revolution, the War of 1812, and the Mexican-American War, little more than a handful of years ago. Fought for the United States and for Virginia.

And now the Warrens were fighting for Virginia against the United States. Fighting for their farms in the Shenandoah Valley.

By geography and fate the Shenandoah was destined to be one of the bloodiest battlefields. The valley was more than one hundred fifty miles long and ten to twenty miles wide. Between the Blue Ridge on the east and the Alleghenies on the west, this region was one of varied scenery and natural wonders.

Unfortunately, it was also the ideal avenue of approach between the forces of the North and South. Both sides now considered the Shenandoah Valley the passport to victory or defeat.

But young Dell Warren had shipped out before the

valley had been invaded. He now regretted his choice to fight at sea rather than on his own soil, where his father and brothers fought this night. But Dell Warren vowed to himself and to God that if he made it through this voyage—now an expedition—he would return to Virginia and fight the enemy on the Warrens' own home ground. Fight to victory—or to the death.

Dell Warren thought he heard something and turned, but too late.

The butt end of a gun crashed against his head, dropping him hard to the ground.

Grizwald motioned back to the other two. Reynolds and Manfried stepped from behind a boulder and moved past the horses toward the far end of the picket line, each carrying a saddle and bridle.

Somewhere in the night a coyote howled and waited for an answer. None came. But Grizwald saw something, someone, coming and whispered to the other two. They followed him around the line of horses toward the other side of the boulder near where Warren had fallen.

The night cloud had drifted past the moon now shedding a soft light on the land below.

Adam Forrester approached the crumpled heap and recognized the unconscious face of Dell Warren. Forrester wore no side arm. He was about to reach down, pick up Warren's rifle, and fire a shot to arouse the camp when the gun barrel touched the back of his head and he heard the cock of a hammer.

"Don't make a sound," Grizwald whispered.

Forrester nodded in silence.

"Too bad," Grizwald continued. "Another two minutes and we would've been out of here."

"Is he dead?" Forrester spoke softly and pointed down at Warren.

"No." Grizwald pulled a knife from its sheath with

154

his left hand. A knife with a long, pointed blade that glinted in the moonlight. "But in your case, we got no choice."

The blade started to move toward Forrester's throat when a shot rang out. A bullet exploded into the left side of Grizwald's head and blew away his right ear and the starboard section of his skull.

At the same time Forrester's derringer discharged. Reynolds's right eye disappeared and the slug lodged in his brain, but Reynolds never knew what happened.

Both he and Grizwald were on the ground, dead as beaver hats.

Manfried was on his knees, next to where his gun had dropped, pleading for his life.

Kevin Connors, still pointing his gun, stepped out of the shadows as the camp sprang to life and sleepy men rushed toward the survivors, some with guns drawn and all asking what had happened.

"Deserters." Forrester waved down at the two bodies and at Manfried, who had buried his head in his palms and was crying and trembling. "Mutineers. Two dead, and I think I'll hang the other one. . . ."

"No . . . no . . . please . . . I'm with you, Captain. . . . I swear . . . I'm with you from now on . . . please . . . please . . . I'll do whatever you say . . ."

"Yes, you will."

Johnny Rink had rushed to Dell Warren's side as Warren was staggering to his feet.

"You all right, Dell?"

Warren managed to nod, then look to Forrester.

"I'm . . . sorry, Captain, they . . ."

"It's all right son. They almost got me too." Forrester pointed at the two bodies. "Somebody throw a blanket over 'em. We'll bury 'em in the morning before we start out." Forrester took a cigar and match out of his pocket and lit up. "Now, I'm going to say something and say it just once. You all volunteered to serve the Confederate States of America. You volunteered in, and now I'm giving you a chance to volunteer out—in the next thirty seconds. It's true you joined up to serve at sea, and now we're on land and that's why I'm giving you this chance. If you stay you're liable to get killed . . . or maybe wind up with a bigger bounty than any at sea. That's all I'm going to say about that. So, if there's any yellow-bellies among you, get out now. But if you stay I don't want to hear any questions, or see any hesitation when you're given an order—any order—or I'll kill you on the spot—any spot." He took a deep puff and looked around. "Thirty seconds are up. Anybody wants out, take a step forward."

Nobody moved.

"That's it, then. Get some sleep. I don't think we'll need any sentry tonight."

The men dispersed, leaving Forrester and Connors standing next to the blanketed bodies.

"Well, Mr. Connors, what do you think?"

"I think that speech you just made sounded sorta . . . patriotic."

"And effective?"

"Looks that way."

"Good. And just remember one more thing."

"What?"

"Sometimes patriotism can be very . . . profitable." Forrester smiled and tucked the derringer back into his belt. Connors leathered his revolver.

"And thanks, Mister Connors." He pointed at the dead bodies. "That makes us even."

"No, Captain. That was for Dakar. I still owe you for Casablanca and that slave aboard the *Jubilee*."

* * *

Gunnison's camp had long since gone silent in the deep night. Campfires glowed and occasionally crackled. Most of the men, including Gunnison, slept out in the open, saddles or saddlebags for pillows.

Dominique had the cover of one of the wagons all to herself.

Four or five of the other men slept under each of two other wagons, and Jeff and Discant, their tunics finally unbuttoned, lay beneath the last wagon.

"Jeff," Discant whispered. "You asleep?"

"No."

"Didn't think so."

"Now you know."

"It's funny what you think about sometimes," Discant said.

"Like what?"

"Like now. You know what I was thinking?"

"How the hell could I?"

"I was thinking how, back at the Academy, I never could get to sleep the night before a test."

"Yeah, well, we might just be in for a few tests out here before this thing is over, with a lot more at stake than some exam."

"I guess so. What about you?"

"What do you mean?"

"I mean, what were you thinking?"

"I was thinking about something I said that I shouldn't have."

"To your father?"

"No."

"Oh, to that girl, Dominique. Right?"

"Right."

"I can't quite . . ."

"Figure her out?"

"Yeah."

"You're right about that, too."

"One's thing's obvious."

"What?"

"Head to heel and hip to hip, she's the best-looking woman I ever saw."

Silence.

"What did you say to her?"

"Never mind."

"Jeff."

"What?"

"I'm . . . I'm glad we had that drink with your father, aren't you?"

Silence.

"You know . . . what he said about who we can trust . . . and who we can't."

"I don't trust anybody, including my dad."

"Jeff, he—"

"Listen. This is an order."

"I'm listening."

"If we do get hit and anything happens to me, see that the cargo gets to the United States."

"Nothing's going—"

"Even if you have to . . ." Jeff paused.

"To what?"

"To kill Gunnison."

Chapter Nineteen

Earlier that evening at China Lil's, just before closing, Lil sat at a table with Captain Rosario Montego. The orchestra had already left and so had most of the customers. Montego sipped his drink and did his best to appear jovial, to distract China Lil from her thoughts as she sat across from him, one hand tightly gripping a tall glass. With the other hand, she glided her fingers along the jade necklace at her throat.

". . . and then, with my fist, I hit him like a boulder from a catapult. She, of course, wanted to get married. I tell you, Lil, the trouble with marriage is women. They just don't . . . Lil . . . Lil, you're not listening, are you?"

"No."

"Neither am I. I'm just talking. I . . ."

Don Carlos Alvarez had risen from his usual corner table, escorting a new companion and potential conquest. She was young, dark, svelte, and beautiful, and from the eager look on her face, did not have any resistance on her mind. After patting her hip, reassuring his return, he left her standing there, and strolled toward Lil and Montego.

"Good evening." He smiled.

"Good night," Montego said.

"Yes," Don Carlos grinned back toward the waiting girl, "yes, it appears to be. A very good night. Very interesting. But then, there are a lot of interesting things in prospect. Don't you think?"

"Like what?" Montego finally looked up.

"Like a Yankee ship in need of repairs landing here at San Angelo, with a captain named Gunnison. But instead of the ship continuing, the cargo is unloaded, a heavy cargo. Who knows what that cargo is? Do you, the captain of the port?"

Montego did not answer.

"Or you?" He smiled at China Lil. "Captain Gunnison's . . . friend?"

Lil did not look up.

"And so the captain and the cargo, the heavy cargo, are on their way overland to . . . who knows where? And here it becomes even more interesting. A Confederate ship, also in need of repairs, comes into port with a captain named Forrester. It appears that they've had an . . . unfriendly encounter.

"The Confederate captain abandons his ship and, without a heavy cargo, begins his pursuit, which probably will end in another . . . unfriendly encounter, after a surprise attack . . . unless. . . ."

"Unless what?" Montego asked.

"Unless," Don Carlos grinned, "a certain rider I saw, leaving on a fast horse, can avoid the Confederate captain and warn the Yankee captain. Now, don't you think all that is interesting?"

Silence.

"Oh, and of course, something else that makes it even more interesting. But then again, you know . . . there's a war going on, and they're all right in the middle of it. Gunnison, Forrester, and a lady named Lessuer. Oh, didn't you know? She insisted on joining them to protect her interests, so I was considerate enough to provide her with transportation."

"In return for what?" Montego asked. "You're not known for your beneficence."

"Beneficence had nothing to do with it. Among other things, I am a man who looks to the future. Now, if I was a gambling man, I don't know who I'd bet on. But then, I never gamble. I only believe in," he looked toward the waiting girl, who obviously was growing impatient, "a sure thing. Yes," Don Carlos concluded, as he turned and started to walk away, "it is a good night."

"If, some good night or day," Captain Montego said, as he watched Don Alvarez and the girl walk toward the door, "that man is found with his throat slit and his vitals missing, I will light a candle . . . no, two candles, and pray that the perpetrator will be rewarded with a long and peaceful life and afterlife."

For the first time that evening China Lil smiled, but only for a moment.

"You know, Lil," Montego went on, "if a man wears a uniform you know he is your friend or enemy, but a man like Don Carlos who wears a smile is more dangerous and despicable then any uniformed enemy. His only cause is himself and his only pleasure is profit— profit and . . ."

"To hell with him," Lil said. "He's not worth thinking about."

"What are you thinking about? As if I didn't know?"

"Right now I'm thinking about whether Roberto got through to Gunnison. If he's not back by morning . . ."

"There probably will be a widow with three fatherless children in San Angelo."

"Don't say that."

"We've got to face the facts."

"If that happens . . . I'll take care of them."

"*We'll* take care of them."

"Rosario, I've been thinking that maybe I should get on a horse and go . . ."

"To protect your interests?"

"To throw my arms around him."

"And then what? Give him something else to worry about? No. He's got enough." Montego reached out, took her hand away from the glass, and held her fingers with his own. "No, my dear, I know how you feel. He's saved both of our lives and we both love him in our own way, but there is nothing either of us can do now except wait."

"And pray."

"That too." Montego nodded.

Chapter Twenty

The winter morning sky was heavy. Gunmetal gray, almost daring the searchlight of the sun to break through. But break through it did, and began to burn into land more forked now.

Ridges. *Rincónes*. Barrancas. Cathedral mountains in the distance. Dry. Desolate.

Land that had been conquered time and again.

Yet remained unconquered.

The caravan moved in its customary formation. Gunnison, Dominique, and Bogartis in the lead. Then Jeff and Discant. The naval contingent interspersed with the crew of the *Phantom Hope* among the four wagons and with Mister Joseph and Rankin at the rear.

"Sonofabitch," Dominique gritted.

"Are you talking to me?" Gunnison said.

"We forgot something last night."

"Prayers?"

"No. Papers. I got so damn mad at your son, the officer and gentleman, that I didn't remind you about drawing up the agreement for the *Phantom Hope*."

"Oh, that."

"Yes, that."

"Well, I've got a few other things on my mind."

"So have I. But that's one of 'em, and I'd just as soon get it off my mind and on paper—with two copies, signed and sealed, tonight."

"If there *is* a tonight," Mister Bogartis muttered.

"What was that you said?" Gunnison asked.

"I said you're doggone right."

"Yeah, that's what you said, all right."

"And, by the way, Captain Gunnison," Dominique went on, "when you do draw up the agreement—"

"Oh, for God's sake."

"No, for *my* sake. Make sure it says that I am to be paid the full amount just as soon as you take possession—"

"I already got possession."

"It doesn't look like it, not out here. . . . I am to be paid the full amount immediately and in gold."

"Gold?"

"Gold!"

"Bouillon or dust?"

"Just so it's gold."

"Anything else?"

"Yes. I would appreciate it if for the rest of this trip you would keep your son just as far away from me as possible."

"Then it looks like he's going to be far away from the both of us."

"That suits me fine." Dominique had been speaking loud enough to make sure that Jeff had heard the conversation. She wheeled her horse and headed toward the rear of the caravan.

"Where are you going?" Gunnison asked.

"Far away from the both of you."

"That suits me fine." Gunnison grinned. "Hope she goes back to San Angelo," he said to Bogartis.

"No such luck," Mister Bogartis replied.

General Carvajal had split his command into two forces. The main contingent, led by him, was high on a ridge. With Carvajal were Andres and Beka, along with Melena, who had insisted on coming at least this far.

The other flank of his army, led by Vega, rode out of sight of the caravan approaching below, toward another ridge across the distance.

Carvajal and his men were double-checking the loads in their pistols and single-shot rifles.

"You were right, Andres," Carvajal said, looking below.

"I was? About what?"

"Those wagons."

"Oh, you mean heavy."

"Very heavy. They won't be able to run very fast. I think maybe they'll leave 'em behind and keep on going."

"Maybe," Beka said.

"And maybe not," Carvajal countered. "Depends what's in them. Could be worth fighting for."

"And dying for?" Andres smiled.

"Maybe," Carvajal said. "We'll find out as soon as Vega gets in position."

"And then," Melena spoke up, "we go back and get that trunk with the clothes and things."

"You and that damned trunk."

"You could have let me go back this morning with a wagon."

"Yes. You'd have a hell of a chance finding it out

there in the desert. Andres and Beka will take you back later."

"Well, I wish you'd hurry up and attack."

"Don't tell me how to general, goddammit. We can't attack till Vega's in position, so just shut up."

"Did you finish your carving?" Rankin asked Mister Joseph as they rode.

"Not quite. Probably finish it up tonight."

"Have you decided what you're going to do with it?"

"Not sure."

"That's a very nice piece of wood. What is it? Oak?"

"Not sure of that either. All I know is it's not part of the true cross."

"Oh, I don't know about that, Mister Joseph. In a way every cross is part of the true cross."

"I guess," Mister Joseph nodded, "that's one way to look at it."

Dominique Lessuer rode her Appaloosa some distance apart from the others.

Jeff Gunnison reined his horse away from Discant and veered back until he was alongside her.

"It's me," he said, "bigmouth."

Silence.

"Look. Last night you said that sometimes I talk too much. You were right."

"I also said that you're a sonofabitch."

· "Well, maybe we can skip that part."

"Why?"

"Because . . . I . . . I was out of line . . . like Mordred."

"And this morning you're back to being Galahad? For how long? Until you think up another Cleopatra remark? I'd rather skip the whole thing."

"I don't blame you."

"Then drift."

"I will. But first, I apologize."

"All right, so you apologize. Duly noted. Now drift."

"Sure. But it's a long way to Vera Cruz and—"

"Vera Cruz isn't the end of the world, sailor boy, but for me it's a new beginning . . . and I figure I've got one coming."

"I guess you've had some bad breaks."

"Who hasn't? But I'm not complaining."

"No. You wouldn't."

"And just one more thing . . ."

"Yes?"

"For your information, even Cleopatra was a virgin once."

Dominique heeled the Appaloosa and rode away from Lieutenant Jeff Gunnison.

Carvajal was still looking toward the other ridge across in the distance.

"I don't see them yet," Andres said.

"Neither do I." Beka squinted.

"That's because they're not there yet." Carvajal kept looking.

"You know what I should have had them do?" Melena said.

"Who do?"

"Andres and Beka," Melena answered Carvajal's question. "I should have had them draw a map."

"Of what?"

"Of where they left the trunk . . . in case they both get killed in the—"

"Goddammit! If you say one more word about that trunk, I'm going to slap you off that horse, and I don't want you talking to those two about it. I'm—Hold on! There they are . . . see 'em?"

Both Andres and Beka nodded. General Carvajal removed his General Santa Anna hat and waved it.

After Dominique rode across to the other side of the caravan, Jeff rode up toward the front of the procession and assumed his usual position next to Discant.

Gunnison glanced back.

"Did you make peace?"

Jeff didn't answer.

"I guess not." Gunnison smiled at Bogartis.

"Captain Gunnison." Discant spoke above the sound of hoof beats and creaking wagons. "I was wondering, sir."

"Wondering what?"

"Do you think it might be a good idea if a few of us went out ahead, to scout and make sure—"

"Number one, you couldn't make sure of anything. Number two, what makes you think they'd attack from the front? Number three, in case of attack it's best to keep our force together. Number four . . ."

"Thank you, sir." Discant smiled. "I see what you mean."

"Them young fellas," Bogartis said, "have got a lot to learn."

"Partly they learn, Mister Bogartis, and partly they die."

"Yeah, well, they seem to be doing all right so far." Bogartis stretched his neck ahead. "I just don't like it."

"Don't like what?"

"It's just too damn . . ."

Gunshots.

". . . quiet."

"Not anymore."

The two armed contingents swept down from both

168

ridges, hoofs pounding, guns firing, dust swirling in their wakes, screaming and yelling.

"Make for that ridge ahead!" Gunnison hollered, and pointed. "Get those wagons up there! Jeff, hold 'em off! Move!" He waved at the wagons.

The drivers went to their whips, slapping reins and cursing. Cookie did most of the cursing.

The wagons rolled toward a protective ridge on higher ground.

Crewmen of the *Phantom Hope* and the navy contingent drew Henrys from their scabbards and took aim.

The two guerrilla forces, led by Carvajal and Vega, converged in an uneven brigade and blasted the fleeing caravan with revolvers and single-shot rifles. They attacked with speed and confidence toward the outnumbered prey as they had done dozens of times before, always with the same result: victory.

But this time they were met with an unexpected contingency. A contingency that diminished their superior numbers.

Repeating rifles.

Jeff, Discant, and the navy men, along with Gunnison's crew, fired their Henrys, cocked, and fired again and again with devastating results while protecting the heavy wagons as they made their way toward the ridge.

Mister Joseph and Rankin were still near the tail end of the wagons. Mister Joseph's rifle spit out a rapid stream of lead with deadly effect. Rankin had a revolver in hand but had yet to fire when he saw the driver of the last wagon take a shot, slump, and fall from the wagon onto the ground. The driverless wagon began to careen and swerve away from the caravan.

Rankin kicked his horse, reining it parallel to the wild-eyed animals pulling the wagon. Alongside the six-up Rankin leaped onto the team and struggled to grab the loose reins that had fallen between the horses. Twice he almost fell off before he took hold of the reins and began the perilous move from horseback back toward the wagon bed.

Mister Joseph rode nearby, firing at the advancing guerrillas.

Rankin jumped, still grasping the reins, onto the bouncing wagon and, still standing, took command of the team. The last wagon fell in line with the other three and made for the ridge as the riders around them kept up their rifle barrage.

Jeff, through the dust and gunsmoke, spotted Dominique. He waved at her and pointed to the ridge ahead. She didn't need any urging as she galloped past him and everybody else as more guerrillas, men, and horses were hit and fell.

All four wagons made it to the ridge. Gunnison and the other men dismounted and formed an effective line of defense that became an offense, peppering away at the attackers, who were confused and decimated by the firepower of the Henrys.

Dominique had grabbed up a Henry and was firing and hitting what she aimed at.

"Jesus Christ!" Carvajal screamed. "What've they got! Back! Back!" he commanded, and wheeled his horse. "Go back!"

The circling guerrillas were in full accord as General Carvajal lead the retreat in a swirl of dust and curses.

Gunnison looked for Jeff and spotted him talking to Discant. Discant nodded, and then Jeff moved away and toward Dominique, who was still holding a Henry.

"Are you all right?" he asked.

"Hell, I'm sitting on top of the world."

"I don't know, we may be sitting on top of hell."

"We gave more than we got."

"Where'd you learn to shoot like that?"

"At finishing school."

"Dominique . . ."

"What?"

"Truce?"

"Huh?"

"I mean between us."

"Well . . ."

"Just to Vera Cruz."

"You said it before. It's a long way to Vera Cruz."

"It's getting longer." He pointed out toward the guerrillas. "So are the odds. Truce?"

Dominique smiled, nodded, and reached into her blouse for a cigarette.

When they were well out of range of the Henrys and behind the shelter of an outcropping of boulders, the guerrillas reined up and General Carvajal swung off his saddle, holstered his pistol, and slammed his hat onto the ground.

Vega, Andres, Beka, and all the rest, some wounded, reeled off their mounts, still flustered, distressed, and discouraged by the unanticipated outcome of the attack.

Melena, who had been watching from a safe distance, also rode up and dismounted. She ran to Carvajal and flung her arms around him.

"Prospero! Are you hurt?"

"No!" He pushed her away, almost knocking her to the ground. "I'm not hurt . . . but look out there." He pointed toward the battleground. "There must be fifteen, twenty fighting men, all dead. Goddammit, they were cutting us down like weeds." He moved toward Andres and Beka. "Why the hell didn't you tell me about those rifles?"

"We didn't know." Andres cringed.

"Why not?"

"Why . . . not?" Andres stammered. "You . . . saw them too. There's no way of telling how many times a gun will shoot by looking—at least not from far away."

"We got too damn close. Somebody give me a drink. I got to think."

Vega handed the general a canteen.

"Not water!" Carvajal shouted.

"It's not water, my general."

"Oh . . . I got to think." Carvajal took a deep swallow.

"Maybe now we wait for the rest of our army," Vega suggested.

"And let them see what happened! What kind of a general do you think I am? We still outnumber them."

"Not as much," Vega observed.

"Enough."

"Prospero," Melena said, "I think Vega's right. I think we ought to wait."

"And I think you ought to shut up. Who's the general around here? You or Vega? Or somebody else? *I'm* the general, and without me you are all nothing. So all of you shut up and listen. . . ."

Rankin was still on the teamster's seat in the wagon with his face bent into both hands, almost as if in prayer.

Mister Joseph walked up to the side of the wagon.

"Mister Rankin, are you okay?"

"What?" Rankin looked up and tried to conceal the tremor in both his hands. "Oh, yes."

"Did you get hit?"

"No . . . no . . . I was just thinking about the driver . . . and all those other men . . . on both sides . . . out there, dead."

"Yeah, well, it's too bad there aren't more of them out there dead, on the other side."

172

"You . . . mean that?"

"I sure as hell do. Here, let me help you down. That was some piece of work you did out there. Saved that wagon."

"I'm not sure I realized what I . . . what I was doing," Rankin said as Mister Joseph reached out his hand to help.

"But you did it." Mister Joseph smiled.

Gunnison and Bogartis walked over to where Jeff and Dominique stood as she lit the cigarette.

"How many of those cigarettes you got?" Gunnison asked.

"I've got a lifetime supply."

"Yeah, well, that might not be too long. But at least we're still partners. Jeff, how many of your men did you lose?"

"I don't know."

"You should."

"There's Jim." Discant was approaching and had heard Gunnison's question. "He'll report to you."

"One dead," Discant said, "one wounded, but not badly."

"And we lost three, right, Mister Bogartis?"

"That's right, but not near as many as them—thanks to these Henrys we kept. What do we do next, Captain Gunnison? Looks bad."

"Well, I'm not making out my last will and testament yet."

"I didn't ask you what you *weren't*, I asked what we *were*."

"We reload and wait—"

"I'll be damned!" Bogartis pointed. "Look! Seems like we don't have to wait any longer."

In the distance below, General Carvajal approached slowly, on horseback, out in the open. He smoked a cigar and held a rifle high above him, a rifle to which was tied a white bandanna.

Carvajal waved the rifle to make sure the white flag could be seen as it fluttered in the air.

"Do you believe that, Captain?" Bogartis asked.

"No."

"Neither do I," Jeff said.

Gunnison started to walk toward his horse. He looked back at Bogartis.

"Hand me one of those Henrys. Make sure it's loaded."

"Aye, sir." Bogartis checked the rifle and tossed it to Gunnison as the captain mounted.

"Thanks."

"What're you going to do?" Jeff took a couple of steps toward Gunnison.

"Talk to him."

"Why?"

"I don't know," Gunnison said. "Got to do something."

Chapter Twenty-one

The followers from both sides watched.

The two leaders in the vast expanse of sandy espadrille rode slowly closer to each other.

They would meet between the two outlying forces. A safe zone. Carvajal would be out of range of the caravan's rifles. Gunnison would be out of range of the guerillas' guns.

The zone would be safe in that regard. But white flag or no, Gunnison and Carvajal would not be safe from each other. White flag or no, each was armed and at the ready—in case of treachery instead of talk.

Carvajal's guerrillas were mounted in fighting formation, divided into three flanks with Vega at the head of the middle force. Melena was mounted next to Vega but had no notion of participating in the battle if the negotiation collapsed.

Despite Vega's failure in his aborted conquest of Melena in bed, in the field of battle he was much more effective, even fearless. If Carvajal fell, Vega expected to take his place with the guerrillas and Melena. His only rival was a Colonel Sebastian who was north on an expedition.

At the ridge with the wagons, Gunnison's contingent also watched and waited, Henrys loaded and aimed, even though they were out of range.

Dominique still smoked, even as she aimed.

Jeff and Discant were on one side of her, Mister Joseph and Rankin on the other.

"Windage and elevation, Mister Rankin, don't forget to allow for windage and elevation," Mister Joseph instructed.

Alan Rankin did not reply.

"What do you think they want?" Discant whispered to Jeff.

"All they can get."

"You don't think he'd give them . . . what's in these wagons, do you?"

"Over my dead body—and remember what I said about Gunnison."

"Let's not even think about that. Right now an awful lot is up to him." Discant pointed toward Gunnison.

"Yeah . . . him and that man with the flag."

Gunnison rode closer, not fast, not slow, still gripping the Henry. He stopped about ten yards from Carvajal, who took the cigar out of his mouth with one hand and held the bandannaed rifle in the other.

"I am General Carvajal."

"What army?"

"The army of President Benito Juárez."

"Does he know that?"

"Of course. Everybody knows."

"I don't see any flag . . . or many uniforms."

"Today we didn't bring a flag, but we got one . . . and you shouldn't judge an army by uniforms."

"What's on your mind, General?"

"I thought maybe we should talk—just until I," Carvajal took a puff, "finish smoking this cigar."

"Talk."

"Good. First, who are you? Who am I talking to?"

"Just a captain."

"What army?"

"No army. A ship."

"You mean a boat?"

"You can call it that."

"But, Captain," Carvajal waved the hand with the cigar, "I can't see any boat."

"There's a lot you can't see."

"Maybe so. But there's something *you* can see—even from here." Carvajal motioned behind him. "We got more men than you."

"We got more lead."

"Maybe." Carvajal grinned. "What else you got?"

"Determination."

"I don't know what that means." The general shrugged.

"Depends on what you got in mind."

"That depends on what you got in those wagons."

"Cargo."

"Cargo?"

"And it belongs to the United States government."

"Maybe not anymore. You are not in the United States, you know. So maybe we take it from you."

"That's where determination comes in."

"I think maybe we make a deal."

"Maybe. Maybe not." Gunnison moved the rifle slightly.

"That's a good gun." Carvajal pointed.

"Name's Henry."

"Henry?"

"I call him Uncle Henry. He's mean . . . and he's got a lot of relatives back there just as mean . . . with a lot of ammunition."

"Good."

"We think so."

"You give us guns and ammunition . . ."

"And what do you give us?"

"We let you and the wagons proceed. Where you going? Vera Cruz maybe?"

"Maybe."

"We let you proceed to Vera Cruz. Good deal!"

"No deal."

"Don't be so hasty, *Capitán*. There's something more you ought to know."

"Then tell me."

"Besides all those men back there, we got reinforcements coming pretty soon. Many soldiers."

"We'll accommodate 'em." Gunnison glanced at the rifle in his hand. "With these."

"I'm almost finished with this cigar."

"I hope you enjoyed it."

Carvajal looked back toward his guerrillas, then at Gunnison.

"We don't want to kill you."

"Then stop shooting at us."

"I don't think so." He smiled and let the cigar drop to the ground.

Carvajal started backing his horse away. So did Gunnison.

Each man kept his eyes on the other.

Discant nudged Jeff. "What do you think?"

"I think the talking is over." He turned to Dominique. "I also think it'd be better if you went farther back."

Double Eagles

"Think again."

"At least," Discant said, "he's still holding up that white flag."

"Yeah," Bogartis nodded, "and there's still a gun tied to it."

The two negotiators were now about twenty yards apart, still backing away. The rifle in Carvajal's hand suddenly leveled down at Gunnison and fired, just missing the target.

Carvajal wheeled his horse and spurred hard. The animal reacted with alacrity, galloping away with breakneck speed.

Gunnison aimed and squeezed the trigger of the Henry, shooting Carvajal's horse from under him. Horse and rider plummeted to the ground. Carvajal wobbled to his feet. The horse didn't.

The general managed to pick up his fallen hat and muttered, "My best goddamn horse." He waved the hat, motioning to Vega and his men to charge as Gunnison rode toward the ridge.

The guerrillas galloped ahead, screaming and waving their pistols and rifles, waiting until they were within range to fire.

Carvajal drew his gun and shot at Gunnison, once, twice, three times, and missed on all three attempts.

Behind the barricade of wagons the defenders braced themselves for the onslaught.

"Wait till they're closer!" Jeff shouted.

"Careful . . . don't hit Gunnison!" Bogartis shouted louder.

"Get ready, Mister Rankin," Mister Joseph said.

More than forty rifles pointed toward the advancing guerrillas as they swept forward in uneven columns.

Gunnison guided his horse between two of the wagons, reined in, and flew off the animal.

"Fire!" he commanded. "Pour it to 'em!"

The guerrillas' rifles and pistols began to explode, and so did the Henrys from behind the line of defense—with good effect.

The guerrilla charge was momentarily discouraged as some of the front-liners swirled and struggled to reload their single-shot rifles. Others grabbed at their leaking wounds.

From the ground Carvajal continued to wave them on, as did Vega from his horse. Quickly, the guerrillas re-formed and advanced again, firing.

But as they did, another band of riders swooped in from the rear, screaming Confederate yells and shooting at the guerrillas in a deadly cross fire.

Leading the charge of the attackers was Adam Forrester, with Connors riding next to him, and right behind, Johnny Rink, Dell Warren, and the rest of the crew from the *Corsair*.

Gunnison had joined the firing line and the firing.

Mister Joseph cocked his Henry and squeezed off again and again until he noticed that Rankin, next to him, had not fired a single shot, nor did he look as if he intended to. His eyes were lidded shut and he seemed to be muttering to himself.

Mister Joseph poked Rankin's shoulder.

"Shoot, goddammit, shoot! What the hell you waiting for? Shoot!"

But Rankin did not shoot. He continued to mutter—and tremble.

Mister Joseph looked at Bogartis, who had seen and heard what happened. They both shrugged and began firing again.

Between the charge of the Confederates and the barrage from the Henrys, almost a dozen guerrilla riders and horses had fallen. Only one Rebel was hit and killed—Manfried.

In the dust and disorder, Carvajal pulled one of his own wounded men off a horse, leaped on with a flying mount, and led the retreat.

"Hold your fire!" Gunnison held up his rifle. "Let 'em come in." He pointed to Forrester and his followers, who had slowed and were making their way up toward the ridge.

"Who's that?" Dominique turned to Jeff. "Another Galahad?"

Jeff didn't answer.

"That's the man who had Captain Gunnison court-martialed," Discant said. "Adam Forrester."

"So that's what he looks like." She lowered her rifle. "I've heard about him."

"Yeah," Bogartis said. "This is a mixed blessing at best."

"I don't think it's any blessing at all, sir," Mister Joseph injected.

"Them's the same one's we beat at sea," Cookie remarked.

"Yeah, well," Bogartis rubbed his jaw, "this is dry land—or hadn't you noticed?"

"Does that change anything?" Cookie wondered, and looked at Gunnison.

Jeff looked at him too. So did the rest of them.

Gunnison began to walk toward the Confederates who had ridden in. The others waited for just a beat, then followed him.

Forrester was the first to dismount, his face pleased and friendly. He moved toward Gunnison.

"Well, Captain, didn't ask for permission to come aboard, but looks like we're all in the same boat."

"And we didn't ask for your help, Forrester."

Andrew J. Fenady

"But you needed it and you got it."

"They'll be back with more."

"I know that."

"Then why don't you get out now."

"Out to where?"

"That's up to you."

"No, that wouldn't be very smart . . . for either of us."

"I might not agree." Gunnison lifted the barrel of the rifle that had been pointed to the ground. "And there's more of us. . . ."

"Take it easy, Tom. Say, can I see"—Forrester pointed to Gunnison's Henry—"one of those?"

"Mister Bogartis." Gunnison motioned.

Bogartis tossed his rifle to Forrester.

"Mighty fine piece of equipment." Forrester looked from the rifle to Dominique and back to the rifle. "Yes, sir. Mighty fine . . . you know the three most beautiful things in the world are a loaded gun, a spirited woman, and . . ."

"And what?"

"Could be . . . a flag"—Forrester shrugged—"a freshly minted coin . . . or something else."

"Get to the point."

"Look, Tom, if the two of us combine forces we might make it. If we split up, no chance for either of us. Not after what we did."

"Make it to where?"

"Now you're talking."

"I haven't said anything yet. To where?"

"Vera Cruz. Then we go our separate ways. North and South."

"Uh-huh."

"Is it a deal?"

"You're the second one who's offered me a deal today. I turned down the first one."

182

"Tom . . ."

"Just what're you doing out here, anyhow?"

"*Corsair*'s no longer seaworthy. You know why."

"Yes, I do." Gunnison looked at Jeff.

"I want to get to Savannah and get another ship. The 'cause,' you know."

"Yes, I know."

"Look, we even left our supply wagon behind, we were in such a hurry to come to your rescue. We got nothing left, so how about a truce? Just to Vera Cruz. They're going to hit us again, and when they do, today'll look like something for drummer boys and old ladies. What do you say, Tom? Truce to Vera Cruz? Not much choice anyhow."

"Just one thing, Forrester."

"Name it."

"I give the orders."

"Why, hell yes, Captain." Forrester smiled, saluted, and walked toward his men, leading them away.

Jeff approached Gunnison.

"You believe all of that?"

"I don't believe any of that."

"Then why . . . ?"

"Because if he doesn't join us where we can keep an eye on him, he might join them." Gunnison pointed toward the guerrillas. "Where we can't."

"You might be right."

"I better be."

Jeff walked away, followed by Discant. Gunnison turned to Bogartis, who was standing near Mister Joseph.

"Well, have you got an opinion, too?"

"Not about that. About somethin' else."

"Go ahead."

"Well, in my opinion, Captain . . . you'd better have

183

a talk with Rankin, right, Mister Joseph?"

"I think so, sir." Mister Joseph nodded.

"Why?"

"Because in a fight he ain't gonna be much good. Wouldn't shoot at them Mexicans when they was comin' at us. Just stood there with his eyes shut, mumblin' to himself. Right, Mister Joseph?"

Mister Joseph nodded again.

"All right, I'll do that." He turned and walked three or four steps before almost bumping into Dominique Lessuer.

"Oh . . ."

"Oh, what?" she asked, still holding the rifle.

"I damn near forgot about you."

"Well, now you're reminded, partner."

"Yes, ma'am. Say, I'm told you're pretty fair with that thunder stick."

"And other things."

"I'll bet." He started to walk away.

"Just a minute."

"What?"

"I was just wondering . . . about Forrester. . . . Are you gonna—"

"I don't know what I'm gonna. . . . Maybe I'll sic you on to him . . . partner."

Just then Cookie walked by.

"Cookie," Gunnison said. "What's for dinner?"

"Huh!" Cookie looked around. "It sure as hell ain't fish."

Chapter Twenty-two

That night in camp Gunnison and Forrester's men had fallen into natural segregation in accordance with their allegiances, North and South. And as in most of the encounters up in the United States, the North outnumbered the South.

There were murmurs and grumbles on both sides, but so far the uneasy truce was holding.

Johnny Rink had taken a harmonica out of his pocket and begun to play a tune that was heard in both the Northern and Southern armies.

Lorena.

Gunnison leaned against a wagon with a tin cup of coffee in one hand and an unlit cigar in the other. Jeff stood next to him, and they both looked out in the direction that the attack had come.

"Guard's posted?"

"For them." Jeff pointed away from the wagons. "I

don't know about . . ." He jerked his thumb toward Forrester's men.

"They won't try anything."

"You don't think so?"

"Not tonight, nor soon. They're worse off than we are. There's fewer of 'em, and not armed as well. No, Forrester'll bide his time."

"For how long?"

"I don't know," Gunnison whispered, and smiled. "But in the meanwhile, I'll keep an eye on him."

Jeff nodded and thought to himself that he also was going to keep an eye on somebody. His own father.

"Captain." Three men approached—Bogartis, Mister Joseph, and Alan Rankin. It was Rankin who spoke. "Sir, I was told you wanted to talk to me."

"I do, and the rest of you men can walk away."

"I'd rather they stayed, sir."

"Have it your way. I'll put it to you straight."

"You always have, sir."

"You've been a good sailor. You did well at the wheel when the *Hope* was in trouble. And Mister Joseph here reported how you saved the wagon, risking your life in the bargain, when the driver was killed. That'll all be in the ship's log . . . when we get back. Now here's the arrow. You have any reservation about killing the enemy?"

"I have . . . reservations about killing anybody, sir."

"When you signed aboard you must've known it might come to that."

"Well, sir . . ."

"Have you changed your mind," Gunnison made a circle with his cigar, "about these men staying?"

"No, sir. Permission to speak freely, sir?"

"Granted."

"I . . . I believe in the Union, sir . . . and in freedom

186

for slaves. I wanted to be of help in any way I could. I thought that aboard ship I could do that without actually . . ."

"Killing anybody?"

"Yes, sir."

"Strange way to fight a war. What if we all felt that way?"

"For the sake of the Union, I'm glad you don't. But I do, sir."

"What is it? Your religion?"

"I can give you no further explanation, sir. Except to say this. I'll do anything else you say. Whatever the odds, the dirtiest job you've got, give it to me no matter the risk, and I'll do it or die in the endeavor. You can hang me for a mutineer if you choose, sir. But I will not willfully kill."

"Nobody," he looked at the others, then at Rankin, "nobody's going to hang you, Mister Rankin. And nobody's going to say anything more about this. Now, get out of here and let me finish this coffee."

They all walked away, except Jeff.

"I don't know . . . ," he said.

"Don't know what?"

"What I would have done in your place. If one of my men . . ."

"What should I do? Hang him?"

"No, but . . ."

"This way I know what I've got, and he might even be more effective than somebody with a gun. You heard what he said. He'd take the dirtiest job. Well, I just might give it to him, and instead of killing, he just might get himself killed. Man has his secret reasons and doesn't want to talk about it. I'm going to leave it at that for now."

"I don't believe in secrets between officers and men."

"Oh, I don't know," Gunnison drank from the cup. "I wouldn't give you a plug nickel for a man who didn't have some secret."

Johnny Rink had finished playing Lorena. Dell Warren, leaning on a boulder next to him, nudged the Texan's elbow.

"Johnny, you know Shenandoah?"

"I think so."

"Let's hear it, okay?"

"Sure."

Rink began to play. Dell Warren started to hum, then sang the words.

> "Shenandoah, I hear you calling,
> Calling me across the wide Missouri.
> Oh, Shenandoah, I'm going to leave you
> Away, you rolling river . . ."

Unlike Lorena, this was not a song sung by both the Northern and Southern armies, and as Johnny Rink played and Dell Warren sang, the murmurs and grumbles grew louder from the Northern part of the camp as some of the other Southerners joined in the singing.

"Hey you! Playing that mouth organ! You! Johnny Goober! You hear me?" a Yank hollered out.

"I hear you." Rink stopped playing and called back. "And the name's Johnny Rink, Yank."

"Rink or Goober or whatever. Quit playin' that damn Rebel song. You hear me?"

"I hear you, bluebelly."

Rink started to play again, and Warren sang.

> "Oh, Shenandoah, I'm going to leave you
> Away, I'm bound
> Across the wide Missouri . . ."

Double Eagles

"Goddammit!" The Yank stood up and took a step toward the Southern group. "I said shut up with that song."

"Okay, then, how'd y'all like this one?" Rink began to play "Dixie" as Warren and the rest of the Southerners sang the words.

> "I wish I was in the land of cotton,
> Old times there are not forgotten,
> Look away . . ."

And the Northern, more numerous contingent struck up another song.

> "Mine eyes have seen the coming
> And the glory of the Lord
> He has trampled out the vintage . . ."

The two choruses rang out against each other, louder and louder.

> "Look away, Dixie land
> Dixieland where I was born . . ."

> "Where the grapes of wrath are stored
> He has loosed the fateful lighting of
> His terrible swift sword . . ."

> "Early on a frosty mourn
> Look away . . ."

The men from both sides had stood up and started to move closer to each other.

> "His truth goes marching on . . ."

> "Look away, Dixieland . . ."

189

A gunshot.

Both sides stopped singing.

Forrester took another puff from his cigar and smiled.

Dominique grabbed up her rifle.

So did Bogartis, Mister Joseph, and Discant.

Kevin Connors drew his side arm.

Gunnison stepped into the middle of the camp, the gun he had fired still in his hand. Jeff stood next to him.

"All right!" Gunnison said. "The concert's over! I don't want to hear any more singing from anybody on either side till this trip's finished—and that's an order." He holstered the gun and started to walk toward one of the campfires. Jeff followed.

"They make a pretty picture together." Connors said to the Reb next to him. "Father and son. You know Captain Forrester had the old man drummed out of the Navy."

"I heard." The Reb nodded.

"I wonder how long his kid'll last?" The first mate grinned.

A hand grabbed Connors's shoulder and spun him around. James Discant smashed a right into Connors's jaw, dropping him almost into the fire. The Reb jumped Discant.

Men from both sides leaped at each other, throwing punches, grabbing, twisting, slugging, wrestling, even biting. Connors sprang up and at Discant.

Rink and Warren were back-to-back in the middle of the fray.

Bogartis, Mister Joseph, Cookie, and Alan Rankin rushed in to break up the melee, all with commands: "Break it up" . . . "That's enough" . . . "Save it" . . .

Another gunshot got their attention—this one from Forrester just as Gunnison and Jeff walked in. Jeff took hold of Discant, and Forrester pushed Connors away.

Gunnison looked Forrester in the eye.

"This is your idea of a truce?"

"Your man," he pointed at Discant, "started it."

"I'll shoot the next man that does," Gunnison said. "On either side."

Captain Thomas J. Gunnison walked away. The men separated into clusters—Union and Confederate.

Vega handed the paper to Melena. He couldn't help noticing that she had put on some weight in the last couple of months. She stood close to him, her breasts swelling over the tight cotton blouse, and shimmering near the campfire—away from the rest of the men and women.

"They described where they left it, so I drew the map," he said. "You ought to be able to find it easy."

"I'll find it. I'll take a wagon when he's away . . . and one of the women to help me with it."

"Melena . . . you won't tell him I—"

"I won't tell him anything until I get back. Then he'll be glad when he sees me in all those clothes . . . and so will you."

"I'd rather see you without any clothes."

"Maybe you will . . . someday. When he went down today with that horse, I thought he was dead . . . for a minute."

"So did I. Did you see how I led the charge?"

"I saw." Melena nodded and patted his cheek. "Nobody lives forever, Vega. Today he was lucky. We were all lucky. Now, you better get back before he misses you—or me."

Gunnison stood alone, looking at the picture in the lid of his watch. He was not aware that Jeff had walked up

191

next to him. Before Gunnison could close the lid, his son caught a glimpse of the faded photograph.

"I've never seen that picture of her before."

"Few people have." Gunnison put away the watch.

"I can't remember her at all."

And I can't ever forget her, Gunnison thought to himself but said nothing. Instead he lit a cigar. Jeff stood watching him and also said nothing.

"You . . . you care for a cigar? I've got another in—"

"No, thanks."

"You don't smoke?"

"Just on rare occasions."

"This is pretty rare. We haven't talked like this in . . . a long time."

"Aunt Martha said you and Mom were married the day you graduated from—"

"That's right. We met at the Academy prom. I was dancing with somebody else. I turned and there she was. Not the most beautiful girl in the room—she was the only girl in the room . . . in the world . . . at least for me. I knew it just as soon as I saw her. There's no sense trying to describe her. I haven't got the words. Nobody has. But you saw the way she looks in the picture." He tapped the pocket with the watch inside. "I went right up to her and told her."

"Told her what?"

"I'm going to marry you. She just smiled, pointed at my uniform, and said, 'Looks like you're already married.' In a way I guess she was right. But we were married anyhow. I should've burned that uniform, but I didn't, even after you were born. She wouldn't have it any other way except for me to go to sea, and once while I was gone she was dead and buried."

"The epidemic. A lot of people died."

"Yeah, but she died without her husband there. He was in the Navy."

"Is that why you hate it?"

"Hate what?"

"The Navy. Trying to pass the guilt on to it, instead of yourself. . . . Maybe that's why you broke the rules . . . everybody's rules but your own."

"Maybe . . . and maybe I talk too much—even to you." Gunnison moved off.

First Mate Kevin Connors was soaking the swollen left side of his jaw with a wet bandanna as Forrester strolled up to him, smiling.

"I never saw you on the deck before—not that way."

"That kid hits like a blacksmith."

"Okay, that's over and done with. From now on peace, quiet, and cooperation with the bluebellies. Pass the word."

"Aye, sir."

"I'll see you later." Forrester started to walk on.

"Where you going, Captain?"

"Going to play friendly."

Someone tapped Jeff Gunnison on the back of his shoulder. He turned, not knowing what to expect. What he didn't expect was Dominique Lessuer.

"I was playing Lake Erie."

"What's that mean?"

"Means I was listening."

"You . . ."

"Oh, I didn't mean to. But there I was by the rock . . . and there he was on the other side . . . and then there you were . . . and so I . . ."

"You could've made yourself known."

193

"But I didn't. Just my nature, I guess. You weren't very . . . cordial."

"Neither was he . . . all those years."

"He tried to be just now . . . and you didn't help."

"Maybe I didn't want to."

"Maybe you ought to grow up."

"You think you can help me grow up?"

"If I really tried," she said. "For starters, how about walking me back as far as the wagon?"

"Let's start."

Gunnison, Bogartis, Cookie, and another crewman were playing poker by one of the campfires. Forrester stepped into the firelight, lit a cigar, and watched as he took a puff.

"Mind if I sit in?"

"There's an open space at the blanket." Gunnison pointed.

"I'll fill it."

"Can I sit down for a minute?" Mister Joseph asked.

Rankin, who was alone, nodded and Mister Joseph sat across from him.

"I want to explain something to you," he said.

"You don't have to explain anything."

"I'm not an informer. But I had to do what's best for the crew . . . and Mister Bogartis saw what happened out there. He told Captain Gunnison, but if he hadn't, I would have. I'd've had to—"

"That's all right. I should've told him myself . . . probably would have before long. Don't worry about it."

"I won't, but I just wanted to know if there's anything I can do to help."

"There's nothing anybody can do to help . . . and if

194

you want to know, I'll tell you why. I guess I have to tell someone."

"Go ahead."

"I'm an unfrocked priest."

"I said as far as the wagon." Dominique smiled. "And here we are."

"You also said 'for starters.' "

"Go slow, sailor boy."

"Don't call me sailor boy, and if I went any slower, I'd back into yesterday."

"Seems to me like you're leaning forward all the way."

"All the way to what?"

"To the wagon . . . for starters. Good night, sailor man."

The poker game was still on as Jeff walked closer to the campfire and Discant came up next to him.

"How you doing?" Jeff asked.

"Hand's a little sore." Discant smiled.

"Not as sore as Connors's jaw."

"Who's winning?" Discant pointed to the cardplayers.

"Let's find out."

They both stepped closer.

"I'm out," Cookie said.

"Me too." Mister Bogartis threw down his cards.

The game had narrowed to a hand between Gunnison and Forrester. Both had all their cash on the blanket. Forrester smiled his enigmatic smile.

"I'll raise you." He looked at his hand, then across at Gunnison.

"How much?"

"A million."

"Table stakes," Gunnison said.

"What the hell, this is a captain's table. No limit for a couple of captains, is there? A million."

"A million what?"

"Dollars."

"Confederate?" Gunnison asked. "Or Yankee?"

"Time'll decide that."

"Guess so."

"You in for the million?"

"I'm in." Gunnison nodded.

"You owe me a million." Forrester laid down his hand. "All blue. Looks like—"

"You owe me a million." Gunnison fanned his cards on the blanket. "Full house."

"It's only money." Forrester tossed away the butt of his cigar and rose. "There's more where that came from. Well. Good night, gentlemen."

Jeff and Discant looked at each other as Gunnison collected what was in tonight's pot.

Carvajal's hut consisted of three crude wooden walls and a slanting roof built against the side of a mountain, which provided the fourth wall.

The contents included a table, three chairs, a carpet over the dirt floor, and a bed, all appropriated from various citizens for use by the general and his guests.

At the moment General Carvajal had two guests— one overnight, Melena; the other Vega, who sat across the table from the general sharing the contents of a now nearly empty whiskey bottle while Melena lay on the bed, both hands behind her head, eyes closed, snoring slightly and still wearing what few garments she had worn all day long.

As Carvajal talked and drank, Vega's eyes surreptitiously swept toward the voluptuous outline on the bed, illuminated only by the single candle in the center of the table.

"I've never seen anything like it before." Carvajal wiped whiskey away from his mustache.

"Like what, my general?" Vega's attention snapped back from the figure on the bed to the man across from him.

"Like those rifles."

"Me neither."

"We're lucky they didn't cut down twice as many of us."

"What kind of a gun is it that shoots so many bullets?"

"I don't know." Carvajal shrugged. "He called him Henry."

"You think they got more guns in the wagons? And ammunition?"

"I don't know, but we'll find out."

"How?"

"When we take them."

"How?"

"How what?"

"How do we take them? We can't get close enough with the men we got, not against those rifles."

"We could stop them with dynamite," Carvajal said.

"But we haven't got any dynamite."

"I know that. So we'll slow them down a little . . . till Colonel Sebastian and the rest of our men get here from the north."

"How do we slow them down, my general?"

"Ah-ha! You see I know how. That's why I'm your general." Carvajal grabbed the nape of the bottle, drank until it was empty, then slammed the bottle back on the table.

The sound caused Melena to stop snoring and turn her body toward the wall.

197

"Melena, get up and take off your clothes. It's time to go to bed," said Carvajal.

Melena propped herself on both elbows for just a moment, then rubbed her eyes, swung her legs off the bed, and pulled off the cotton blouse, with nothing underneath but the mounds and dips of tawny brown flesh outlined in the candlelight.

Vega stole as long a glance as he could get away with while he backed out of the hut.

"Good night, my general."

After Vega closed the creaky door Carvajal blew out the candle, unbuckled his gunbelt, took off his clothes, and lay in bed with Melena.

"You know something?"

"What?" she responded.

"You're getting fat."

Chapter Twenty-three

The four-wagon caravan, now supplemented with the crew of the *Corsair*, proceeded across the dry, tortured landscape toward a narrow pass between two mountains in the distance.

From atop one of the two escarpments Vega looked through a pair of field glasses, then tapped General Carvajal, who leaned against a boulder and smoked a cigar while his men cut powder out of bullets from their bandoliers and piled the powder under the edge of the boulder.

"There they come, my general." He handed Carvajal the field glasses, who took them while still smoking and looked in the direction Vega pointed.

"Good." Carvajal grinned. "Work faster, more powder."

Bogartis rode at the head of the wagon train next to Gunnison, Jeff and Discant behind them with the navy contingent.

Dominique kept to herself astride the Appaloosa while the rest of the caravan crept along after them.

Mister Joseph rode next to the wagon that Rankin now drove. They hadn't said a word to each other since last night.

"How you doing?" Mister Joseph decided to ask.

Rankin just nodded and snapped the reins.

"I . . . uh . . ." He took the carved cross out of a pocket and held it up for a moment. ". . . finished it last night."

"Looks good." Rankin glanced at it, then looked ahead again as Mister Joseph put the cross back into his pocket.

They were both at a loss for further conversation, so neither said anything more.

Johnny Rink looked around at the landscape, then at Dell Warren riding next to him.

"You know, Dell, I was just thinking."

"What?"

"This country looks a lot like some parts of Texas."

"It sure as hell doesn't look anything like Virginia. Virginia's mostly green."

"Parts of Texas are too. Ever been there? Texas, I mean."

"Never have."

"You know that it used to be part of Mexico."

"Yes, I know."

"My daddy fought against them, the Mexicans I mean, for Texas's independence . . . and then again in the war that followed, on the side of the United States."

"Mine fought in that war too."

"All the way from Virginia?"

"All the way from Virginia."

"And now," Rink said, "here we are fightin' on the

Confederate side against the United States. Try to make sense out of that."

"I have."

"How so?"

"Well, we're still fighting for independence."

"We are?"

"States' independence. Virginia, Texas, and the rest. Doesn't that make sense?"

"I guess."

"What do you mean, 'you guess'?"

"I guess it has to—otherwise we wouldn't be here."

First Mate Connors's oversize jaw was still sore, and the left side had turned a dirty shirt blue. As usual he was at Captain Forrester's side, now on horseback as they rode near the second wagon.

Forrester cupped a palm against the hot, dry air and lit a cigar. He tossed away the burnt match and looked down at the deep ruts the heavy wagon wheels left on the ground. The captain pointed the wet end of the stogie down toward the tracks as he looked at Connors and smiled. Connors nodded.

"Those wagons," Forrester said, "could use a set of sails and a swift wind."

"Don't think that'd help much, Captain."

"No, not out here. All the men under control?"

"I passed along the word. No more trouble with the Yanks. They'll behave—until you give a different order."

"Good." Forrester then pointed the lit end of his cigar ahead toward Dominique, whose flowing red hair bounced loosely on her shoulders beneath the brim of her hat. "Ever see hair as all-fired red as on that filly?"

"Not that I recall."

"Me either . . . oh, maybe once. There was that belle in Galviston—but that's where the comparison ends.

201

Wasn't near as . . . Think I'll just amble ahead and get better aquainted with that eye candy."

"Aye, sir."

Discant glanced back as Forrester's horse came abreast of Dominique's. The ensign nudged Jeff.

"Looks like Captain Forrester's maneuvering toward Mademoiselle Lessuer."

"He'll likely find breakers ahead," Jeff said without looking back.

Captain Adam Forrester tipped his hat as his horse flanked Dominique's Appaloosa.

"Good day, Miss Lessuer."

Silence.

"I couldn't help noticing the beautiful brilliance of your tresses shimmering in the sunlight—"

"Oh, Christ!"

"How's that?"

"Cyrano de Bergerac in Mexico. Please spare me."

"Consider yourself spared." Forrester smiled. "And I note that you are an exponent of plain talk. I admire that in a woman . . . among other things."

"Well, just forget about the other things."

"Erased from the tables of my memory . . . where you are concerned."

"Now he's doing Shakespeare. Hamlet, no less."

"Hamlet couldn't make up his mind. I always do. I heard about you back in San Angelo."

"And I've heard about you . . . in a few places, including New Orleans."

"Ah, New Orleans. A beautiful city."

"A sewer by the sea."

"If you say so. Speaking of New Orleans, I knew your father. He was a fine man."

"He was a scalawag."

"He was a fine scalawag." Forrester grinned. "I remember a card game in a certain house in the French—"

"Look, Ahab, go find your Moby Dick someplace else or you'll get a harpoon through your ball cock."

"My, my. Such strong talk from somebody who doesn't weigh as much as that Mexican saddle."

"Well, that's one saddle you'll never straddle, Ahab, so keep riding."

"Good day." Forrester tipped his hat once more and smiled. "Parting is such sweet sorrow."

Captain Forrester rode ahead. As he passed the two naval officers he offered a salute to which they did not respond.

"Looks like you were right about those breakers," Discant said to Jeff. "Doesn't seem like he fared too well."

As the caravan approached the pass, Forrester pulled up alongside of Gunnison.

Unseen by any of the nearing contingent below, Andres and Beka packed more black powder under the boulder that rested at the edge of the high mountain shoulder.

"That's enough," Carvajal said, still smoking. "That ought to do it."

"Well, Tom." Forrester smiled at Gunnison. "The truce seems to be holding. Troops are downright compatible this morning. Nothing but peace and quiet."

Bogartis, riding on the other side of Gunnison, grunted and mumbled something indiscernible.

Forrester took a deck of cards out of his pocket, let the reins droop over the saddle horn, and shuffled the deck.

"About that million I owe you."

"What about it?"

"What about another try?"

"You want to play poker now?"

"Let's make it simple and fast. High card. Double or nothing."

"Draw." Gunnison nodded.

Forrester turned up a face card.

"Jack of diamonds."

Gunnison took the next card, looked, and then displayed it.

"King of clubs."

"What do you know," Forrester said. "That's two million I owe you."

The caravan moved closer toward the gorge flanked by a high rock wall slanting up to the craggy top.

As the caravan pushed into the ravine, with the four wagons lumbering like a procession of old elephants on their way to the graveyard, Carvajal at the crest of the mountain glanced down, took a deep puff of his cigar, then flicked the ash off the hot end of the stogie.

He motioned for his men to move back, away from the boulder. They readily complied. Carvajal took one last puff, tossed the cigar toward the heap of gun powder as he ran like hell and dove for cover like the rest of them.

The powder beneath the boulder exploded.

Chapter Twenty-four

In the pass below, Gunnison and everybody else heard the smack and echo of the explosion and looked up toward the sound.

The huge, dislodged boulder teetered on the high edge of the slope, but as yet, failed to fall.

"Get those wagons moving!" Gunnison shouted and waved.

So did Bogartis, Jeff, and Discant. They rode back toward the wagons, motioning to the drivers and yelling for the teams pulling the wagons to pick up speed.

"Push, goddammit! Push!" Carvajal screamed at his men, and they complied by slamming their shoulders against the quivering boulder and straining with all their collective effort. As they did, the boulder quivered even more.

"Knock on it!" Gunnison yelled at the drivers.

The teamsters didn't need urging. They knew if the boulder tumbled it would bring down with it more rocks and dirt, enough to obstruct passage and probably destroy the wagons. The drivers responded to Gunnison's yell with yells of their own and whips.

The first wagon made it into the heart of the pass and was straining to get through as the other wagons pulled closer while the riders from North and South milled around them.

Jeff spotted Dominique. She had fallen back near the last wagon, motioning encouragement to the driver. Jeff waved for her to get to the front, but she was too occupied to notice.

Gunfire from above.

Carvajal and those of his men who were not pushing at the boulder let loose a barrage with rifles and pistols. They were too high and far away to be very effective except for adding to the confusion and dust swirling below.

Gunnison, Bogartis, Jeff, Discant, Forrester, Connors, Mister Joseph, Johnny Rink, Dell Warren, and all the men on both sides were now together on the same side, trying to get the wagons and themselves into and through the pass as gunshots from above kicked up dirt all around them.

Cookie's wagon and Rankin's had reached safety on the other side of the ravine, and the third was close behind, but the last wagon had fallen back with a wobbly wheel.

Up above the boulder still wobbled, and the men pushed harder, hard enough to dislodge, then send it tumbling down the hard skin of the escarpment with gathering momentum as it rolled in its descent.

Three wagons made it through the rocky funnel—but not the last wagon.

The driver looked up and saw it coming, but there

was nothing he could do to prevent the inevitable except to jump, and that's what he did.

The cannonball boulder caromed against the rear wheel, crushing it and part of the wagon bed. The wagon careened and keeled over, with heavy boxes flying and flipping like feathers in a sirocco.

One of the boxes hit a rock and splintered open, spewing a cascade of gold coins that splattered into the air, then onto the ground among some of the surprised riders nearby.

But even more surprised was Carvajal, who looked down through his field glasses.

"Gold!" he cried. "Those bastards have got gold! That's what they're carrying in those wagons! Gold!"

"We attack, my general?" Vega asked.

But as he did a barrage of bullets blasted upward, ricocheting around the rocks, Carvajal, and his men, who all ducked back.

"No!"

"No? Why no?"

"Not yet. In a day or two Sebastian will be back with more men—"

More bullets exploded around them.

"They can't get very far in the shape they're in. Let them collect their gold. We'll get it all at once—"

More bullets.

"For now we wait. Stay down before somebody gets killed."

The guerrillas had disappeared from the rim of the mountain and Gunnison had ordered his men, most of whom were now around the wrecked wagon, to stop shooting but stand at the ready.

"Are you all right?" Gunnison asked the dazed driver who had made it to his feet.

207

Andrew J. Fenady

"Yes . . . sir." He managed to nod, then say, "I'm sorry about the wagon."

"Couldn't be helped." Gunnison dismounted. So did Bogartis, Jeff, Discant, Dominique, and Forrester, all looking at the damage—and the double eagles.

Then Bogartis looked up at the mountain.

"Why ain't they comin' after us?"

"They will when they're good and ready. They know we can't get very far." Gunnison walked closer to wagon. "Damn!"

"What are your orders now, Captain?" Jeff asked.

"Mister Bogartis, you think you can repair that wagon?" Gunnison pointed.

"No," Bogartis replied without hesitation.

"All-right, then, box up that stuff," he waved his hand at the scattered coins, "and load it and the rest of those crates into the other three wagons."

"They're overloaded now," Jeff said.

"Yes, they are."

"That'll slow us down even more."

"Yes, it will. But have you got any better notion in that manual between your ears?"

Lieutenant Jeff Gunnison walked away, followed by Ensign Discant. Dominique smiled as she stepped closer to Captain Gunnison.

"You're full of surprises . . ." She looked at the gold coins on the ground. ". . . partner."

"That's just cargo. Doesn't belong to me . . . or to you."

"I didn't say it did. But if I knew you were carting gold, my price would have been a lot more than ten thousand."

"Your price for what?" Forrester smiled.

"You keep out of this," Dominique said to Forrester,

208

then turned to Gunnison. "Maybe we ought to renegotiate."

"You might," Gunnison looked up toward the rim of the cliff, "have to negotiate with somebody else."

"She might at that," Forrester said, still smiling.

"We can stay here all day and talk about nothing, but that's not what we're going to do. We're going to do just what I said." He turned to Forrester. "Unless you want to call off that truce here and now."

"Hell, no." Forrester shook his head. "You're still the captain."

Gunnison started to move away.

"Say, Captain." Forrester held up a double eagle. "It practically flew right into my hand."

Gunnison reached out, grabbed the coin away from Forrester, and walked past Bogartis and Dominique.

"Candida, have you ever seen clothes like this in your life!" Melena exclaimed as she pulled the garments out of the open trunk and held some against her body.

"Never!"

They had had no trouble finding the trunk. Melena had brought Candida with her in the wagon to help. Candida was older, closer to forty—and heavier, closer to two hundred. She was as pleasant as she was plump. Twice a widow and still willing. So far no one in the camp had chanced to challenge the odds by becoming number three. But Candida's hopes, like her smile, never dimmed.

"I don't even know," she beamed, as she held up an undergarment, "what some of these things are."

"Neither do I," Melena said. "But I'm going to put them all on. Here, help me get the trunk into . . ."

She trailed off as she saw the riders approaching, more than a dozen of them. Melena went for the pistol strapped at her hip until she recognized the leader.

"Sebastian!" she called out, and waved the revolver as the riders came closer and reined up.

Sebastian called himself a colonel in General Carvajal's guerrilla army, and that was all right with General Carvajal as long as Colonel Sebastian took orders and executed them proficiently. So far he had done both satisfactorily. Carvajal had sent him on a mission to the north with fifty men. Sebastian, who was younger, vied with Vega for Carvajal's approval and the title "second in command." So far Carvajal was noncommittal, but when it came to dangerous assignments, he was more inclined to send Sebastian, who was smarter if not braver.

"Where's the rest of your men?" Melena asked.

"They'll be along later with the artillery and the loot," Sebastian said. "What the hell are you doing out here?"

"Help us get this trunk in the wagon." Melena smiled. "I'll tell you on the way back." She held up a pair of silk stockings and twirled them.

General Carvajal and his men dismounted and clustered around the broken wagon and the boulder.

They had waited up above on the cliff, smoking and watching, as Gunnison's men boxed up the scattered coins and transferred the fallen crates onto the other three wagons. They waited longer, until the caravan with its deadly rifles had traveled far ahead, almost out of sight. Then they rode down to make a closer inspection.

Through his field glasses, Carvajal was still looking toward the northeast and the dust of the disappearing caravan.

"What do you think now, my general?" Vega asked.

"I think," Carvajal lowered the glasses, "we go back and wait for Sebastian."

"Yes, my general."

Andres and Beka had been rummaging through the wreckage of the wagon. Andres picked up a couple of objects, showed them to Beka, and then called out as he moved closer, while Beka followed.

"General Carvajal!"

"What?"

Andres placed two coins into Carvajal's hand. Carvajal put one of the coins in his mouth and bit, then smiled.

"Real gold?" Beka asked.

"Yes." Carvajal nodded. "Real gold."

"Much gold for President Juárez," Andres said.

General Carvajal neither said a word, nor nodded, nor reacted in any way.

"You think," Vega pointed at the pass, "all those other wagons are filled with gold?"

"I think so." Carvajal spoke slowly as he put both the double eagles into his pocket. "I also think . . ."

"Yes, my general?"

"They don't have . . ." General Carvajal looked in the direction of the caravan. ". . . very long to live."

Chapter Twenty-five

An unsettling quiet prevailed over the camp that night, a quiet broached by muted speculation and more often than not the word "gold" whispered by crewmen of both the *Phantom Hope* and the *Corsair*.

Jeff and Discant leaned against the wheel of one of the wagons, each with a tin cup of coffee.

"It does boggle the mind," Discant said, looking at the wagon.

"What does?"

"Knowing how much gold is in this wagon and the other two."

"Trouble is, now everybody knows—not just the few of us who knew up to today."

"Yeah," Discant nodded, "how does that poem go? 'Gold! Gold! Gold! Hard and yellow, bright and cold.' And this much gold can turn anybody hard and cold."

"Except us." Jeff smiled.

The two had been almost inseparable since the Acad-

Double Eagles

emy. Jeff was a year older and much more serious than James Discant, who in many ways had been a child of adversity. Abandoned at birth, raised in a Carolina orphanage, he had been found in a bassinet in front of a church with a note: "Please take care of my baby. I can't. I named him James Discant." In spite of such shadowy origins the boy grew to be the brightest and most optimistic in the orphanage, and through the good offices of one of the orphanage's patrons he received an appointment at the Academy, where he met Jeff Gunnison. While the two were different, one serious, the other cheerful, they complemented each other and became best friends. Since graduation, Jeff had done his best to get Discant assigned to him and usually succeeded, as in the case of the *Phantom Hope*.

"Right. Except us," Discant responded.

"This time, Jim, we've really got to cover each other's backs. Between the crews of the *Corsair* and the *Hope* and—"

"There's another unknown quantity." Discant smiled and pointed.

Dominique Lessuer was walking alone toward one of the other wagons.

"You want me to cover your back where she's concerned too?" Discant said, still smiling.

"I'll see you later." Jeff dumped the dregs of the coffee cup and handed it to Discant.

At Carvajal's camp the subject also was gold.

Around the campfire Sebastian had just finished his report emphasizing the success of his mission, as Carvajal, Vega, and Melena listened. Besides the dozen men who had come back with him, the rest would return soon with spoils and the piece of special equipment he had taken with him.

213

"Good." Carvajal nodded. "I got to figure out the best time and place to surprise them."

"I've got a surprise for you inside," Melena said.

"I know you went and got that trunk even after what I told you."

"You tell me a lot of things, but this time you'll be glad. Wait till you see what I got."

"I've seen everything you got."

The men all laughed.

Dominique took one of the knives from Cookie's cutlery on the back of his wagon and moved away.

Gunnison sat alone, a bottle in one hand, a double eagle in the other. He poured a drink and stared at the coin, then closed his fingers around it. He looked up at the sound of Forrester's voice.

"Fifteen million in gold, Captain. Right in the palm of your hand."

"Shut up, Forrester."

"Just passing the time of night."

"Pass it some other way."

"All right." Forrester came closer, then sat.

"That wasn't an invitation."

"Aw, come on, Tom." He pointed to the coin still in Gunnison's hand. "We're both on the same page."

"Yeah, but in different books."

"Well, then," Forrester held up a deck of cards, "I owe you two million. One card, double or nothing. Just to pass the time of night."

Gunnison shrugged.

Forrester delt two cards facedown, one to Gunnison, one to himself.

Gunnison turned up a four of diamonds.

Forrester grinned and turned up his card.

A deuce of clubs.

"You win again, Captain. I owe you four million."

"You knew we were hauling that gold, didn't you?"

"Yep."

Gunnison passed Forrester the bottle.

"What do you intend to do with that knife?"

Dominique turned.

"I said—"

"I heard you. Caught a splinter from that wagon."

"Let me take a look."

Dominique pulled down the front of her blouse, revealing a fierce gash on the upland of her breast.

Jeff took a good look.

"I've seen worse."

"Worse what?"

"Never mind. Just give me the knife."

"Help yourself." She handed him the knife and pulled the blouse a little lower.

"Mister Rankin . . ."

"Yes?" Alan Rankin turned and faced Mister Joseph.

"I thought you might want to have this." He extended the carved cross.

"I thought that was for someone in your family."

"I can always carve another one. Please take it."

"Thank you . . . and . . ."

"And what?"

"I'd like to tell you what happened."

"That's none of my business."

"No, but it's mine, and I want to tell you, since you were so . . ." He looked at the cross. ". . . since you gave me this . . . if you don't mind."

Mister Joseph just nodded his head and smiled.

"Years ago, when I was a young priest, there was this young couple, both friends of mine, who had asked me to marry them. Of course, I agreed. The night before the wedding she was brutally murdered. All the evidence pointed to him. Blood. The weapon. He was convicted and sentenced to hang. But another man who had coveted her came to me and he confessed, to wipe the sin from his immortal soul. He knew that I could not break the sanctity of the confessional. But I did. I had seen another man hang, and it was ghastly. I could not see that young boy hang for something he did not do. So I broke the law of the church in order to save his life."

"But—"

"I know what you're going to say. But there are no exceptions in the eyes of the church. I made my choice knowing that the church would have no choice. All my life I wanted to be a priest. I still do."

"You are a priest, and you always will be. You made the right choice."

"Thank you, Mister Joseph." Alan Rankin extended his hand.

Jeff had heated the knife blade in the fire. He turned toward Dominique.

"I hope you've got a steady hand," she said.

"You know I can't . . . probe, unless you hold that . . . thing still."

"Thing?"

"Could you cup it underneath with your hand so it doesn't . . . jiggle? Or you want me to do it for you?"

"You just go ahead. That . . . thing won't jiggle."

"Yes, ma'am."

Jeff proceeded to probe.

"Your dad told you about the gold, didn't he?"

"He had no choice. You're jiggling."

"Work around it. Doesn't it tempt you? The gold, I mean."

"Hell, I'm already rich. Make almost a thousand dollars a year, and that'll probably double in ten years unless I trade it in for a tombstone."

"Pretty dumb trade."

"Sometimes it can't be helped."

"And sometimes you sound like your father."

"What about you? Your father was a Southerner. New Orleans, wasn't it?"

"And other places."

"Then your sympathies must be with . . ."

"Myself. But there's a lot about the South I like."

"What're you doing in Mexico?"

"My father was sick, finally remembered he had a daughter. Sent for me. By the time I got there he was dead."

"I'm sorry. . . . Hold still."

"Don't be . . . and don't cut that off."

"That'd be a major operation."

"Anyhow, I thought I'd inherit a fortune."

"But you didn't?"

"After the debts, all I had left was his interest in the *Phantom Hope*—Ooww!"

"Sorry. Splinter broke. Only got half of it."

"Well, don't stop."

"I won't. Do you have to smoke so much?"

"It takes the place of . . . Never mind. Keep digging."

Forrester was digging at Gunnison.

"Are you dumb enough to take that gold to a country that drummed you out of its navy? Disgraced—"

"Well, I'm not going to let you take it to Savannah."

"I got no such notion."

"And you haven't got the gold, either."

217

Andrew J. Fenady

"No. But we have."

"We?"

"Look here, Captain, in this world there are those who prey and those who are preyed upon. The eagles and the chickens. Now, you and me . . . we're not chickens. We're eagles. Double eagles."

"Two of a kind, huh?"

"Who knows how this disagreement between the states is going to turn out, and who cares? But you and me, we can be the masters of our own destiny. You follow me?"

"*Follow* you?"

"Well, that's not what I meant. I'll follow you so long as we go in the same direction."

Jeff held the blade up with the splinter on its edge.

"Got it!"

"Congratulations."

"Can I," he removed the splinter from the blade and held it between his thumb and forefinger, "keep this as a memento?"

"Of a successful operation?"

"I hope so. But it's going to leave a scar."

"Then," she covered her breast with the blouse, "that'll be our little secret."

"I hope so," he repeated. "Stay here. I'll get something to kill the infection."

"In Vera Cruz," Forrester was saying, "there are United States ships. But there's another port to the south. . . ."

"Alvarado," Gunnison said.

"You've already thought about it, huh?"

"Maybe."

"Sure you have. There's neutral ships for hire in Alvarado, and no U.S. Navy."

218

"So?"

"So the two of us could pull it off, sail away to Spain or any place and live like rajas. Versus that you can't come up with any better notion."

"I thought you were in the Confederate Navy. . . ."

"For half of fifteen million—"

"Half?"

"I'm not greedy. A third."

"You forgot a couple of in-betweens."

"Such as?"

"A couple of crews. Can you handle your men?"

"I'll take care of the ones who won't go along. Your son is all we have to worry about."

"Yeah, and the Mexican Army."

"With you and me on the same side," Forrester smiled, "who's worried about an army?"

Jeff Gunnison wasn't smiling. He had heard enough of the conversation. More than enough. He had a hard time not throwing up as he turned and walked.

A few yards away, as Jeff moved past Bogartis and Cookie, looking dazed and straight ahead, Cookie leaned toward the first mate.

"Mister Bogartis, have you ever been in love?"

"Nope. I been a sailor all my life."

Dominique stood up as Jeff approached empty-handed.

"What's the matter? Couldn't you find any . . ."

He kept walking past her without looking at her or saying a word.

In the hut, Carvajal sat on a chair by the table, drinking and laughing as Melena stood naked by the trunk, cursing and flinging clothes across the room.

"I told you you're getting fat." He grinned. "Nothing fits."

Andrew J. Fenady

"Shut up!"

"Be careful," he said, "or you'll be sorry."

"These things belong to some skinny ass who's nothing but bones!"

"They would've fit you last year."

"They would have fit me when I was twelve years old." She picked up one of the dresses from the trunk. "Maybe if I let this out a little . . ."

"Trouble is, you let yourself out more than a little."

Carvajal stood up and took off his gunbelt, then started to unbutton his pants.

"Never mind the clothes. Get in the bed. I got work to do tomorrow . . . and tonight."

Andres passed Beka the bottle.

"Beka . . ."

"What?" Beka drank from the bottle.

"How many wars have we fought?"

"I don't know." Beka shrugged and drank. "I think maybe it's all the same war. . . ."

"What do you mean?"

"I mean, it just starts and stops for a while and starts all over again."

"Just so we're here when it finally stops."

"Somebody has to be." Beka passed the bottle back. "Presidente Juárez says—"

"How do you know what he says? Have you ever seen him? Or heard him?"

"No, but I was told. He says we fight for democracy."

"Me," Andres said. "I fight so I won't have to fight anymore."

"I don't understand."

"Me either," Andres replied.

*　　*　　*

Dominique thought of going after Jeff and finding out what had happened during the time he left and came back. But he didn't come back—instead he walked past as if she weren't there, as if nothing were there. As if he were alone in his thoughts and in the world.

She had decided it was best to leave him alone, at least for tonight, and see what would happen tomorrow. Instead, she lit a cigarette and smoked, until she felt a presence, then turned, hoping it was Jeff. It wasn't.

"I've been thinking," Forrester said, "about you and me."

"I know all about me . . . and enough about you."

"Not nearly," said Forrester. "You ought to let me tell you the story of my life. I've got six or seven versions, but what you don't know is that I'm the only one around here who knows what he's after."

"What's that?"

Forrester came closer and spoke confidently.

"You've heard of soldiers of fortune? Me? I'm a sailor of fortune."

"Yeah," she inhaled, "but you don't have a fortune."

"Not yet. But that's what I'm after. And I'm going to get it."

"Captain Gunnison . . ."

"I just left him. He's confused."

"And Jeff?"

"He's just a kid, blinded by duty. So that leaves me . . . and you."

"Where does it leave us?"

"Paris. London. Name it. Fun and games. With a fortune. Play it smart. I could use you. . . ."

"I'll bet."

"No, I mean as a distraction . . . when the time comes."

"Keep talking."

221

"We'll talk later. You think it over." He smiled as he put his arms around her. "Meanwhile, here's something to remember."

Forrester kissed her. Dominique didn't resist. She co-operated until, in a swift, sharp movement, her knee battered his groin and he jerked back in surprised agony.

"Something for you to remember . . . while I think it over."

Dominique walked away.

With his hand Forrester soothed the sore spot and smiled.

While Discant slept next to him under the wagon, Jeff stared straight up into the darkness.

He was not smiling. He was thinking. Thinking about what he had to do.

Chapter Twenty-six

The valley yawned wide and greener than the land behind, with splashes of wildflowers scattered from the valley platform upward along the tilting flanks of the pitted hills.

A good place for an ambush. Good for the ambushers. Not good for the ambushed.

Gunnison rode alone at point, his eyes facing the horizon. He was aware of the movement along the left ridge, and then the rider coming alongside.

"More of 'em every hour," Mister Bogartis said, nodding to his left.

"Yeah, I know."

"Could be anytime now."

"Could be, or could be they're just trying to make us nervous."

"They already done that."

"Go back and tell Dominique to move to the other side of the wagons."

"Good idea. Anything else?"

"Just keep a watch back there."

"Aye, aye, sir." Bogartis peeled off and fell back toward the others.

Johnny Rink and Dell Warren rode near the rear of the wagons.

"Dell?"

"Yeah?"

"You ever had one of them twenty-dollar gold pieces? One of them double eagles?"

"Yep."

"More than just one?"

"Yep."

"I only seen one once—before that box split open. What is it that makes gold so . . . so . . ."

"Precious?"

"Yeah . . . precious."

"Well, Johnny, you can make things out of it."

"You can make things outta wood—it ain't precious."

"Yes, but wood's just about everywhere. Gold is hard to find, so somebody's got to pay for the labor of finding it."

"Well," Rink pointed to the wagons, "somebody found a whole hell of a lot of it somewhere."

After Bogartis spoke to Dominique, she crossed to the right side of the caravan, then rode ahead toward Jeff and Discant. As the Appaloosa came nearer, Discant discreetly left some distance between him and the lieutenant.

"Would it make any difference," she said to Jeff, "if I quit?"

"Quit what?"

"Quit smoking. Is that what bothered you last night?"

"No."

"Well, something did. All of a sudden you had that

224

heart-bowed-down look. You want to tell me what happened?"

"No."

"I see. You want to tell me *anything*?"

"No . . . except . . . just keep out of the way."

"The way of what?"

"Gunnison and me."

"Oh, we're back to that. It's all right with me. Captain Forrester thinks I'm good company. Last night he—"

"You're free, bright, and twenty-one. Do whatever you want, but right now just leave me alone."

She wheeled the Appaloosa and rode back past Discant and then past Forrester and Connors. As she did, Forrester tipped his hat and smiled. Without acknowledgement, Dominique kept riding.

"Captain," Connors said. "You think Gunnison'll go along? To Alvarado, I mean?"

"He doesn't have to go along that far. Just till we take over. Don't worry about a thing." Forrester smiled and rode ahead toward Gunnison.

"When do we turn south, Captain?" Forrester asked as he pulled alongside.

"I'll tell you when," Gunnison said.

"Want us to take care of the kid?"

"What do you mean 'take care of'?"

"He won't get hurt permanent, that's part of the deal."

"I'll take care of him my own way."

"Anything you say, Captain."

This time Gunnison swung off and rode back to Jeff and Discant.

"Jeff," he said, "there's a mission beyond that stream ahead. Let the men and horses water up and then we'll head for it. The padres'll put us up for the night. I've stayed there before."

Jeff made no reply, didn't even look at his father.

"Yes, sir," Discant said.

Gunnison rode off toward the point again, but looked back over his shoulder and saw that Jeff was now talking to Discant.

From the ridge Carvajal looked down through his field glasses. On his right side stood Vega, on the left Sebastian. Besides the guerrillas from the camp and more of Sebastian's men who had caught up with them, Carvajal had ordered Melena and the other women to accompany them with food and other supplies. He had told them that they were not going back to camp until they got what they came for.

As he lowered the field glasses Melena came between Vega and the general, who ignored her presence.

"That's the place to hit them." Carvajal pointed to the stream.

"But the cannon—" Sebastian started to say.

"Out in the open we don't need the cannon. I'll take the middle. Vega, you take the right. Sebastian, the left."

"Yes, my general," Vega said, and nodded.

Sebastian just nodded.

At the stream the horses were being watered, canteens replenished, people refreshed.

Gunnison, shirtless, was kneeling some distance away from the rest, dipping his kerchief into the water and sponging it onto the back of his neck.

As he rose and started to turn he took a wallop on the jaw and crashed back, half in, half out of the water. He quickly shook off the effect of the unexpected punch and looked up at his son.

"What the hell is all that about?"

"That's to let you know," Jeff said, "that you're not going to get away with it."

Bogartis, Dominique, Discant, and most of the others had realized what was happening and quickly moved closer to the two men.

"Get away," Gunnison navigated to his feet, ". . . with what?"

"The Navy was right about you. You're just a—"

Jeff swung again, but this time Gunnison was ready. He moved his head just enough, then sailed a left hook into Jeff's jaw. The lieutenant bounced off a tree and sprang back into what had the makings of an interesting contest.

Jeff was faster and sharper, Gunnison slower but stronger. Each struck effectively. Each was down, then up.

The lieutenant was not quite up when Gunnison smashed a left into his midsection and followed with a hard right cross to the jaw.

Dominique covered her eyes as Jeff managed to grab on to his father, who seemed reluctant to hit his son again but was about to as Bogartis, Discant, Mister Joseph, Rankin, and a few others managed to pull them apart.

Forrester, Connors, Johnny, and Dell just stood and watched.

Both Gunnison and Jeff were pumping for air. Jeff turned to Discant and pointed to his father.

"Get his gun. Arrest him."

"I don't think," Gunnison said, "that he's going to carry out that order—at least till he checks with his superior."

Nobody moved.

"And who's that?" Jeff wiped his face. "You?"

"Nope." Gunnison pointed to Forrester. "Him."

Jeff stood frozen. So did most everybody else, as Gunnison went on.

"Somebody tipped off Forrester when the *Hope* was sailing with a cargo of Henrys. Somebody fouled up the rudder just before the attack . . ."

Jeff realized that Gunnison was beginning to make sense. He shifted his gaze to Discant. So did everybody else except Forrester, who seemed apt to make a move. Connors, Johnny, Dell, and the rest of the Confederates stood ready to follow Forrester's lead.

". . . and only Discant knew about the fifteen million in gold when the rifles were dumped. So he's the only one who could've sent word to Forrester . . ." Gunnison leveled his look at the Confederate captain. ". . . because Forrester already knew when he joined up with us. But," Gunnison pointed toward a moving dust cloud in the distance, "this is not a good time to talk about it, 'cause here comes that bastard with his whole damn army."

"Great sufferin' water lilies!" Bogartis boomed as everybody on both sides reacted to the imminent danger. They all ran for horses, wagons, and rifles.

Gunnison grabbed his shirt.

"Get to the mission!" he yelled. "Knock on it!"

Chapter Twenty-seven

The swirling dust cloud was spearheaded by Carvajal at the point, Vega at the right wing of the shaft, and Sebastian at the left.

The attackers far outnumbered their prey, but General Carvajal had made two miscalculations. He thought that Gunnison and the caravan would stand and fight in the open at the stream. And he miscalculated the distance from which the attackers would be spotted—a distance great enough to give Gunnison and company enough time to make a run for the cover of the walled mission. And that's exactly what they were doing.

"Jeff!" Gunnison hollered as he mounted. "You and your men cover us with your Henrys long as you can!" He waved at the wagon drivers. "Make for those walls!"

Once again the enmity between the forces of the North and South was washed away by the sudden necessity of staying alive. Blue and gray melded under the guidon of survival. Forrester, Connors, Rink, Warren, and the other Confederates rallied with the Yanks to forestall and repel the common enemy long enough to gain the sanctuary of the fortlike mission.

The galloping guerrillas had something else in mind. The three-pronged attackers, led by Carvajal, Vega, and Sebastian, swooped from the flank of the hill onto the flatland with rifles firing, guns blasting, even a few sabers gleaming in the sunlight as the battalion advanced.

Hate also gleamed in General Carvajal's jet-black eyes—hate and the hunger for victory over the intruders who had dared to impinge on his domain and had up to now outmaneuvered, outwitted, and even humiliated him in front of his army of peasant partisans. Hate—and greed. Greed for gold, some of which he would deliver to the government of Juárez, and as much of it as he could secrete for the security of his future no matter what the outcome.

Carvajal cursed and fired his pistol at the fleeing wagons. But there were those from the caravan who did not flee. They turned and fired, with their repeating Henrys taking a heavy toll.

Gunshots—smoke—yells—hoofbeats—dust—blood. Casualties on both sides—but disproportionate due to the Henrys. Horses and men fell. Some rose. Others were wounded, gasped for breath, and died.

Jeff, with Discant and the other Navy men nearby, still mounted, cocked and fired again and again as the guerrillas wavered, milled, and dispersed while casualties mounted.

Cookie and the other drivers, reins in one hand, whips in the other, yelled at the wagon teams, prodding them faster toward the open gates of the mission.

As the wagons neared the gates, Gunnison and Bogartis whirled their horses back toward the battle. Rankin's wagon was the last to reach safety. Forrester rode alongside Dominique, both still firing accurately at the pursuers. Mister Joseph found himself between Johnny Rink and Dell Warren, all three blasting away, Mister Joseph with his Henry and Rink and Warren with revolvers.

Connors looked around for Forrester, who was nowhere in sight. Back in the field, Connors suddenly cringed and grasped at his stomach in pain and shock.

By now Carvajal was no longer at the head of the guerrillas. He had sought shelter behind the cluster of some of his men, including Vega and Sebastian, who were still foolish enough to keep up the attack.

Jeff ordered his men to make for the mission, and as he did, Discant was hit and dropped hard from his horse. Jeff spun his mount around amid the gunfire.

Discant looked upward toward the lieutenant. There was little hope in Discant's agonized face. But Jeff spurred his horse closer to Discant, who managed to get to one knee. Jeff jammed the Henry into its scabbard and managed to reach down and pull the wounded man onto the horse with him. Gunnison fired and shot down a guerrilla who was closing in and taking aim at his son.

More shots from the Henrys cut down more of the beleaguered attackers in what was becoming a much too costly and obviously failing endeavor.

Jeff, on his horse riding double with the wounded Discant, bouncing but still holding on, made it to the gate of the mission with Gunnison, Bogartis, Mister Joseph, and the naval contingent following and firing back at the guerrillas. Their gunfire now was augmented by the caravan forces who had taken refuge behind the walls and had also set up an effective barrage of lead from their Henrys.

The guerrillas were in disarray.

Carvajal reined in his horse as he watched more of

his men being hit and realized that he was in imminent danger of sharing their fate. Both Vega and Sebastian rode close to him and anticipated the only logical command left to their leader.

"Go back!" General Carvajal screamed. "Go back!!" He jerked the reins hard as the bit tore into his horse's mouth and his oversize spurs cut the flesh of the horse's flanks.

As Carvajal led the retreat, the gunfire from the mission ceased. Both Vega and Sebastian looked back at the carnage left behind.

Carvajal did not look back.

The gates of the mission were now closed. The wounded, including Discant, were taken to one of the mission rooms where Jeff, Dominique, and Rankin were setting up what would serve as a field hospital, a field hospital with no doctor and little of what could be called medicine.

Gunnison had dismounted and stood near his horse, looking around at the grounds of the mission. It was not what he had expected to see.

Forrester and his men also had dismounted, all but Connors, who was still mounted near them. They were all within hearing distance as Bogartis, Mister Joseph, and Cookie approached Gunnison.

"Mission's been abandoned," Mister Bogartis said.

"I can see that," Gunnison nodded.

"And looted," Bogartis added. "Nothing here but a few sheep grazing."

"Round 'em up, Mister Bogartis. We'll eat 'em. Might be here for a long time."

"What do we eat when we run out of sheep?" Cookie asked.

"Horses. And we start rationing the water right now."

"Eat horses?!" Cookie scratched his whiskers. "Who'll pull the wagons?"

"We will."

"I can see you're in no mood to make sense," Cookie said, and walked away.

"Think they're discouraged?" Bogartis pointed toward the hill where the guerrillas had retreated.

"Think they're mad."

"How many you figure there's left?"

"Too many."

"Yeah. What's next?"

"I don't know, but it looks like we've dropped anchor for a while."

"We've been in worse places, haven't we, Captain?"

"No."

"You know something? You're right."

"Well, come on." Gunnison motioned to Bogartis and Mister Joseph as he walked away. "Let's reconnoiter."

Adam Forrester had watched and listened. He took a cigar out of his pocket and then a match, and turned to Connors, who was still mounted.

"Mister Connors . . ."

Forrester sensed something was wrong. Connors's eyes stared straight ahead, but vacant, his face ashen.

"Kevin . . ." Forrester took a step closer, and as he did the first mate slipped off his horse and hit the ground flat and facedown.

Both Rink and Warren rushed to the fallen man, turned him over, and brushed the dirt from his face as Forrester knelt beside him. Connors's eyes were now closed.

"Kevin . . . can you hear me? It's me, Adam. . . ."

"I hear you, Adam." Connors's eyes flinched open. He tried to smile through the penetrating pain. "Nothin' . . . you can do . . . this time. . . . I'll see you in . . . in . . ."

233

Andrew J. Fenady

"Hell," Forrester said as Connors died. Then Captain Adam Forrester rose. "Damn."

He put the unlit cigar in his mouth and took a step back.

"I'm sorry, sir," Dell Warren said, just above a whisper. "I know you were good friends."

Forrester said nothing.

Both Warren and Rink rose to their feet. There was another moment of silence before Warren cleared his throat and spoke.

"Sir."

"Yes?"

"I, uh . . . what do you think, sir?"

"About what?"

"Our chances of surviving."

"Surviving?" A remarkable transformation occurred in Forrester's face and demeanor. From mourner to commander in less than an instant. "Listen, son. I'm not even thinking of surviving."

"You're not?" Warren asked, and glanced at Johnny Rink.

"Hell, no. I'm thinking about prevailing. And that's just what we're going to do."

"Yes, sir." Warren smiled. "I was hoping you'd feel that way."

"There is no other way."

"Yes, sir!" Johnny Rink brightened. "What are your orders, sir?"

"When the time comes, just follow my lead. Until then, we just play along with those Yankees."

"You bet." Johnny grinned. "And sir, I was wonderin' about somethin' . . ."

"Speak up."

"Well, sir. Since we're all in here together against

them Meskins out there, you think you can talk to that Yankee captain about . . ."

"About what?"

"About maybe lettin' us use some them Henrys the next time them Meskins come after us? We could do a site more damage than with pistols and single-shot rifles, sir."

"Son, that's a damn smart suggestion. I should've thought of it myself . . . and those Henrys could come in handy later on. I'll talk to Gunnison. Good thinking."

"Thank you, sir. Anything else?"

"Yes." Forrester looked down at the body of his first mate. "You two get a blanket. Cover him up and put him someplace for now."

"Yes, sir." Rink nodded.

"Captain. . . ." Dell Warren hesitated.

"What is it?"

"May I ask you one more question, sir?"

"Go ahead."

"Is it true, sir? What Captain Gunnison said. Is Mister Discant one of us?"

"Yes, he is. We couldn't have come this far without him."

"It's strange, isn't it, sir? I mean, how the lieutenant went back and . . ."

"A lot of strange things happen, Mister Warren. The trick is to take advantage when they do. Remember that."

"Yes, sir. . . . How bad was Discant hit?"

"Bad."

Captain Adam Forrester moved away, leaving the two Confederates with the body of First Mate Kevin Connors.

He walked to the side of one of the wagons, struck a match on the rim of a wheel, and lit the cigar. He looked

Andrew J. Fenady

back at the body as Warren and Rink covered it with a blanket.

For more than a dozen years since that night in Dakar, the two men had shared bottles, battles, and even women. On continents hot and cold, on seas calm and stormy, they had seldom been apart more than a few feet for more than a few hours. It was a rogues' alliance that neither ever spoke of. The word "friend" was never mentioned by either of them. They never shook hands. They never slapped each other on the shoulder. They never even touched each other. But each of them knew he could rely on the other until the end. The end for Connors had come on a Mexican desert when Forrester was riding beside a woman named Dominique Lessuer and his first mate had stayed behind to fight.

The only man Captain Forrester would never double-cross was dead.

He inhaled the smoke from his cigar and let it curl inside his lungs until it hurt, then he slowly breathed it out of his mouth and nostrils, watching it disappear against the sky.

Only then did it occur to him that until that last minute the two men had never called each other by their first names.

Inside the room that had been set up for the wounded, Ensign James Discant lay barely conscious on a table, but aware that Jeff and Dominique were standing at his side. Alan Rankin had done his best to stanch the bleeding from the bullet still inside Discant's body.

"Jeff . . ." Discant's eyes widened and tried to focus. "Jeff . . ."

"Don't talk." The lieutenant leaned closer and touched Discant's shoulder.

"It won't make much dif . . . difference . . . and some things have to be said. . . . Listen, Jeff."

236

"All right." Jeff looked up at Dominique, then back at Discant.

"When . . . when war broke out I was . . . going to leave the service and join the South. . . . They said I could do more good as . . . as . . . there's no other word for it . . . spy."

"I understand."

"No, you don't. . . . Maybe I don't either . . . but my friends . . . my roots . . . Carolina . . . couldn't betray them . . . so I betrayed . . . Jeff . . . ?"

"I'm here."

"Why? Why'd you come back . . . for me . . . you knew your father was . . . right . . ."

"I guess I forgot about those last few minutes. Remembered other things. I don't know, maybe all of a sudden that other war seemed awfully far away. You take it easy now, Jim, please."

Discant managed to smile.

Captain Gunnison, Bogartis, and Mister Joseph had entered the room and listened to most of what was said.

"He's asleep." Rankin moved toward Gunnison and Jeff, and Dominique followed. "I've done all I could, but if I tried to get that bullet out he'd die for sure."

"You a doctor, Mister Rankin?" Gunnison asked.

"No, sir."

"Too bad. We need a doctor. But we also need people who can handle a gun. Under the circumstances, have you changed your mind about that?"

"No, sir."

"I'm beginning to think—"

"Excuse me sir." Mister Joseph took a step forward. "May I speak?"

Gunnison nodded.

"Mister Rankin, please, why don't you tell them? You told me."

237

Andrew J. Fenady

"I thought that was in confidence."

"It was, and I won't break that confidence, but it can't make that much difference to you now. Not here. Let me tell them."

"Whatever it is, Mister Joseph," Gunnison said, "I could order you to—"

"I would not obey that order, sir," Mr. Joseph said.

Gunnison's eyes narrowed and he was about to speak, but Rankin spoke first.

"I was once a priest . . . who broke one vow. I will not break another. I will not kill."

"You won't have to, Mister Rankin," Gunnison said, and started to turn away.

"Sir."

"What is it, Mister Rankin?"

"For two years I did missionary work in Africa. We treated the sick. I'd like to stay here and do whatever I can . . . with your permission, sir."

"Permission granted."

Buzzards had begun to circle over the battlefield.

Gunshots from the mission and from the hillside scattered them for a time until the temptation to feast on the bodies below overtook them again and they winged back and circled again until more gunshots were fired.

When Carvajal, Vega, Sebastian, Andres, Beka, and the rest of the guerrillas—those who were not dead and left behind—made it back to the hillside where Melena and the other women had watched and waited, General Carvajal swung off his horse cursing and screaming in a fit of black anger and rancor, springing up, down, and rocking sideways like a chimpanzee.

He proceeded to fling his Santa Anna hat on the ground, stomped it, then kicked it into the air. He tore

238

Vega's sombrero from his head and abused it even more.

Finally he seemed to simmer. He stood, still shuddering perceptibly, but less violently.

"Goddamn those bastards! They'll pay for this! I'll get every last one of them and make them eat their own gizzards. I'll—"

"Prospero." Melena held out the Santa Anna hat she had retrieved and brushed off with the palm of her hand, then whispered. "You're going to give yourself a heart attack. Besides, you're not behaving like a general."

"What?"

"Would Napoleon kick his hat and make such a demonstration in front of his army? What if President Juárez saw you like this?"

"You're right!" Carvajal's demeanor changed instantly into that of a general, maybe even Bonaparte. "Gimme that goddamn hat!"

Carvajal had left instructions at his headquarters, with those who were not fit to fight, that when Sebastian's contingent showed up they were to move out immediately and join up with the main body of guerrillas.

Thirty of Sebastian's men, all armed, had ridden into the main camp, received and followed the general's orders, and had arrived at the hillside shortly after the kicking and stomping demonstration had ceased.

"Where's the rest?" Carvajal barked. "Where's the cannon?"

"A wheel broke. They're trying to fix it."

"Goddamn!" Carvajal looked up at the sky. "Look at those feathered sonsofbitches!"

"General Carvajal." Sebastian came forward. "Can I make a suggestion?"

"Suggest."

"In private."

Carvajal led Sebastian a few feet from the others. Vega sneered as they walked away but said nothing.

"What?"

"Do you intend to attack again?"

"Damn right."

"Will you wait for the cannon?"

"It might never get here."

"Then those bodies out there . . . ours and theirs . . ."

"What about them?"

"They make the men . . . queasy."

"So?"

"So queasy men don't fight good. Not with dead bodies in the way. I have an idea that would help . . . and maybe I could get some information that will help us too."

"What's your idea?"

Chapter Twenty-eight

Cookie had made coffee in the huge pot he carried in his mobile kitchen. Enough coffee to go around—more than once. Strong coffee. Cookie would not compromise where coffee was concerned. He didn't mind watering the soup at times, or stretching the stew, cheating when it came to flour in the bread. But his coffee was inviolate, sacrosanct. Some of the crew called it tar. But not to his face.

Jeff and Dominique stood on the steps just outside the main entrance to what had been the church at the mission and sipped the potent liquid from tin cups.

"Did you have any idea about Rankin being a . . . priest?" she asked.

"No, but he did seem different than the rest of the crew. And when there was a death aboard ship, he . . . he did recite a Catholic prayer, and well, there was always a sort of, I don't know what to call it . . . tranquillity . . . pathos . . . something different."

Andrew J. Fenady

"All Catholics are a little different. . . . Used to be one myself."

"A Catholic?"

Dominique nodded.

"Used to be?"

"Maybe I still am, but I haven't been near a church in years."

"You're pretty near one now." Jeff pointed to the open door of the church.

"Yeah," she smiled, "but I'm drinking coffee instead of taking communion."

Gunnison, Bogartis, and Mister Joseph stood behind the wall, but on an elevation, observing the terrain. Bogartis and Joseph drank coffee while Gunnison looked through his telescope.

"What're they doing?" Bogartis asked.

"Looks like they're setting up field headquarters. Well out of range."

Bogartis muttered something as he took a swallow from the cup.

"What did you say?"

"I said I hope they stay that way."

Forrester, who had heard most of the conversation, stepped up onto the elevation.

"You know damn well, Captain," Forrester pointed, "they're not going to stay out there, not with the gold we've got in here."

"No, they're not." Gunnison lowered the telescope. "But we've got a wall between us . . . and our Henrys."

"There's something else between us," Bogartis said. "There's them damn buzzards again."

"Fire a couple of rounds, Mister Joseph."

"Yes, sir."

Mister Joseph cocked and fired twice, scattering the vultures.

Double Eagles

"Speaking of Henrys, Tom," Forrester pointed to Mister Joseph's rifle, "there's something I'd like to talk to you about."

"Let me guess, Forrester. You want some of 'em for you and your men."

"Good guess, Tom. Makes sense. We could be a lot more effective against the enemy. . . ."

"And speaking of the enemy, take a look at what's coming out there."

"I'll be keelhauled!" Bogartis exclaimed. "Another white flag."

"Yeah." Gunnison nodded. "But this one's not tied to a rifle."

"That don't look like that so-called general."

"Because it's not," Gunnison said.

Sebastian, mounted but unarmed, was making his way across the battlefield, carefully avoiding bodies of fallen men and horses, and holding a long pole with a white cloth attached. His face was calm, his manner confident.

Word had spread throughout the mission, and Yanks and Rebs alike awaited the messenger's proposal and Gunnison's response.

Sebastian stopped just outside the gate, looked up, and spoke in a clear, precise voice.

"I am Colonel Sebastian Rojas of the army of Presidente Benito Juárez. I am unarmed. May I come inside and talk?"

"I am Captain Thomas J. Gunnison of the good ship *Phantom Hope*," came Gunnison's voice. "I am armed, and no, you can't come inside. But I'll come outside . . . and talk."

"Very good, Captain," Sebastian replied.

"Open the gate, Mister Bogartis," Gunnison said.

243

"And get me my horse. I don't favor looking up to Colonel Peaceable out there."

Jeff and the rest of the contingent watched as the gate opened and his father rode just outside the wall where Sebastian waited.

Colonel Sebastian Rojas saluted. Captain Thomas J. Gunnison did not return the gesture.

"If you're here to surrender, Colonel, I think we can do business. Otherwise . . ." Gunnison shrugged.

"I am here on behalf of General Prospero Carvajal . . ."

"You look more like an officer than he does. Fate doesn't always make the right men generals. Go on."

". . . on a humanitarian mission."

"That usually means you need something."

"We both do, Captain."

"What?"

Sebastian pointed to the dead bodies, then up to the flapping vultures.

"We propose a truce."

"I've heard that refrain before."

"Not under these circumstances. . . . A truce while your men and ours retrieve the dead before . . ." Sebastian pointed again at the birds.

"A worthy notion—under the right conditions."

"Name your conditions, Captain."

"We'll get our people first . . . and whatever rifles were left behind. After that you can do the same."

"Why not at the same time?"

"Because those are my conditions."

"I see."

"And when it comes to humanitarian, do you think it humanitarian to want to kill us, when all we want is to keep what's ours and travel in peace until we can get out of here?"

"I am a soldier, sir, who obeys orders."

"That's another refrain I've heard before."

"A man must do what he must do."

"No," Gunnison said. "A man must do what he *thinks* he must do."

"You have my word, Captain. I'll do what I can on your behalf, but first . . ."

"You heard my conditions. Are they acceptable . . . to your superior?"

"I can safely say so, Captain."

"Then you can safely get the hell out of here while the getting's good."

Sebastian smiled and saluted.

This time Gunnison returned the salute.

Sebastian wheeled his mount and rode away with the white flag fluttering above the dead bodies.

Two hours later the battlefield was cleared of the corpses from both sides.

The humanitarian mission was completed.

Chapter Twenty-nine

General Carvajal had been reluctant to agree to Gunnison's terms in clearing the battlefield. He had wanted his men to retrieve the bodies first, along with some of the Henrys. But Sebastian was able to persuade him otherwise, barely.

Carvajal figured they would eventually have the rifles and the gold. So he went along with Gunnison and Sebastian. But he was still stewing.

Carvajal also was upset that Sebastian had been unable to gain entry into the mission and more closely appraise the situation. But again he figured that ultimately he and all his men would be inside and Gunnison and all his men would be dead.

"No more white flags!" he screeched defiantly. "From now on we show 'em nothing but our battle flag!"

"We've wrapped the four bodies in blankets, sir," Mister Joseph said to Gunnison. "And dug the graves."

"Thank you, Mister Joseph."

"Will there be any kind of . . . ceremony, sir?"

"Soon as we can get to it."

"Yes, sir."

Jeff and Dominique approached Gunnison and Bogartis, who stood next to him.

"How's Discant?" Gunnison asked.

"Not good," Dominique replied as she inhaled the cigarette. "The ex-padre's doing all he can, but looks like a lost cause."

"Yeah, there's a lot of lost causes these days."

Forrester, Warren, and Rink came up behind Jeff and Dominique.

"Have you been in to see him?" Gunnison asked Forrester.

"See who?"

"Your man Discant."

"Uh, yes, but he was asleep. I'll go back later."

"You better not wait too long."

"I won't. Tom, about those rifles . . ."

"Just a minute." Gunnison raised his telescope and looked toward the hillside. "Uh-huh."

"What're they doin' now?" Bogartis asked.

"Now, Mister Bogartis, they're showing us their colors." He handed the first mate the telescope.

A Mexican flag had been raised on a makeshift pole at the highest point of the hill.

"Too bad we haven't got a flag with us, Captain." Bogartis lowered the telescope. "We could make this war official."

Gunnison already was moving. He made his way over to his horse. He reached into his saddlebag and pulled out a neatly folded American flag, then started to walk back past Jeff and Dominique. Gunnison handed the flag to the first mate.

"Show 'em our colors, Mister Bogartis."

"You bet . . . sir!"

Carvajal looked through his field glasses, Vega and Sebastian on either side of him, Melena, Andres, and Beka nearby. They were all grouped directly beneath the Mexican flag.

"You see what the sonsofbitches are doing?" Carvajal exploded.

"What, my general?" Vega strained to see.

"They're raising their flag on our land. They're insulting us. That's what they're doing! I'm going to make that Gunnison eat it!"

Dell Warren and Johnny Rink had walked up to Gunnison and saluted. Gunnison returned their salutes.

"Captain," Warren said. "May we make a request, sir?"

"Why not?"

Jeff, Dominique, Bogartis, and even Forrester watched from a distance as Warren and then Rink spoke to Gunnison.

Rink pointed to the Union flag flying atop the wall of the mission, then spoke some more.

Gunnison nodded.

"Mister Bogartis," he called out.

A drapery of silence covered the hillside where the bodies of the dead guerrillas had been returned.

Earlier the surviving guerrillas had watched as the Americans had set out from the mission and retrieved what the Mexicans could make out were less than half a dozen of the dead. When the enemy bodies were taken to the mission, the guerrillas descended onto the field with two wagons and later returned with more than two dozen human carcasses, many of them brothers, fathers, husbands, and sweethearts of the men and women on the hillside.

Within an hour, amid tears, prayers, and wailing from some of the women, the bodies had been deposited into a shallow common grave and covered with Mexican soil.

Andres sat alone on a flat stone, his head buried into the palms of both hands, when he heard Beka's voice.

"What are you doing?"

"I don't know," Andres answered without looking up.

"You don't know what you're doing?"

"I think I'm thinking."

"About what?"

"About what I'm doing here." Now Andres lifted his head out of the bowl of his palms and looked toward the fresh mound of earth a few yards away. "You saw them."

"I smelled them, too."

"They're killing us five to one."

"Maybe six or seven . . . but we'll take them."

"After more of us get buried over there."

"We're soldiers. We're not supposed to think about that."

"Maybe so, but that's what I was thinking about—that hole in the ground. Beka . . ."

"What?"

"You're not married."

"And I'm not going to be, not till this is over."

"If . . . if I join them," Andres pointed to the mound, "do what you can for Marrisa and the baby. Besides the hundred pesos, I've got some more money in my trunk back at—"

"Stop! It's bad luck to talk like that. We came into this together and we'll go out together—but just in case . . . I'll do what I can."

"Thanks." Andres rose to his feet. "What do you think Carvajal is going to do next?"

"I don't know." Beka shrugged, then pointed in another direction. "But right now I think he's throwing up."

Melena, holding a bottle of whiskey by its nape, walked toward General Carvajal, who leaned against a tree with one hand and clutched his stomach with the other, retching, his head bowed.

"Drink some whiskey," she said, and held out the bottle. "It'll settle your stomach."

Carvajal grabbed the bottle and drank, then coughed and drank again.

"You should not let them see you like this."

"Like what?"

"Like puking."

"I wasn't, and you shut up about it!"

"Yes, my general." Melena's voice mimicked Vega's.

"That's right, I'm your general and everybody else's around here. And if anybody doubts it, they're going to find out different." He smashed the bottle against the tree and started to move. "Get out of my way!"

Johnny Rink and Dell Warren scrambled down from the wall while everybody else watched.

"This is the damndest, craziest war I ever fought," Bogartis said to Gunnison.

"It might get crazier, Mister Bogartis."

"That was very thoughtful, Tom." Forrester came up to the two men. "But it would be a lot more thoughtful to hand us some of those Henrys."

"One thing at a time," Gunnison replied, still looking up toward the top of the wall.

*　　*　　*

Carvajal peered through his field glasses as Vega, Sebastian, Melena, and the others stood by him. His expression was one of perplexity as he lowered the glasses for a moment, then raised them and looked again.

What he saw, and what the others could make out even from this distance, was the Stars and Stripes waving over the mission—and next to the American flag, also waving, the Stars and Bars, battle flag of the Confederacy.

"Those bastards!" Carvajal shoved the field glasses at Vega, who was the closest. "Now they got two flags flying over our country."

"Yes, my general." Vega nodded and handed the glasses to Sebastian.

"I'll show them something! We're going to hit 'em right now! Kill every damn one of 'em under both flags!"

"Now?" Sebastian was incredulous, stunned.

"Right now!"

"General Carvajal, sir," Sebastian pleaded, "why not wait for the cannon?"

"Because the goddamn cannon might never get here, and because they don't expect us to attack so soon and because I say so!"

"Yes, my general." Vega nodded.

"One of you leads the attack. Whoever does becomes second in command."

"I will lead, my general!"

"Good!"

"No." Sebastian handed Carvajal the field glasses. "I will lead. I will go."

"Good. Both of you lead. Both of you go! Give the order to mount up!"

Chapter Thirty

To the north, hundreds of miles away, across the breadth of a nation divided, in some cases brother against brother, father against son, battles were being fought with bullets and bayonets, rifles and swords, hand to hammering hand.

Billy Yanks, their dirty blue uniforms steaming from sun and rain, clashed against screaming, rampaging Johnny Rebs, fighting and clawing for every yard and foot and inch of a nameless bridge, or a fertile green field turned red out of uniforms blue and gray.

Men, barely out of boyhood, from cold harbors of the north, snowbound backwoods of Wisconsin, meadows in Michigan and valleys in Vermont, charged against their former brethren—rich and poor, out of fields and farms, from plantations and shacks, across the flowing waters of the Mississippi, the Missouri, the Red, and the Shenandoah—Southerners who had heeded the call of the Confederacy.

In places many of them had never even heard of—
Harpers Ferry, Big Bethel, Bull Run, Wilson's Creek,
Paducah, Glorietta, and scores of other blood-bathed
groves and basins, on land and at sea—they ripped each
other to shreds and shards, each force fighting under its
own flag, the Stars and Stripes or the Stars and Bars.

And here, hundreds of miles from that divided nation's border, above a beleaguered mission wall, those
two flags fluttered side by side.

"Here they come!!!" Mister Joseph hollered from one
of the mission walls and dropped to a firing position.

"Mister Bogartis!" Gunnison ordered. "Break out
some Henrys to those Rebs!"

"Aye, sir." Bogartis hurried away. "Damndest war I
ever seen."

Nearly a hundred mounted men in two formations—
one led by Vega, the other by Sebastian—came galloping off the hillside onto the open field—pregnable, un-
shielded and completely exposed—charging toward the
inevitable fusillade that would come from the waiting
marksmen shielded behind the whitewashed walls of
the centuries-old mission.

Faster they rode into firing range of the Henrys until
forty rifles, triggered by Yanks and Rebels, exploded
almost simultaneously, then again and again, tearing
into human and horse flesh, bullets blasting into bones
and organs of the oncoming cavalry.

And still they came.

No one had realized the folly of Carvajal's command
more than Sebastian. As he led his flank of the attackers
he wished that, instead of being a good soldier and obey-
ing that command back at the hill, he had taken out his
gun and killed Carvajal. Most likely it would have meant
his own death, but more than likely he would have saved

the lives of the men who were being killed all around him.

In that instant he determined that no matter what the consequences, if he lived, he would kill Carvajal—if he lived.

But he didn't.

From the wall, it was Forrester who took dead aim with a Henry at the man who led the left flank of the attackers, and who squeezed the trigger, sending a bullet into Sebastian's forehead and blowing most of his brains out of the back of his skull.

And still they came.

The mission marksmen, Henrys hot, kept firing. Gunnison—Bogartis—Jeff—Dominique—Mister Joseph—Cookie—Forrester—Rink—Dell—and the rest.

From the top of the hill, through his field glasses, Carvajal watched as Vega waved his men on. But the charge was broken and the guerrillas rode in disarray in all directions.

Andres was hit in the leg. He and the horse both went down hard. He staggered to his feet with blood and bone showing through his left pant leg. Beka reined in his horse and jumped off, running toward Andres, who was hit again, this time in the chest. He dropped to his knees first, then on his face.

Beka came close, picked his friend off the ground, and began to carry him back across the battlefield.

Forrester smiled, took aim, and fired twice.

Beka was hit. Shot in the spine. Both he and Andres fell. Andres was already dead. Beka started to make the sign of the cross. He touched his forehead, then his trembling hand moved down toward his chest. He never made it.

Two of Jeff's men had been hit, three of the Rebels. But the guerrilla casualties were massive. Almost a third of their numbers lay dead, still more than fifty yards away from the mission, when the survivors turned back and fled toward the hillside.

Vega, now second in command, was one of the survivors.

After he led the remainder of the contingent back to the hillside, he dismounted, stood in front of Carvajal, and shrugged.

There was a moment of silence before General Carvajal spoke.

"Sebastian was right," Carvajal said. "We should've waited for the cannon."

Forrester smiled and patted the Henry in his hand as he looked at Gunnison.

"I found me a new friend," he said. "Must've dropped seven or eight of those idiots."

"That was crazy." Bogartis shook his head. "Suicide."

"Yeah," Gunnison agreed. "But I didn't see General Carvajal among 'em." He turned to Jeff. "How's the ammunition?"

"Low," Jeff replied.

Chapter Thirty-one

The long, late-afternoon shadows slanted from the bullet-pocked walls of the mission toward the slender trenches of earth that would receive the remains of nine Northerners and Southerners who had fought and died side by side in a land some of them had never seen before, a land all of them would never leave.

Everyone inside the mission who was able to stand stood at the rim of the graves that had been dug adjacent to the old missionary graveyard.

Gunnison, Bogartis, Cookie, Mister Joseph, and the rest of the *Phantom Hope* crew. Jeff and what was left of the Navy contingent. Dominique Lessuer, Forrester, Rink, Warren, and the remaining Rebels. And Alan Rankin.

Captain Gunnison had asked Rankin to speak some words as they all bowed their heads. All but Forrester, whose eyes never left the blanket-wrapped body of First Mate Kevin Connors.

"Hear us, O Lord, as we gather to say an earthly farewell to fallen comrades. To those sons of the soil and sea, Union and Confederate, whose bodies we leave to rest far from the homes they knew and loved. Far from the sea that beckoned them from those homes, but whose souls are with you forevermore. They died as soldiers in the armies of men. But they live eternally in the legion of the Lord.

"One generation passes away, and another generation cometh; but the earth abides forever.

"The sun also rises. The wind goeth to the south, and turneth about to the north. All the rivers run into the sea; yet the sea is not full.

"The thing that has been, it is that which shall be; and that which is done is that which shall be done; and there is no new thing under the sun; and there is nothing apart from God.

"As the sun sets this day into the long night of those we leave behind we await the morning of the eternal sunrise that will find us, your children, O Lord, in your garden of Paradise. Amen."

"Amen," all the others repeated. All but Adam Forrester.

Then they walked away—except for those assigned to the burial detail.

Rankin hurried toward the room where Discant and the other wounded lay.

Jeff took hold of Dominique's hand. Mister Joseph climbed back up to what had become the watchtower. Cookie repaired to his wagon to start on the supper. Gunnison stood in the center of the courtyard. The captain checked the time from his watch and let his gaze shift to the picture on the open lid.

"Captain Gunnison!" Mister Joseph called from the tower, and pointed out across the field.

It was beyond belief to think that the guerrillas would attack again so soon after such a disastrous charge, after leaving behind so many dead from their ranks.

It had to be something else.

It was.

Gunnison, Bogartis, then Jeff, Dominique, and Forrester climbed to where they could get a clear view of the field.

Without a truce, without a white flag, just as the sun was slipping behind the curving hills, Carvajal had sent out two wagons with a detail, to pick up the bodies strewn across the ground outside the mission.

"What are your orders, Captain?" Bogartis asked.

"What do you think are my orders, Mister Bogartis?"

"Maybe they've had enough," Bogartis said. "Maybe they'll pick up their dead and go away."

"You don't really believe that, do you?"

"No, I don't." Bogartis scratched his whiskers. "I was just pretendin'."

"Well, let's just pretend we don't notice 'em and let 'em go about their business . . . and don't say it."

"Say what? Oh, bein' a crazy war, you mean?"

"All wars are crazy," Gunnison said, and walked away.

Bogartis followed.

"Your father's quite a man." Dominique squeezed Jeff's hand.

Forrester shook his head slightly and left the two of them behind.

Later that night after supper, Gunnison and Bogartis stood near a wagon drinking coffee. Gunnison had heard what Dominique had said to Jeff: *Your father's quite a man.* He wondered if his son agreed. He wondered if after all those years they would, in fact, be father and son again. Nothing would be worth the lives that this expedition had taken on both sides. He wondered if the war being fought at home was worth the lives that would be forfeited on both sides . . . if all the wars ever fought . . . but that was no way to think. Worth it or not, wars would be fought as they had always been fought. And as Rankin had quoted from the Bible, "There's no new thing under the sun."

Still, Gunnison couldn't help wondering what his son thought.

"We can take one more charge, Captain," Bogartis said. "Maybe two."

"I know."

"Hope *they* don't." Bogartis spilled out the dregs of his cup and moved off as Forrester appeared riffling a deck of cards.

"I heard what he said."

"You hear everything."

"I try. But he's right."

"So?"

"So," Forrester shrugged, "maybe we ought to make a deal. Give 'em the gold right now. That's what they want."

"I thought you wanted to live like a raja."

"But I don't want to die like a fool. Show me a hero and I'll show you a tragedy."

"Even if we made a deal, don't you think they'd double-cross us after what it's cost 'em?"

"I'd say it's an even bet."

"You're a gambler." Gunnison pointed to the cards in Forrester's hand.

"Sure I am." He smiled. "I owe you four million, don't I?"

"High card," Gunnison said. "Double or nothing."

"The odds are really against you this time, Tom." Forrester extended the deck.

Gunnison drew a card.

"Seven," he said. "Draw."

Forrester picked a card and turned it up.

"Looks like a four from here." Gunnison handed his card back to Forrester.

"So it does. And looks like I've got to go along with you—at least till your luck changes."

Forrester put the deck into his pocket and started to walk away, but turned back and smiled.

"Oh, one more thing, Tom."

"What?"

"About giving up the gold . . ."

"What about it?"

"You know I was just testing you."

"Yeah, I know. I've been tested before."

Earlier that afternoon Dominique had spread a blanket in a cubicle near what had become the hospital room. She had placed a few of her personal possessions in one of the corners. The cubicle had probably served as spartan quarters for one of the former priests.

Jeff had walked her to the hallway that led to both the hospital room and the cubicle.

They stood near each other in the darkness except for the candles that reflected out of the open door to the hospital room and the moonlight that splayed through the arched windows of the mission. The glow from the candles and moonlight haloed around her form and face and glistened through her red hair, making it appear even redder.

She put her arms around him softly in an invitation for him to respond. He accepted the invitation but held her firm and close.

Her face was nearer to his than it had ever been, and moving ever so slowly closer.

"Thanks for walking me home." She smiled, their lips

almost touching. "Sorry I can't ask you in."

"Why not?"

"This is a church, you know. Or didn't you think I'd notice?"

"We could go outside someplace."

"And talk about 'old times'?"

"I wasn't thinking about talking."

"I can tell."

"How?"

"By the way you—"

The kiss was long and tender . . . and then not as tender. It was fired by the pent-up craving that both of them had held in check up to now.

Their bodies melded, and each could feel the other's every plane and curve coursing into a form that became one—until she pulled away.

"Lieutenant . . ." she whispered. "I think we'd better call it a night."

"That's not what I call it."

"Lust?" She managed to smile.

"Partly."

"What else?"

"I'm not sure, Red."

"Neither am I." She whispered again. "And I want to be, Jeff. Who knows? I might even die a virgin."

"Not if I can help it." This time he smiled.

"You can. But not like this."

"Some other church? Some other time? With a ring? Is that what you mean?"

"I'm not sure what I mean. And you said you're not sure either."

"I'm sorry I said it."

"No, you're not. Because you have to be honest, like your . . ."

261

"Like my father? That's what you said back at the stream. That he was honest."

"So I did. Let's say good night, Jeff. Please."

"Sure." He nodded. "Good night, Dominique." He turned and walked up the hall toward the outer door.

"That was a beautiful scene," came Forrester's voice as he stepped from the doorway of the hospital room. "All that was missing was a balcony."

"You are a sonofabitch, Mister Forrester."

"I never said otherwise." He stepped closer. "But I was just visiting an old comrade. Too bad he's unconscious, however—you two put on a better show."

"It wasn't for your benefit."

"I enjoyed it, nevertheless."

"Well, the show's over, Mister Forrester."

"Oh, no it's not. There's a whole last act to go, and if you play it smart, we'll take the curtain call together . . . along with that pot of gold."

"You still think so?"

"You're your father's daughter. He would've played it smart. Besides," Forrester nodded toward the outer door, "he's just a boy in a man's uniform. Uniforms don't mean anything to me."

"What does? That pot of gold?"

"That . . . and other things. Just don't forget what I said, Red."

"I won't." Dominique started to walk toward the cubicle but turned back. "And Captain Forrester . . ."

"Yes."

"My father . . . he didn't die so smart."

The last time Gunnison had looked up at the North Star was in the garden with China Lil in San Angelo. Just a few nights ago. Not that far, as miles are counted. But a lot of dead men ago.

"What're you thinking about?" Jeff moved up close

262

behind his father, then beside him, and pointed to the North Star. "Were you out at sea?"

"No. To be honest, I was back in San Angelo, thinking about the night before we left."

"Somebody just said that you were *always* honest. Seems like you're everybody's hero."

"Not *everybody's*," Gunnison said pointedly. Then, after a beat, "That somebody who said it . . ." Gunnison motioned back toward the direction where Jeff had come from. ". . . somebody with red hair?"

"Very red. That last night in San Angelo . . . somebody with a jade necklace?"

Gunnison was silent.

"She and I had a little talk," Jeff went on. "Told me how you met. You were quite a hero there too."

Gunnison shrugged.

"She didn't tell me the story behind that jade necklace—but I remember you saying that everybody's got to have some secret."

"No secret. Not much of a story. Saw it in a window in Hong Kong. Thought of her for some reason. Bought it. Gave it to her. That's all. No more to it than that."

"There is as far as she's concerned."

"Too bad."

"Can I ask you one more question?"

"Who's stopping you?"

"If we get out of this . . . and when the war's over . . ."

"Those are two mountains to climb."

"I said 'if.'"

"Yeah?"

"What're you going to do?"

"There's a nice little place up in California called Santa Barbara. . . ."

"I've heard of it."

"I've been there. Might go back someday and watch a few sundowns." Gunnison withdrew the gold watch and sprung open the lid. "Sundown's the most satisfying part of the day."

"That all depends."

"On what?"

"On who you watch it with . . . don't you think?"

Gunnison snapped the lid closed.

"She said something else," Jeff added.

"Who?"

"China Lil. She told me that I'd never have a step-mother."

"So?"

"So maybe that's why she holds on to that necklace you gave her . . . instead of a ring, which is what she wants."

"Well, Jeff," Gunnison said after a pause. "It's a way past sundown. Maybe we better turn in."

"I guess so . . . and thanks."

"For what?"

"For being . . . honest."

After the bodies had been retrieved, Carvajal had broken out the liquor and distributed it with a lavish hand. He wasn't sure of his next move, and neither were the men and women of the hillside camp. But he knew that time was on their side. He would fill that time by giving his men all they could drink and allowing them to enjoy the company of the women as much as they wanted.

They did both. Long into the night. Carvajal sat by himself and smoked as the others sated themselves into oblivion. Melena watched and waited from a distance until he beckoned, as she knew he would.

Vega had found himself a suitable companion, but he looked from time to time toward Melena, until she rose and walked with that unmistakable walk toward Carvajal and the blankets he had spread under a tree in the distance. He watched both of them silhouetted against the night sky as they removed everything they wore, then crawled between the blankets.

Vega rolled back against his companion and reached for her. But in the darkness he imagined that he was reaching for Melena.

Hours later the night was at its darkest just before first light, when Vega ran toward the rhythmic movement of the blankets beneath the tree.

"General Carvajal!" he shouted again and again.

Carvajal's head came out from the blanket in a fury.

"What's the matter with you, man? Have you gone crazy?"

"No, my general!"

Melena appeared out of the blanket, uncovered to her waist.

"What the hell is it?" Carvajal demanded.

"It's good news, my general!"

Chapter Thirty-two

The sun rose veiled by a morning mist clinging to the slopes of the uplands. Crystal droplets trickled from skeletal limbs of crooked trees on the banks of the hills.

Within the hour the land and everything on it was warm and dry, then hot and still and silent. Mystic.

From a distance the mission looked like a painting without a frame. Nothing moved except for the two flags that fluttered from their poles.

But within the walls there was movement and a heavy air of expectation. Expectation of the worst.

Breakfast had been served, not exactly served . . . dished out. Coffee and some sort of mush that Cookie had concocted, along with biscuits of uncertain ingredients. Coffee strong. Mush spongy. Biscuits mealy. But nobody much complained or cared. They were concerned with what was to come.

The what was almost certain. Attack. The when, uncertain. Any minute . . . or later, when food and water were low and nerves were taut.

Jeff had waited outside as Dominique came through the door and onto the steps of the building.

"Morning."

"Good morning, Jeff."

"Dominique, if I was out of line last night I—"

"You were fine." She smiled. "I stopped by to look in on Jim this morning. Mister Rankin's doing all he can . . . but that isn't going to be enough. He's awfully weak."

"Want to get some coffee?"

She nodded and took his hand.

The Rebel contingent, what was left of it, stood by one of the wagons, dipping their biscuits into their coffee cups and making the most of their morning meal. Captain Forrester was among them, but he stood cradling a Henry and watching as Jeff and Dominique walked in the distance.

"Captain," Rink said, "I heard 'em say we was low on ammunition."

"Son," Forrester smiled, "we're low on everything," he tapped the side of the wagon with the barrel of the Henry, "except gold and . . ."

"And what, sir?"

"Desperation."

"I'm not sure what you mean, sir."

"I mean what I said before . . . and you tell the rest of 'em . . . when the time comes . . . just follow my lead."

"Yes, sir." Rink nodded as Forrester walked away. Then Rink looked at Dell Warren. "Desperation? That ain't so good, is it, Dell?"

Dell Warren just smiled and bit into a biscuit.

Cookie was on his way toward Gunnison and Bogartis, who stood in the middle of the compound. Forrester fell in close behind.

"Pretty damn soon," Cookie said to Gunnison.

"Pretty damn soon, what?"

"We're gonna have to start eatin' them horses. Slaughtered the last of the sheep last night. Cooked everything but the fur and hoofs."

"Some of it tasted like fur to me," Bogartis remarked.

"It ain't funny," Cookie grumbled.

"I know it's not," Gunnison said.

"Ain't much water left either . . . except in that stream way out there."

"What the hell are they waiting for?" Forrester said. "Wouldn't you think they'd charge again and make us use the last of our cartridges?"

"That's one way to do it," Gunnison replied. "Or . . ." He never finished.

A mortar shell exploded twenty yards from the mission and to the right, sending up clods of dirt and rock.

"Captain!" Mister Joseph yelled from the watchtower.

Another shell exploded, closer and more to the center.

Gunnison hurried toward the higher level, where he could get a better look at the hillside, followed by Bogartis and Forrester, then Jeff.

Gunnison looked through his telescope.

"That's what they were waiting for. Their artillery to catch up to them."

"Well, it sure as hell did," Bogartis said as another mortar exploded at closer range.

"What've they got?" Jeff asked his father.

"Take a look." Gunnison handed him the telescope while another shell burst more accurately.

"One light mortar," Jeff said. "And it's sitting out of range of our Henrys."

"Well, that breaks it," Forrester squinted. "They're zeroing in with every shot."

Mister Joseph climbed down from the tower and hurried toward Gunnison and the others.

"Dominique, get inside," Jeff said.

She shook her head and didn't move.

The next shell exploded against the wall of the mission, hurtling chunks of stone and mud in all directions and leaving a jagged hole in the barrier.

Carvajal, a few yards to the side of the cannon, was holding his field glasses with one hand and his belly with the other. Laughing. He tossed the glasses to Vega. Now Carvajal's guerrillas were relaxed, unmounted, most of them unarmed, smiling and enjoying the fireworks.

The mortar was halfway up the hillock on a level spot, with its gun crew in the open, but in safety, out of rifle range.

The gun, a bronze Cochorn, Model 1041, with the tube weighing just under 300 pounds, had handles on both sides of the bed, allowing two men to carry it for short distances if necessary. The crew consisted of six men. The cannon fired a 24-pounder shell, weighing 16.8 pounds with a half-pound of powder—delivering a maxim range of 1,200 yards with accuracy.

The shell had to be loaded carefully to ensure that the fuse pointed outward when the projectile came to rest at the bottom of the bore. If not, the force of the propellant could drive the fuse into the shell, causing the cannon itself to explode.

But this crew knew what it was doing. They loaded efficiently and fired effectively.

The next burst smashed into the mission wall closer

to the gate and two of the defenders fell wounded from the result of the debris.

"We've got to knock it out," Gunnison said to no one and everyone.

"There's no way." Forrester shook his head. "The bastards've got us."

"Maybe not." Gunnison removed the gold watch and chain from his pocket, unsnapped the clasp, and handed it to Jeff. "Hold this."

Gunnison moved away—past Bogartis, Dominique, Forrester, and Mister Joseph.

Still holding the watch and chain, Jeff looked through the telescope toward the mortar again. Its muzzle was tilted high, being loaded, then fired.

Gunnison was now on horseback, with the reins in one hand and a Henry in the other, moving toward the entrance of the mission.

"Open the gate!"

Two men unlatched and pulled open one of the twin gates.

"He's crazy!" Forrester muttered.

"Theoretically," Jeff said, "it could work."

"I'm going with him." Mister Joseph started to move.

"Mister Joseph!"

The black man turned back toward Jeff, who hit him square in the jaw with his right fist and handed the watch and chain to Bogartis with his left. "Hold this."

Jeff grabbed Bogartis's Henry and bolted toward another horse, as Gunnison rode out of the mission like his saddle was on fire.

Dominique opened her mouth to say something—but didn't.

The gun crew spotted Gunnison, immediately lowered the muzzle of the mortar, and fired at the zigzagging lone horsemen.

The shot was long and detonated to the right. But by then Gunnison was not alone. Jeff had ridden out of the gate and was trying to catch up. And right behind Jeff was Forrester, aboard another horse galloping onto the field.

The mortar blazed again, with the shell landing between the veering riders, sending clods of earth and rocks splattering among the horsemen.

Gunnison let the reins fall over the pommel of his saddle, cocked the lever of his Henry, and fired again and again. Jeff covered him, shooting at the gun crew. So did Forrester.

Carvajal screamed with rage at Vega and the guerrillas, who had expected nothing so foolhardy and audacious.

"Shoot the riders! Shoot the goddamn riders!"

The guerrillas scattered for their rifles.

Jeff and Forrester were still zigzagging and shooting at the gun crew. But Gunnison wasn't aiming at the crew. He cocked and fired repeatedly.

One of the bullets hit the mark.

A shot smashed into the lowered muzzle of the mortar, exploding the loaded shell, blowing up the cannon—and with it, what was left of the crew.

"Get 'em!" Carvajal screamed. "Go after 'em! Kill 'em!"

Vega and a dozen others scrambled toward their horses and started to mount.

Gunnison, Jeff, and Forrester whirled their animals, while still firing, and rode like hell back toward the mission.

One of the last shots tore into Vega's throat and he tumbled onto the hillside, gushing blood.

Half a dozen other guerrillas had made it to their horses and were riding and firing across the open field.

Andrew J. Fenady

But as soon as they rode into range, three of the pursuers fell victim to the sharpshooters from the mission. The other three turned back as Gunnison, Jeff, and Forrester rode through the gate.

Carvajal and Melena both knelt beside Vega. She pressed her palm against his throat in an effort to arrest the blood that spouted from the ruptured artery. The effort was in vain.

Vega opened his eyes, saw Carvajal leaning over him. He managed to reach up and touch Melena's hand.

"My general . . . ," he whispered, ". . . Melena." Then his voice came stronger. "God damn . . . both of you." Vega's eyes closed, and he died still touching Melena's hand.

The defenders at the mission cheered as Gunnison, Jeff, and Forrester reined in and dismounted.

Dominique ran to Jeff and threw her arms around him.

"Where's my watch?" Gunnison smiled at his son.

"He's got it." Jeff pointed to Bogartis.

"Well, Captain," Forrester said, "you bought us a little time."

"Not just me." He looked at Jeff and smiled again. "Thanks."

Jeff nodded and walked away with Dominique. As he passed Mister Joseph, he touched the black man's elbow.

"Sorry about that poke."

Some time after the cannonading started Alan Rankin had come out of the hospital room and was standing next to Mister Joseph as Jeff had spoken to him.

"What did he mean by that?" Rankin asked. "What poke?"

"Oh, nothing. Just a family matter." Mister Joseph

rubbed his jaw and managed to smile, even though it hurt.

"Forrester." Gunnison turned toward the Confederate captain. "Weren't you the one who said 'show me a hero and I'll show you a tragedy'?"

"I did, Tom . . . and this isn't over yet."

"Well, anyhow, thanks."

"That's all right, Tom—and coming from you that's as good as gold . . . almost." He smiled and walked away, still holding the Henry and heading toward Johnny Rink and Dell Warren, who stood a few yards away.

Bogartis handed the watch and chain to Gunnison.

"Is it still ticking, Mister Bogartis?" Gunnison snapped open the lid and looked inside.

"Yeah, and you're damn lucky *you* are, Captain. You know, I didn't think either one of them two'd come after you."

"Neither did I." Gunnison closed the lid and put the watch into his pocket. " 'Specially one of them." He moved off.

Mister Bogartis stood there, scratching his whiskers, and wondered which one of them Gunnison meant.

Forrester kept walking as Rink and Warren fell into step with him, one on each side.

"Captain, sir," Rink grinned, "I never seen the like of it. They couldn't a done it without you. You sure saved his bacon."

"I wasn't thinking of his bacon."

"Huh?"

"I was thinking of our gold."

"I don't quite understand, sir," Warren said.

"I'd rather deal with Gunnison than those guerrillas."

"Don't you think," Dominique said to Jeff as they

walked along the side of a building, "you ought to sit down someplace and take it easy?"

"I'll take it any way it takes." He smiled. "I've been thinking . . ."

"Think some more. You're still dizzy. Let's sit down on these steps," she said, and pointed.

"Sure."

Dominique pulled a cigarette and match out of her blouse, struck the match against the steps, lit the cigarette, and inhaled.

"Aren't you ever going to quit?"

"Quit what?" She exhaled.

"Quit smoking."

"I'll quit when you quit."

"Quit what?"

"Quit asking."

"I quit."

"Then so do I." She inhaled again and smiled. "After I finish this one."

"You make up your mind that easy?"

"Sometimes." Dominique let the smoke sift out of her mouth. "But I don't think you've made up your mind . . . about a lot of things."

"What do you mean?"

"About him, for one. First you were going to beat him up and put him under arrest. Then you ride out there, maybe save his life and certainly risk your own. *Have* you made up your mind?"

"About him? Nope. About you? Yep."

"What about me?"

"First off," he pointed to her breast, "you're a good patient."

"Had a good doctor."

"Maybe the doctor ought to check on the operation, make sure—"

"I think the patient and the doctor both need a little more time."

"To do what?"

"To reflect." She smiled. "Wouldn't want to do anything impetuous all of a sudden."

"You mean like a church . . . and a ring? Because if that's what it takes . . ."

"I mean . . . you're still dizzy."

"Maybe so, Red, but it's not just from that ride."

"Slow down, Galahad, I'll be around." She flipped the cigarette away.

"Sure, we'll take our time." He looked across at the beleaguered mission and smiled. "We've got all our lives."

Chapter Thirty-three

There was blood on the moon. Or so it seemed. The waxing moon glowed with a reddish hue still reflecting the last rays of the sun that had just set.

From a bleak rim of a distant hill the night cry of a lone wolf called out for a lost mate.

The two forces, one on the hillside with superior numbers, the other inside the battered mission with superior rifles but little ammunition, settled in for the long night—for many on both sides, what might be the last night.

For Ensign James Discant it would be the last night. Discant was dying.

Jeff and Alan Rankin were at his side. As was sometimes the case with dying men, he seemed to rally just before the end. The penultimate force within gathered its final earthbound strength. Discant opened his eyes.

"Jeff . . ."

The lieutenant leaned closer and touched Discant's

hand. There was the faint trace of a smile on the ensign's face.

"Jeff . . . I'm sorry . . . we couldn't be . . . on the same side . . ."

Jeff tightened his grip on Discant's wrist.

"Maybe, my friend . . . ," Discant said, ". . . maybe someday there'll only be . . . one side again."

"I hope so."

"Jeff . . . Forrester? I want . . ."

"Dominique's getting him."

"I'm here, Jim."

Forrester and Dominique stood near the entrance to the room.

"Talk to . . ." Discant raised a hand weakly.

"It's all right, Jim," Jeff said, and let go of Discant's wrist. "You go ahead and talk to him. We'll be back."

Jeff and Rankin moved toward the doorway. Jeff nodded to Forrester, then left the room, followed by Dominique and Rankin.

Forrester went to Discant's side, leaned down, and smiled as the dying man looked up at him.

"Son, you're going to . . ."

"No . . . sorry, sir . . . can't help . . . no matter what happens . . . get gold to . . . South. . . . I . . ." Discant breathed his last.

"Sure I will . . ." Forrester straightened and muttered so no one could hear. ". . . you poor dumb bastard."

Jeff, Dominique, and Rankin waited in the hallway as Forrester came out of the room, shook his head slightly, and walked toward the door.

"Say, Johnny." Warren pointed to Rink's Bowie knife. "Can I borrow that Arkansas toothpick?"

"Sure." Rink unsheathed the knife and handed it to Warren.

Warren pulled a long cigar out of his pocket and proceeded to cut it in half. He gave the knife back to Rink with one hand and offered him a halved cigar with the other.

"Smoke," he said.

"That's your last cigar, Dell."

"Go ahead, smoke." He placed it in Rink's hand, took out a match, and struck it. "I wish it was made out of fine Virginia leaf." Warren lit Johnny's half, then his own. "Howsomever, these Mexican cigars aren't bad," he puffed, "once you get used to them."

Rink puffed and nodded.

"The Lord and war," he said, "sure do move in mysterious ways."

"Mind chewing that a little finer?"

"Well, here we are—you, one of the gentry of Virginia, and me, a dirt farmer from Texas, the two opposite ends of the Confederacy, and we wind up squat in the middle of Mexico."

"We haven't wound up yet. But we sure as hell might, maybe tomorrow."

"Yeah."

"You know, Johnny, if I wasn't buried in Virginia, I'd want to be buried at sea."

"Not likely. Not if we die tomorrow. Dell, what do you think Captain Forrester's got in mind?"

"I don't know," Warren said. "But I've heard and seen some things about Captain Forrester that don't sit too well."

"Me too. But you can't believe everything you hear . . . and besides, he is our commandin' officer . . . isn't he?"

"He is . . . long as the commands he gives benefit the Confederacy and not himself."

"He said to follow his lead."

"I will . . . so long as it leads to Savannah."

"Tom," Forrester was saying to Gunnison, "you want to hear something funny?"

"Can't imagine what that would be."

"That damn fool Discant died thinking I was still going to try to get that gold to the South."

"Yeah. That is funny."

"Well," Forrester shrugged, "at least he died proud, thinking it was for something."

"What about you, Forrester?"

"What about me?"

"Don't you have any pride in what you're supposed to be fighting for?"

"The Bible says 'pride goeth before a fall.' " Forrester smiled.

"Not exactly. It says 'pride goeth before destruction—and a haughty spirit before a fall.' "

"You know your Bible, but what's the difference? A fall is a fall. And if you mean do I have any pride or feelings about the 'cause,' or states' rights, or slavery . . ."

"Well, do you?"

"There's always been slaves, there always will be. Goes back to the Code of Hammurabi, and before. Egypt, Greece, Rome, all the great empires had slaves."

"And they all fell. What if you were one? A slave."

"Then I'd fight like hell. But I'm not. And as for states' rights, *might* makes right."

"Does it?"

"Sure. 'Eagles suffer little birds to sing.' And speaking of eagles . . . about those . . ."

Forrester spotted Jeff and Bogartis approaching.

"Have 'em dig another grave," Gunnison said to Jeff, who nodded.

"Plantin' and prayin'," Bogartis grumbled. "Pretty soon there ain't gonna be anybody left to pray."

"Well, I'll say good night, gentlemen." Forrester walked away.

"There's a couple of things I'd like to talk to you about." Jeff looked at his father.

"I can take a hint," Bogartis muttered, and moved off.

"Let's see if we can scare up a drink," Gunnison said to his son.

"Andres, Beka, Sebastian, Vega, and all the rest," Melena said in the darkness as she lay on the blanket next to Carvajal, "all of them dead."

"They died for a good reason."

"They died because you ordered them to die."

"Somebody has to give the orders."

"Who gives you orders?"

"Not you, so shut up."

"Yes, my general."

"And after tomorrow . . ." Carvajal paused.

"After tomorrow, what?"

"I will be the most famous general in Juárez's army. More famous even than Zarazoga and Diaz."

"First you've got to take the mission and the gold."

"I'll take them both. We outnumber them four to one."

"You sure that's enough? They still got those rifles."

"Rifles are no good without bullets. They haven't got enough bullets. So tomorrow I lead my army to victory and to gold, much gold."

"How much gold for Juárez . . . and how much for you?"

"Enough for Juárez to make me a hero in his eyes . . . and enough for me to make me rich. The richest general in any army. You'll see."

"Will I see any of the gold?"

"You will share in the gold and the glory."

"What do you mean?"

"I mean that you and all the other women who can ride will mount up and charge with us."

"Prospero, you are crazy."

"All great generals are a little crazy. I need everybody who can ride to draw their fire—use up their bullets. Then we take them and the gold." Carvajal laughed.

"You think the women will do as you order?"

"If they don't, I'll use some bullets on them. But they will charge with us for Mexico, and so will you."

"Yes, my general."

"Come here."

"Yes, my general."

As Carvajal reached for her, Melena reached for a knife she had hidden beneath the blanket, grabbed it, and thrust it toward his heart. But Carvajal's hand was at her wrist; then, with both his hands over hers, he twisted until the blade pointed at her breast. He forced with all his strength until the blade plunged into her chest up to the hilt.

"Confusion to the enemy," Gunnison said as he and Jeff sat across from each other and lifted their cups.

Jeff nodded, and they drank.

"What's on your mind, Lieutenant?"

"For one thing, that flag that was in your saddle-bag . . ."

"What about it?"

"How long have you had it with you?"

"Since it was taken down from the mast of the *Confidence*."

"Why?" Jeff asked.

"Why was it taken down?"

"Why did you carry it?"

"I don't know. Maybe figured it might fly on some

281

other mast of some other ship, some other time."

"I see."

"Do you?"

"I do." Jeff nodded. "I see something else, too."

"What?"

"That I've been somewhat of a stuffed shirt sometimes."

"Somewhat?" Gunnison smiled. *"Sometimes?"*

"Most of the time."

"That's closer." Gunnison took a swallow of whiskey.
"Is that what you wanted to talk about?"

"Something else, too."

"What?"

"Dominique Lessuer."

"Talk," Gunnison said, and drank again.

The two other wounded men had been asleep in the
hospital room when Mister Joseph had asked Alan Rankin if he might come outside and talk for a few minutes.
Rankin said he thought the sleeping patients would be
all right. They went out the door and sat on the mission
steps.

Mister Joseph looked directly into Rankin's eyes and
spoke softly.

"I want to make a confession."

"But I'm not a priest."

"That's all right, I'm not a Catholic. I'm a Methodist,
but under the circumstances, you'll have to do, if you
don't mind."

"Not if you think it will help."

"I think so."

"Then go ahead."

"Have you ever heard of Harriet Tubman and the Un-
derground Railroad?"

"Yes. She smuggled a great many slaves out of the
South."

"That's right. They called her 'The Conductor.' When my wife, daughter, and I ran away she arranged our passage to a safe house—only it turned out not to be safe. When another slave and I went for supplies, the house was raided. We got back in time to see our families being dragged out. I wanted to go and help them, or at least be with them. But he said it was hopeless, and I let him talk me into standing there and watching the terror in their faces and hearing my little daughter calling out for her daddy as they loaded them and the rest of the runaways into a cart to be taken back to the owners. Owners! I swore to myself that night that someday I'd go back and try to get them out again, but I never did . . . and I've never seen them since, but every night I see their faces and hear my little daughter crying for her daddy to help her . . . and my wife being pushed into that cart . . . while I stood there."

"But you couldn't have helped."

"I could have tried. I could have been whipped again like I was whipped before . . . and beaten . . . and I would have been with them. Instead, I ran away to sea where I'd be safe. I've never told anyone until now. That's what I wanted to confess. But there is no absolution for that—for cowardice, is there, Father?"

"God must think there is . . . and so must you."

"How? By saying Hail Marys?"

"By what you think and do. It's never too late."

"For what?"

"For absolution. You're not a coward. I've seen that, more than once. If we get out of this, you'd want to help them then, wouldn't you?"

"Of course I'd do anything—if we get out."

"Then there's a simple solution. Pray that we get out."

"Then what?"

"If we do . . . have you ever heard of Robert Gould Shaw?"

"No."

"He's a white man, a Harvard graduate, and the last I heard he was forming a black brigade, the Fifty-fourth Massachusetts Volunteer Infantry." Alan Rankin smiled. "And it most certainly will be heading south."

"So will I—if we get out."

"Then start praying."

"I already have." Mister Joseph rose from the steps and extended his hand as Rankin also rose. "And thank you, Fa—"

"Don't call me that, please."

"Thank you, Mister Rankin. You've helped me a lot."

"And vice versa, Mister Joseph, vice versa."

"Beg pardon, sir," Dell Warren said. "Can we talk to you for a minute?"

Adam Forrester turned and faced Warren and Johnny Rink, who stood beside him. Warren held a folded article of clothing in his hands.

"Certainly, fellas." Forrester took a drag of his cigar. "Just enjoying a good cigar before turning in."

"Yes, sir." Rink smiled. "We just enjoyed the last of ours." He looked at Warren. "Actually his."

"How's that?"

"Well, 'ol Dell cut his last cigar in half, split it with me, and we smoked her up."

"You did that, Mister Warren? Shared your last cigar with your comrade?"

Warren shrugged.

"Greater love hath no man . . ." Forrester flicked the ash from his cigar.

"Excuse me, sir?" Rink frowned.

"Never mind, that's another horse. But here . . ." He reached into his pocket and removed two long stogies.

"I've got a couple of extras. I'd like to share 'em with you two."

"That's very kind of you, sir," Warren said as they accepted Forrester's offer.

"Nothing's too good for a couple loyal comrades of the Confederacy. Now, what's on your mind, boys?"

"Well, sir, we heard about Discant," Warren said.

"Yes. Very regrettable."

"We also heard that you was with him when . . ." Rink didn't finish.

"I was, and he died like a brave soldier to the end . . . uh, loyal to the cause."

"Yes, sir," Rink said. "We figured that."

"And sir," Warren added, "you think that the captain will be burying him in the morning, before . . ."

"Yes." Forrester nodded. "I imagine so."

"Well . . ." Warren hesitated. "We thought that you . . . that is, that he . . ." Warren extended the article of clothing he held in his hand.

"What's that?"

"It's a naval tunic, sir, Confederate," Warren said. "Mine. I don't have any need of it anymore, and we thought he might want to . . . be buried in it."

"That's very thoughtful of both of you." Forrester took the tunic. "I'll make sure that he is."

"Thank you, sir," Warren said.

"No. I thank you, and boys . . ."

"Yes, sir?" Rink's face moved forward just an inch.

"You won't forget what I said, you and the rest of the men."

"There's only seven of us left, sir . . . and you."

"I know that. All the more reason we've got to stick together—no matter what happens."

"We will, sir." Rink nodded. "You can count on us, sir."

"I know that." Forrester smiled. "Good night, gentlemen. Enjoy your cigars."

"Yes, sir," both men said as they saluted.

Forrester returned their salutes and watched them turn and walk away.

Then he looked down at the Confederate tunic and shook his head ever so slightly.

"We've got a couple of options we'd like to talk to you about," Gunnison said to Dominique Lessuer as Jeff stood next to him.

"It's good of you, both of you, to let me in on them."

"We haven't . . . yet."

"But you're going to, otherwise you wouldn't've asked me to me to come out here in the moonlight and listen."

"You want to light up while you listen?" Gunnison pointed to where she usually kept her smokes and matches.

"I quit smoking. What're the options?"

"Well." Gunnison looked at Jeff, then back to her. "One of them is, in the morning before they hit us, you ride out with a white flag. At least you'll save your life."

"What about the ten thousand you owe me?"

"If I gave it to you in gold, they'd just take it away. But I've got another idea." Gunnison smiled. "Suppose I gave you my IOU?"

"You know," Dominique smiled back, "what you can do with your IOU."

"Yeah, I didn't think that option would sail."

"You were right. What's the other one?"

"The other one is," Jeff said, "you take your horse tonight, now, sneak out of here while those guerrillas are asleep, and ride like hell to Vera Cruz. They wouldn't spot you, and even if they did they wouldn't go after one lone rider, because you sure as hell couldn't bring back any help. Now, that option makes plenty of sense."

"Maybe to you, but not to me."

"Why not?"

"Because no matter what you say or do, both of you, I'm staying here and I don't want to hear any more about anymore options except that one, so just shut up."

"You're a damn fool," Jeff said. "This could be your last chance."

"Yours too." Dominique smiled, took him by his arm, and led him away.

Cookie handed Bogartis a piece of rock candy.

"Here's the last of it."

Bogartis took the candy and grinned at him.

"Thanks. Why don't you eat it yourself?"

" 'Cause I know you got a sweet tooth, and besides, I ain't got no teeth."

Bogartis cracked off a chunk as Gunnison approached.

"Well, Captain," Bogartis said as he chewed at the candy, "looks like tomorrow'll be the last dustup."

"Looks like." Gunnison nodded and pointed toward the guerrillas' camp. "Guess it's their turn to remember the Alamo."

"Yeah," Bogartis bit into another chunk, "we'll give 'em somethin' to remember."

Gunnison nodded again.

"Say, Captain," Bogartis grinned, "I saw them two young'uns headin' away together."

"So?"

"So," Bogartis grinned wider, "what do you suppose they got in mind?"

"Well, Mister Bogartis, was I them, under the circumstances, I know what I'd have in mind."

Chapter Thirty-four

Both flags, the Stars and Stripes and the Stars and Bars, had been raised into the dawning sky and now flapped in the morning breeze.

The gentle strains of "Dixie" rose from behind the mission walls in soft accompaniment to the words spoken by Alan Rankin as everyone in the mission, except the wounded who lay in the hospital room, stood near the open grave. Present were Gunnison, Bogartis, Cookie, Jeff, Dominique, Mister Joseph, and the remaining crew of the *Phantom Hope,* along with Forrester, Dell Warren, Johnny Rink, and the five other Rebels who had survived.

" 'And he opened his mouth and taught them, saying, "Blessed are the poor in spirit for theirs is the kingdom of heaven. Blessed are they that mourn for they shall be comforted. Blessed are the meek for they shall inherit the earth. Blessed are they that thirst after righteousness: for they shall be filled. Blessed are the peacemakers for they shall be called the children of God. Rejoice and be exceedingly glad: for great is your reward in heaven." '

"O Lord, we commend unto you this soldier who, at last, has found peace. Amen."

"Amen," said all the others, including Johnny Rink, who lowered the mouth organ and tucked it into his pocket.

The body of James Discant, wearing a Confederate tunic and wrapped in a blanket, had already been lowered into the freshly dug grave and the mound of earth was being shoveled into the space below as Gunnison and the others turned away.

Forrester whispered to Gunnison as they walked.

"I'm going along with you, Tom, but just remember, I've got an interest in that fifteen million." He peeled away as Rankin and Mister Joseph came up beside Gunnison.

"Captain?" Rankin said.

"Yes?"

"Have you got an extra rifle?"

Gunnison stopped walking.

"What?"

"I asked if you had an extra rifle."

"I heard you, but . . ."

"I'm no longer a priest. I realized that."

"Well, you just gave a pretty good imitation back there."

"He deserved that and needed it. That's not what you need now. Not to get out of this."

"Suppose we do get out, then what? For you, I mean."

"I'll do missionary work, without a robe or a collar."

"And with a rifle?" Gunnison smiled.

"If necessary."

"Mister Joseph."

"Yes, sir."

"See to Mister Rankin's request, then get back up there." Gunnison pointed to the watchtower.

"Yes, sir." The two men left as Bogartis approached.

"Ammunition distributed?" Gunnison asked.

"What's left of it. Six rounds for each man, plus whatever they already had. They better shoot damn accurate."

Jeff walked with Dominique back from the grave. She took his hand.

"What you said about the 'rest of our lives' . . . today might be it."

"Dominique, you should have left."

"And miss last night?" She smiled. "By the way, sailor man, are you after my money?"

"What money?"

"The ten thousand your father owes me, remember?"

"Forgot all about it. Why, you got plans for it?"

"I don't know," she shrugged, "might open up a school."

"You? A schoolteacher?"

"Partly."

"What's the other part?"

"Well, if you don't know," she squeezed his hand, "then nobody does."

Mister Joseph had climbed back onto the watchtower, rifle in hand.

The defenders of the mission had all assumed their customary defensive positions with rifles at the ready. And now there was another defender with them. Alan Rankin looked up at Mister Joseph and motioned slightly with one hand as he held a rifle in the other.

Mister Joseph nodded, then turned back toward the hillside.

Gunnison and the rest of them watched as the ascending sun flooded the field, brightening the sand and stone that had already been soaked in the blood of fallen men and horses.

Just over a thousand yards away, across the sloping expanse of the hillock, General Carvajal had deployed his guerrillas into three phalanxes—men and women, everyone who could ride—armed and mounted.

And this time, astride his mount, Carvajal himself was at the head of the center column.

As the sun moved behind a drifting cloud formation, every living thing seemed to fall into a heavy, almost suffocating silence.

The forces within the mission, rifles pointed, fingers touching triggers.

The mounted guerrillas, holding reins, and their breaths—waiting for the command they knew would come.

Silence on both sides, as if any sound might betray the dwelling fear every soldier feels before he looks into the face of death.

And then:

The paralyzing silence was encroached. Not suddenly, nor explosively, but gradually by an indefinable rasping that might have been the reverberating echo of distant thunder, but wasn't.

Still, no one moved as the muffled drone became a rumble, with nothing yet in sight, and grew relentlessly louder.

All defenders within the mission, Gunnison, Bogartis, Jeff, Dominique, Forrester, and the rest of them, turned their eyes then their faces toward the approaching sound.

Carvajal and his troops, who were all closer to the sound, moved their mounts and faced a nearby hillside summit wherefrom came the rumble.

Over the rim, to the northwest, in an endless column of fours, preceded by a corps of drummers, an army appeared and approached. And with it the swelling sound of drumbeats, hoofbeats, and footfalls.

Gunnison's telescope was trained on the advancing army. But by now all the others within the mission could see as well as hear the countless formation of mounted and marching men.

Near the front of the formation moved a coal-black carriage drawn by a team of horses, just as black.

"Those aren't any guerrillas," Gunnison said, lowering the telescope. "Those are regulars."

"Yeah." Forrester nodded. "Looks like every uniform in Mexico is out there. Their whole damn army."

"For a while there," Bogartis added, "I didn't think we could be any worse off, but it 'pears we are."

The black carriage, escorted by two riders, pulled away from the long column and waited at the base of the hillock as Carvajal rode to meet it.

"Looks like," Bogartis said, "they're gonna chew the fat of confabulation."

Jeff moved closer to Gunnison.

"What do you think?"

"No sense thinking," Gunnison said. "At least not yet."

As his horse pulled up alongside the carriage, which had stopped, Carvajal saluted both the escorts and whoever was inside. He leaned closer to the open window and began talking. He motioned toward the mission then back up toward the guerrillas on the hill, and then again pointed at the mission.

After a couple of minutes, a time that seemed much longer to those inside the mission, the carriage, Carvajal, and the two uniformed riders began to move in the direction of the gates.

Not fast. Not slow.

The defenders, except for Gunnison, their Henrys still aimed, waited and watched as the carriage and the three mounted men approached.

"Tom," Forrester said, "I got one of the guerrilla's eyeballs smack in my sight."

"Put it down. All of you, lower your guns," Gunnison ordered, and added, "But hold on to 'em. Open the gates, Mister Bogartis."

Bogartis gave the signal, and both gates swung open as everybody watched and waited until the carriage and the three riders came through and stopped.

Gunnison approached, looked at the riders. The expression of hate and rancor was still smeared across Carvajal's face.

The other two men wore the uniforms of generals, both men handsome, resplendent, their look noncommittal. They both dismounted, and so did Carvajal as the carriage door opened.

A man stepped out, short, stocky, dressed in black, wearing a frock coat. An Indian.

His face was bronze, and though not old, was lined with deep creases. His straight black hair was swept hard across his large forehead. In his hand he carried a stovepipe hat.

"Benito Juárez," he said.

Gunnison stood face-to-face with a legend. The Abraham Lincoln of Mexico. In the instant before he spoke, Gunnison looked into the deep, ebony eyes of the man who stood in front of him, the man who had ignited the flame of democracy in a country ruled by tyrants for centuries. An Indian, born in Oaxaca, who at the age of fourteen could neither read, write, nor speak Spanish, who worked as a servant and was sent to a Franciscan seminary and turned to law instead of the priesthood and became a strong defender of Indian rights. Who rose to civil judge, then governor of Oaxaca. Who fought against the tyrannical Santa Anna and was exiled to New Orleans, worked there in a cigarette factory, then returned to help defeat and exile the same Santa Anna. Who barely escaped a firing squad to become the president of his country, only to flee Mexico City after his forces lost a pitched battle at Silao at the hands of his reactionary enemies who curried the favor of foreign governments. Governments whose intent it was to once again plunder the resources of a country that had been plundered by the conquistadores and many others since. At the time of President Juárez's worst defeat Lincoln had sent him a message expressing hope "for the liberty of your government and its people." But now, that hope for liberty of the government and the people had further dimmed as Juárez had been forced once again to flee from Mexico City. All this raced through Gunnison's mind as he spoke to President Benito Juárez.

"Tom Gunnison . . . Mister President."

The President of the Republic of Mexico nodded in acknowledgment, then looked toward his generals.

"General Zaragoza, Porfirio Díaz, and—"

"We've already met your other general," Gunnison said, and pointed to the fresh graves at the cemetery, "and so have they."

"The misfortunes of war . . . ," Juárez said.

"Far as I know, sir, your country and mine are not at war."

"My *presidente*," Carvajal took a step forward, "it is as I told you. . . ."

"Yes, General Carvajal, you have told me. Now I would like Tom Gunnison to tell me."

Gunnison's men, Dominique, Forrester, and the Rebels glanced at each other, then waited for the captain to state their case.

"Very simple, Mister President. I'm carrying a cargo from San Francisco to Baltimore. Had ship trouble, so we're taking a shortcut to Vera Cruz and another ship."

"The cargo is for the war in the United States?"

"That's right."

"And you are on the side of President Lincoln?"

"We are."

"I see." Juárez looked up at the two flags flying side by side atop the mission wall. "I also see *two* flags."

"Yes," Gunnison glanced at Forrester. "A temporary accommodation necessitated by our misfortunes here in Mexico. But I assure you, sir, that the cargo will be delivered to the government of the United States."

"And the cargo is . . . ?"

"Gold."

"The machinery of war," Juárez said slowly, "is fed with gold."

"And blood."

"Yes." Benito Juárez nodded. "Even now the French are sending an army to spill more blood. We have heard that Louis Napoleon intends to crown his cousin Maximilian, the Archduke of Austria, as emperor of Mexico. If so, Maximilian will find that he wears a phantom crown."

"Sir, on what basis can Napoleon claim—"

"Napoleon makes that claim because of gold."

"Gold?"

"Money that Louis Napoleon and his allies loaned our enemies."

"You beat those enemies."

"Ah, but Napoleon and his allies demand we pay our debts. So the French Army will present us with a bill . . . at the end of a bayonet."

"And you don't intend to pay?"

"We can't pay, Captain Gunnison. The Republic of Mexico is bankrupt. But it is still a republic."

"How big is the bill?"

"Twelve million. Captain Gunnison, how much gold do you carry?"

"Fifteen million."

"That much."

Juárez looked at his two generals, Zarazoga and Díaz, as Carvajal took another step and smiled.

"You see. What did I tell you, my *presidente*. If we had this gold—"

"General," Juárez interrupted, "you know the debt is a convenient pretext." He turned to Gunnison. "Just one more excuse for Louis Napoleon to overthrow the Republic and set up a monarchy as he has in France."

"But with fifteen million," Carvajal persisted in his argument, "we could buy enough guns and ammunition to . . ."

"Yes." Juárez nodded. "We could."

There was an uneasy silence. The followers of both Gunnison and Juárez stood motionless for a moment until Gunnison spoke.

"Didn't this Napoleon ever hear of something called the Monroe Doctrine?"

"Yes, of course," Juárez nodded, "but so long as the United States is fighting a civil war, he knows your country is unable to enforce the Monroe Doctrine."

"Maybe, and maybe not."

"If President Lincoln tried, it would give Europe an excuse to support the Confederacy."

"The French are landing at Vera Cruz?"

"Yes."

"How soon?"

"A week. Ten days."

Gunnison looked from the face of President Benito Juárez toward the wagons loaded with gold, then back to Juárez again.

"Are there still American ships in Vera Cruz?"

"The *Saratoga*, the *Wave*, and the *Indianola*."

"Uh-huh." This time Gunnison glanced toward his son before turning to Juárez. "Well, then, we'd better get to Vera Cruz before the French do."

Juárez did not answer. He stood silent for a moment as General Porfiro Díaz spoke for the first time.

"Are you so sure Presidente Juárez will let you go . . . with the gold?"

"I am," Gunnison said.

"Why?"

"Because," he looked again into the eyes of the man who held the fate of Mexico in his hands—and also the fate of the Americans within the mission, "President Juárez has to choose between the gold . . . and something else."

"Captain Gunnison," Juárez said as he reached inside the pocket of the frock coat and produced an envelope. "You are a farsighted man. I carry with me a letter far more valuable than the gold you carry."

All eyes at the mission, including those of Juárez, went to the envelope he held in his hand as everyone waited for him to continue.

"From President Abraham Lincoln, addressed to Benito Juárez, President of the Republic of Mexico." Juárez repeated, "The Republic of Mexico. So long as he recognizes us, there is still hope, and someday—soon, I pray—when your war is ended, there will be help from our brothers in the north."

"So do I," Gunnison said. "But somebody's going to have to do some explaining about," he pointed to the graves where the Americans were buried, "that."

Andrew J. Fenady

"Captain," Juárez spoke slowly, sincerely, "in your report, I ask you to include my regret," he regarded Carvajal for just an instant, "for the excesses committed by some of the guerrillas who support us. I have received other reports concerning the activities of General Carvajal in this area—activities that will be . . . curtailed, I assure you."

"Thank you, Mister President," Gunnison said, and immediately changed the subject. "You . . . can't defend Vera Cruz?"

"No. Nor Mexico City." Juárez put the envelope carefully back inside his pocket. "But the Republic is not a place. It is the will of the people to defend their constitution. Until we have gathered our strength and are able to defeat our enemies, that carriage will be our capital—and the will of the people will be our shield."

"Sir. You are a farsighted man."

"No. I am a simple Indian who was elected President of Mexico."

The President of Mexico extended a creased brown hand, clasped gratefully by Captain Gunnison.

"Captain, you are in need of supplies and medicine for your wounded. We will leave an adequate supply out there," Juárez nodded toward what had been the battlefield, "to help you reach Vera Cruz." Benito Juárez turned and walked toward the black carriage.

As the sound of the drums faded and the dust wake of the army disappeared from the rim of the hill, for the first time since the mission was occupied there was relief, smiles, and even laughter on the faces of the survivors.

Adam Forrester loosened the grip on his Henry and moved closer to Gunnison.

"Captain," he said, "I've got to give it to you. You sure knew how to play that hand. Almost had me be-

298

lieving you were going to Vera Cruz. How about that!"

"Yeah, how about it?" Jeff took a step forward and away from Dominique.

"Tell him, Tom." Forrester was still grinning. "Or do you want me to?"

"How about it?" Jeff repeated.

"All right, *I'll* tell him." Forrester turned serious, his face grim, his voice edged with irony. "Sonny, you've been had. We're heading south to a port called Alvarado. The old pelican and me—we made a deal. The war's over. You hear me?" Then he smiled again as he looked back at Gunnison.

"I hear you," Jeff said. "I want to hear it from him."

Then he moved another step and raised the Henry just a little.

Dominique, Bogartis, Cookie, Mister Joseph, Rankin, the rest of the crew of the *Phantom Hope*, as well as Forrester, Johnny Rink, Dell Warren, and the other Confederates, all fastened on Gunnison, as Jeff stared at his father.

"Alvarado or Vera Cruz?" he asked.

Chapter Thirty-five

"Vera Cruz."

Jeff trembled, not visibly, but inside. Within the framework of his body he shuddered like a man suddenly awakened from a consuming nightmare. The faint trace of a smile hooked the edges of his lips.

But Adam Forrester was not smiling. He stood tense and coiled, ready to spring.

"We made a deal!" he rasped at Gunnison.

"*You* made a deal," Gunnison said. "A deal which you wouldn't've kept. The war's not over, Forrester, but the game is—and you got no more cards."

"Looks like you're right." Forrester relaxed, smiled, and tossed the Henry to Bogartis. He started to move, but abruptly whirled, grabbed Dominique, pulled her close, and with the other hand drew the derringer from his belt and pointed it at her head. "Except for *this* card."

Forrester cocked one of the hammers of the derringer.

"I wouldn't want to kill her, but kill her I will." He looked at the other Rebels who were standing in a group.

"Are you boys with me?"

None of the Confederates moved. Then Dell Warren shook his head.

"In that case, I'll settle for one of those wagons. She's coming with me as far as Alvarado."

"I don't think she wants to go." Gunnison glanced at Dominique. "Do you?"

Dominique didn't answer, but her eyes moved toward the twin barrels of the derringer pointed at her head.

"I'll say it one last time. One wagon . . . or I'll pull the trigger and blow her brains out."

They all stood, unmoving and silent, watching Gunnison with the Henry in his hand, and waiting for his decision.

"Go ahead," Gunnison said in a matter-of-fact voice. "But as you do . . . I'll kill you."

Neither Forrester nor anybody else had anticipated that decision. Forrester cocked the other hammer of the derringer.

"You're bluffing."

"Then pull both triggers . . . and die."

It was obvious that Forrester wasn't sure of what he was going to do.

"Or put the gun down," Gunnison said, "and live."

"I guess." Forrester regarded Gunnison for just a moment more, then shrugged. "I'll settle for living."

He lowered the derringer, smiled, and started to turn away from Dominique, who still stood between the two men and saw Forrester's gun hand begin to rise as he spun back toward Gunnison. But before he could squeeze she lunged, pushed Forrester off balance, and fell to the ground.

Forrester fired and missed. Gunnison's Henry was level and smoking after the burst of his shot. Adam Forrester dropped, and as he did the deck of cards spilled from his pocket.

Johnny, Dell, and the other Confederates did not move. Jeff walked quickly to Dominique and put an arm around her as Gunnison came close to Forrester and knelt beside him.

Forrester managed to look up at the man who had shot him, then at the cards.

"Pick a card Tom," he murmured, "double or—"

"Nothing," Gunnison finished.

The wagons moved northeast. The savage terrain had changed from rugged ridges and barren rocks to a verdant, more hospitable landscape.

Gunnison held up a hand, motioning for the caravan to come to a stop.

As Mister Joseph reined up next to Alan Rankin in the driver's seat of the wagon, Rankin tossed him the cross the former slave had carved.

"When you see her," Rankin said, "give this to your daughter . . . from both of us."

Mister Joseph smiled and nodded.

Gunnison rode back a short distance and pulled up near Johnny Rink, Dell Warren, and the rest of the Confederates.

"Alvarado's in that direction."

"Sir?" Warren said, then glanced at Rink.

"Well, go ahead." Gunnison pointed south. "And I hope our paths don't cross again . . . till the war's over."

"We'll make damn sure they don't, sir." Johnny Rink grinned, and the Confederates all saluted, spurred their mounts, and let go a Rebel yell, galloping away.

Jeff, Dominique, and Bogartis watched as the Rebels

rode and Gunnison came up close to where they waited.

"You can put that in your report, Lieutenant." Gunnison took out his watch, snapped open the lid, and looked inside.

"Permission to speak freely, Captain?" Jeff smiled.

"Go ahead."

"You can't go on living with a ghost." He nodded toward the watch. "Time to let go."

"You could be right about that." Gunnison unfastened the clasp, closed the lid, and handed the watch and chain to his son. "Here, it was going to be yours someday. Now's as good a time as any."

"What about that lady with the jade necklace?" Jeff put the watch in his pocket.

"What about her?"

"She's still waiting for a ring."

"Guess I could do worse."

"So could she." Jeff smiled. "So could she."

"One question, partner," Dominique said.

"Just one?"

"Would you have let Forrester kill me?"

"I would." Gunnison nodded, then looked at Jeff. "But I'm not so sure about *him*. And say, speaking of rings . . . you know, being a captain, I'm legally authorized to perform marriage ceremonies."

"Have you ever done it?" Jeff inquired.

"Not yet. But got to start sometime, so why don't you go ahead and ask her?"

"All right, I will." He turned to Dominique and pointed toward her hat. "You think our kids'll have red hair?"

"Maybe some will . . . and maybe some won't."

"Some?! How many you figure we're going to have?"

"Have three," Gunnison said.

"Don't you think it's about time you quit giving me orders?" Jeff smiled.

"Maybe so. Maybe you're right about that too, son."

As they rode on, Bogartis lifted his head high as if looking for or sensing something ahead. He rose from the saddle, practically standing in the stirrups, leaning forward, breathing deeply.

"Captain . . ."

"Yes, Mister Bogartis," Gunnison said. "It's the sea."

G. G. BOYER

WINCHESTER AFFIDAVIT

The New Mexico Territory is bleeding in the throes of the Amarillo War, named for the vast estate known as the Amarillo Grant. The estate manager's *segundo* leads a group of night riders known as the Whitecaps, who use violence and mayhem to brutally clear the grant of "squatters," homesteaders and ranchers just trying to make lives for themselves. Cleve Bandelier, former cavalry officer and widowed father of two, leads the group of ranchers that the Whitecaps are forcing off the land. But Cleve will need all the strength and courage he can muster if he hopes to stand up for long against the corruption, brute force . . . and murder.

Dorchester Publishing Co., Inc.
P.O. Box 6640   ___5066-8
Wayne, PA 19087-8640   **$5.50 US/$7.50 CAN**
Please add $2.50 for shipping and handling for the first book and $.75 for each book thereafter. NY and PA residents, please add appropriate sales tax. No cash, stamps, or C.O.D.s. All orders shipped within 6 weeks via postal service book rate.
Canadian orders require $2.00 extra postage and must be paid in U.S. dollars through a U.S. banking facility.

Name _____
Address_____
City_____ State_____ Zip _____
I have enclosed $ _____in payment for the checked book(s).
Payment **must** accompany all orders. ❏ Please send a free catalog.
     CHECK OUT OUR WEBSITE! www.dorchesterpub.com

MORGETTE IN THE YUKON

G. G. BOYER

Dolf Morgette is determined to head west, as far west as a man can go—to the wilds of Alaska to join the great gold rush. He's charged with the responsibility of protecting Jack Quillen, the only man alive who can locate the vast goldfields of Lost Sky Pilot Fork. For Morgette, the assignment also holds the possibility of a new life for him and his pregnant wife, and perhaps a chance to settle a score with Rudy Dwan, a gunslinging fugitive working for the competition. But a new life doesn't come without risk. Morgette's journey has barely begun before he's ambushed. Soon he's beset at every turn by gunfighters, thieves and saboteurs. If he's not careful, Morgette may not have to worry about a new life— he may not survive his old one.

___4886-8 $3.99 US/$4.99 CAN

Dorchester Publishing Co., Inc.
P.O. Box 6640
Wayne, PA 19087-8640

Please add $2.50 for shipping and handling for the first book and $.75 for each book thereafter. NY, NYC, and PA residents, please add appropriate sales tax. No cash, stamps, or C.O.D.s. All orders shipped within 6 weeks via postal service book rate. Canadian orders require $2.50 extra postage and must be paid in U.S. dollars through a U.S. banking facility.

Name_____
Address _____
City_____ State _____ Zip_____
I have enclosed $ _____ in payment for the checked book(s).
Payment <u>must</u> accompany all orders. ❏ Please send a free catalog.
CHECK OUT OUR WEBSITE! www.dorchesterpub.com

JANE CANDIA COLEMAN
BORDERLANDS

In this thrilling collection of brilliant short stories, award-winning author Jane Candia Coleman takes us on an exciting tour of the different borderlands of the Old West, some real, some emotional, borderlands that mark endings . . . but also beginnings. From settlers on the Montana-Canada border to Pancho Villa's bold attack on New Mexico, these tales tell of daring and courage, adventure and danger. They feature journeys made by people looking for a better life, to escape an old life—or simply to stay alive.

Dorchester Publishing Co., Inc.
P.O. Box 6640   ___5070-6
Wayne, PA 19087-8640 $4.99 US/$6.99 CAN
Please add $2.50 for shipping and handling for the first book and $.75 for each book thereafter. NY and PA residents, please add appropriate sales tax. No cash, stamps, or C.O.D.s. All orders shipped within 6 weeks via postal service book rate.
Canadian orders require $2.00 extra postage and must be paid in U.S. dollars through a U.S. banking facility.

Name _____
Address_____
City_____ State_____ Zip _____
I have enclosed $ _____in payment for the checked book(s).
Payment **must** accompany all orders. ❏ Please send a free catalog.
       CHECK OUT OUR WEBSITE! www.dorchesterpub.com

MOVING ON
JANE CANDIA COLEMAN

Jane Candia Coleman is a magical storyteller who spins brilliant tales of human survival, hope, and courage on the American frontier, and nowhere is her marvelous talent more in evidence than in this acclaimed collection of her finest work. From a haunting story of the night Billy the Kid died, to a dramatic account of a breathtaking horse race, including two stories that won the prestigious Spur Award, here is a collection that reveals the passion and fortitude of its characters, and also the power of a wonderful writer.

___4545-1 $4.99 US/$5.99 CAN

Dorchester Publishing Co., Inc.
P.O. Box 6640
Wayne, PA 19087-8640

Please add $1.75 for shipping and handling for the first book and $.50 for each book thereafter. NY, NYC, and PA residents, please add appropriate sales tax. No cash, stamps, or C.O.D.s. All orders shipped within 6 weeks via postal service book rate. Canadian orders require $2.00 extra postage and must be paid in U.S. dollars through a U.S. banking facility.

Name_____
Address_____
City_____ State_____ Zip_____
I have enclosed $_____ in payment for the checked book(s).
Payment <u>must</u> accompany all orders. ☐ Please send a free catalog.
    CHECK OUT OUR WEBSITE! www.dorchesterpub.com

Legend

LOREN D. ESTLEMAN, ELMER KELTON, JUDY ALTER, JAMES REASONER, JANE CANDIA COLEMAN, ED GORMAN, ROBERT J. RANDISI

For the first time, these amazing talents—combined winners of 14 Spur Awards!—have joined forces, and the result is truly the stuff of legend. Together they recount the life of Lyle Speaks, from his hardscrabble boyhood in Texas to his later years as an aging cattle rancher in Montana, years in which his colorful past may yet come back to haunt him. From one end of the West to the other, Lyle's exploits made him famous—admired by some, feared by others. But now Lyle wants to set the record straight. No matter what the cost.

___4496-X $5.99 US/$6.99 CAN

Dorchester Publishing Co., Inc.
P.O. Box 6640
Wayne, PA 19087-8640

Please add $1.75 for shipping and handling for the first book and $.50 for each book thereafter. NY, NYC, and PA residents, please add appropriate sales tax. No cash, stamps, or C.O.D.s. All orders shipped within 6 weeks via postal service book rate. Canadian orders require $2.00 extra postage and must be paid in U.S. dollars through a U.S. banking facility.

Name_____
Address_____
City_____ State_____ Zip_____
I have enclosed $_____ in payment for the checked book(s).
Payment <u>must</u> accompany all orders. ❑ Please send a free catalog.
CHECK OUT OUR WEBSITE! www.dorchesterpub.com

THE ACTOR

ROBERT J. CONLEY

Bluford Steele had always been an outsider until he found his calling as an actor. Instead of being just another half-breed Cherokee with a white man's education, he can be whomever he chooses. But when the traveling acting troupe he is with arrives in the wild, lawless town of West Riddle, the man who rules the town with an iron fist forces them to perform. Then he steals all the proceeds. Steele is determined to get the money back, even if it means playing the most dangerous role of his life—a cold-blooded gunslinger ready to face down any man who gets in his way.

___4498-6 $4.50 US/$5.50 CAN

Dorchester Publishing Co., Inc.
P.O. Box 6640
Wayne, PA 19087-8640

Please add $1.75 for shipping and handling for the first book and $.50 for each book thereafter. NY, NYC, and PA residents, please add appropriate sales tax. No cash, stamps, or C.O.D.s. All orders shipped within 6 weeks via postal service book rate. Canadian orders require $2.00 extra postage and must be paid in U.S. dollars through a U.S. banking facility.

Name_____
Address_____
City_____State_____Zip_____
I have enclosed $_____ in payment for the checked book(s).
Payment <u>must</u> accompany all orders. ☐ Please send a free catalog.
        CHECK OUT OUR WEBSITE! www.dorchesterpub.com

BRANDISH

DOUGLAS HIRT

FIRST TIME IN PAPERBACK!

Captain Ethan Brandish has finally given up his command of Fort Lowell, deep in Apache territory. But the vicious Apache leader, Yellow Shirt, has another fate in store for him. He and a group of renegade warriors attack a stage station and ride off just before Brandish arrives. But the Apaches are still out there—watching and waiting—and Brandish must risk his own life to save the few wounded survivors.

___4323-8 $4.50 US/$5.50 CAN

Dorchester Publishing Co., Inc.
P.O. Box 6640
Wayne, PA 19087-8640

Please add $1.75 for shipping and handling for the first book and $.50 for each book thereafter. NY, NYC, and PA residents, please add appropriate sales tax. No cash, stamps, or C.O.D.s. All orders shipped within 6 weeks via postal service book rate. Canadian orders require $2.00 extra postage and must be paid in U.S. dollars through a U.S. banking facility.

Name_____
Address_____
City_____ State_____ Zip_____
I have enclosed $_____ in payment for the checked book(s).
Payment <u>must</u> accompany all orders. ❑ Please send a free catalog.

TROUBLE MAN

ED GORMAN

Ray Coyle used to be a gunfighter. And when he gets word his boy has been killed in a gunfight in Coopersville, he has to go there—to bring the body home. But when the old gunfighter steps off the train, he brings his gun with him, along with something else . . . trouble.

___4440-4 $4.99 US/$5.99 CAN

Dorchester Publishing Co., Inc.
P.O. Box 6640
Wayne, PA 19087-8640

Please add $1.75 for shipping and handling for the first book and $.50 for each book thereafter. NY, NYC, and PA residents, please add appropriate sales tax. No cash, stamps, or C.O.D.s. All orders shipped within 6 weeks via postal service book rate. Canadian orders require $2.00 extra postage and must be paid in U.S. dollars through a U.S. banking facility.

Name_____
Address_____
City_____ State_____ Zip_____
I have enclosed $_____ in payment for the checked book(s).
Payment <u>must</u> accompany all orders. ❑ Please send a free catalog.
CHECK OUT OUR WEBSITE! www.dorchesterpub.com

GRAVES' RETREAT ED GORMAN

Cedar Rapids in 1884 is a place where ~~Les Graves has a~~ chance to finally earn the respectability he has always wanted and to marry the woman he loves. Then his brother T. Z. comes into town, bringing with him trouble with a capital T. It seems that T. Z. and his friend Neely have big plans for the local bank where Graves happens to work. And they are counting on Graves' help to pull off the heist. All Graves gets in return for his loyalty is a hard cot in a drafty cell—until a rivalry between two local sheriffs gives him one shot at freedom. But before Graves can return to his peaceful life and the pursuit of the woman of his dreams, there are a few more twists in the trail. . . with trouble around each bend.

___4655-5 $3.99 US/$4.99 CAN

Dorchester Publishing Co., Inc.
P.O. Box 6640
Wayne, PA 19087-8640

Please add $1.75 for shipping and handling for the first book and $.50 for each book thereafter. NY, NYC, and PA residents, please add appropriate sales tax. No cash, stamps, or C.O.D.s. All orders shipped within 6 weeks via postal service book rate. Canadian orders require $2.00 extra postage and must be paid in U.S. dollars through a U.S. banking facility.

Name_____
Address_____
City_____ State_____ Zip_____
I have enclosed $_____ in payment for the checked book(s).
Payment <u>must</u> accompany all orders. ❑ Please send a free catalog.
        CHECK OUT OUR WEBSITE! www.dorchesterpub.com

ATTENTION BOOK LOVERS!

CAN'T GET ENOUGH
OF YOUR FAVORITE WESTERNS?

CALL 1-800-481-9191 TO:

- ORDER BOOKS,
- RECEIVE A FREE CATALOG,
- JOIN OUR BOOK CLUBS TO SAVE 20%!

OPEN MON.-FRI. 10 AM-9 PM EST

VISIT
WWW.DORCHESTERPUB.COM
FOR SPECIAL OFFERS AND INSIDE
INFORMATION ON THE AUTHORS
YOU LOVE.

 LEISURE BOOKS
We accept Visa, MasterCard or Discover®.